THE STALKER
BETWEEN THE STARS

I smelled the strange winds that roar between the worlds, bearing the odours of darkling planets and the souls of sundered stars. I felt about me the emptiness of remote and infinite vacuums of space, and their coldness. I saw, blazing on a panoply of jet, unknown constellations and nameless nebulae stretching out and away through the light years into unthinkable abysses of space.

Then, winging through the nearer star-spaces, I spied that enigmatic coffin-shape recognized of old, and again, as in delirious dreams, I heard my lost friend's voice calling to me as across limitless voids.

I yelled in spontaneous response, calling out to him again and again; but then, swelling out of the darkness in the wake of Crow's weird craft, bloating up in a green glow, filling my entire view in an instant, there came . . .

A shape!
Cthulhu!

By the same author

BRIAN LUMLEY

The Transition of Titus Crow

GraftonBooks

A Division of HarperCollins*Publishers*

GraftonBooks
A Division of HarperCollins*Publishers*
77–85 Fulham Palace Road,
Hammersmith, London W6 8JB

A Grafton UK Paperback Original 1991
9 8 7 6 5 4 3 2 1

Copyright © Brian Lumley 1975, 1991

ISBN 0-586-20838-0

Printed and bound in Great Britain by
Collins, Glasgow

Set in Times

This novel
was written in open
admiration of the greatest
macabre author ever,
Howard Phillips Lovecraft,
and is dedicated to the
tremendous concepts
of his now famous
Cthulhu Mythos.

Author's Note

In respect of Art Meyer's Prologue to this work: he is in fact mistaken on one point, though of course he could hardly be expected to have foreseen it! For where he has it that, 'no single word of the author's original text has been altered', I personally would beg to differ.

When I originally submitted *Transition* to DAW Books back in 1973 or '74, it ran about 25,000 words too long for Don Wollheim's editorial tastes. He asked me to cut it and gave me a deadline. Alas, I was a comparative newcomer, a beginner, still learning the business of writing. And I don't suppose anyone ever learns all of it . . . but, instead of a scalpel I used a hacksaw, and then compounded the crime by losing or destroying the excised material. The novel suffered as a result, which was my fault entirely.

What's more, now that Grafton Books see fit to reprint *Transition*, I've been at it again – but this time I hope my surgery has been somewhat less brutal. Assuming that many or most readers of this current novel will have read the previous book, *The Burrowers Beneath*, I've removed several lengthy discussions of that earlier work to allow for a faster pace and 'tighter' read. All of which will meet, I hope, with your approval . . .

Brian Lumley,
Brixham, Devon –
Dec. 1986

LONDON OCCULTIST
BACK FROM THE DEAD!

Mr Henri-Laurent de Marigny, son of the great New Orleans mystic Etienne-Laurent de Marigny, is literally 'back from the dead', having been pronounced missing or dead in 1976 along with his friend and colleague Mr Titus Crow, late of Leonard's-Walk Heath. Speculation is now rife as to whether Titus Crow may also still be alive following Mr de Marigny's amazing reappearance after an absence of almost ten years, since the freak lightning storm of 4 October 1969 that utterly destroyed Blowne House, Mr Crow's residence. Until now it was also believed that the storm had killed the two friends. An element of doubt has always existed with regard to their 'deaths', for no bodies were ever found in the ruins of the house following the storm, despite the fact that the occultists were believed to be in residence.

De Marigny's return yesterday morning was as dramatic as his disappearance. He was fished out of the Thames at Purfleet more dead than alive, saved from almost certain death by drowning by Mr Harold Simmons of Tilbury, who dragged him aboard his barge from the precarious refuge of a buoy. Mr Simmons reports how, despite de Marigny's battered and bruised condition and the fact that all his limbs were broken, the occultist clung to the buoy like a limpet, even making an exhausted, delirious attempt to fight his rescuer off. 'He looked like he'd been hit by an express train,' Mr Simmons reports, 'but he certainly wasn't ready to give in!' Mr de Marigny, identified initially through certain documents he carried, is now recovering in hospital . . .

The *Daily London News*
5 September 1979

Contents

Prologue

At Miskatonic University, the morning of 20 March 1980, just six days before the Fury, Professor Wingate Peaslee, then head of the Wilmarth Foundation, called me into his office for a final briefing on Foundation affairs before he left for Innsmouth, where he intended to supervise personally what was then Project X, since known as Project Cthylla.

As vice-president of the Foundation (and in my capacity as Peaslee's right-hand man and understudy) I was of course already very well informed in all aspects of Foundation work; therefore my briefing was not protracted. Wingate was uneasy. Though at that time our organization had already enlisted the aid of many 'sciences' of previously dubious authenticity, we were only beginning to investigate precognition; in this lay the source of the professor's disquiet. Within the space of the last week he had received no less than three separate warnings from psychically endowed persons within the Foundation, all of them forecasting doom – forecasting, in fact, the Fury! Could he afford to ignore them?

The question with prognostication is of course this: Will the foreseen event come about as a direct result of external and uncontrollable influences, or will it be brought about by internal forces attempting its avoidance? Would Project X bring about a disaster, or would the disaster be brought about by the abandonment of the project? Another problem is this: How does one avoid what will be, what has been foreseen? There again, and perhaps on the brighter side, there was always the chance that those warning visions of doom had been deliberately planted by the CCD in the minds of the three Foundation psychics in an attempt to hold up the Innsmouth operations. These were some of the problems that worried Wingate Peaslee; they were among the reasons for his deciding to supervise Project X personally.

That same morning he had received by airmail a parcel from London containing a number of notebooks, various documents and tape recordings. The parcel was from a personal friend of the professor's and a former member of the Foundation, Henri-Laurent de Marigny. Similarly that morning a communication had arrived from the British chapter of the Foundation consisting of a brief and cryptic note from the psychic Mother Eleanor Quarry. Peaslee showed me the note. It said simply this: 'Titus Crow has been back. He is no longer here. I believe that this time de Marigny has followed him. Wingate, I think we are in for terrible trouble.'

Typical of the brilliant British psychic and cryptic as it was, nevertheless the first three sentences of this note meant much to both Wingate Peaslee and to myself; the last sentence was more obscure, unless it was yet another warning of approaching doom.

Peaslee then told me how he would dearly love to explore the contents of the parcel from de Marigny himself but simply had no time at present to do so. I was given that task. Perhaps, in retrospect, it would have been better if Peaslee had not gone to Innsmouth but had attended to the parcel instead. Who can say?

First I read the notebooks, a task I completed on the morning of 24 March. I began to listen to the tapes late on the night of the 25th, pressure of work keeping me from them until then. I had barely started when, just after midnight, there came the first subterranean rumblings, the first grim warning that this was to be the day of the Fury!

Fortunately, before the Fury struck with its full force, I was able to place manuscripts and tapes alike in my office safe. When I retrieved them from the debris of Miskatonic four days later, the notebooks and documents were still intact; the tapes had suffered somewhat.

So much for a prologue. As background material toward an understanding of the forces behind the Fury, and as a personal account of his own involvement with the CCD and with Titus Crow, Henri-Laurent de Marigny's work is required reading. In it, as in the transcriptions from the tape recordings of Titus Crow's narrative, which follow it – and as in de Marigny's recently reprinted earlier account of the Wilmarth Foundation's work, *The Burrowers Beneath* – no single word of the author's original text has been altered.

Arthur D. Meyer
New Miskatonic,
Rutland, Vermont

Part One

1

But What of Titus Crow?

(From de Marigny's notebooks)

My first thought on awakening, particularly on finding myself in a hospital bed, was that it had all been a nightmare, a horrific dream perhaps engendered of whichever drugs I had been given to assist in my recovery from –

My recovery from what?

Plainly I had suffered some terrible accident or attack of incredible ferocity. My arms and legs seemed to be in splints; I was bandaged top to bottom and barely able to move my head. There was a lot of pain, so much that I could specify no single area of my body for its origin, it was everywhere. I was patently lucky to be alive! Exactly what, then, had happened to me? I could remember nothing. Or was there . . . something?

Yes, there was something. I could remember water pulling me down, and strange hands tugging at me.

Then, turning my head as far as my various wrappings and bandages would allow, I saw the vase of flowers by my bed, close enough for me to read the message on the attached card:

> To a dear and valued friend,
> long lost but found again –
> get well very soon,
>   W. Peaslee

Peaslee! Professor Wingate Peaslee, head of the Wilmarth Foundation! Fragmentary visions of past events tumbled chaotically in my painfully fuzzy mind as I read

17

the man's name. But at least I knew now that they had been no nightmares, those horrible scenes reviewed subconsciously by my mind's eye immediately prior to waking – no dreams but *memories* of my past experiences as a member of the Wilmarth Foundation. My eyes, peering through slits in swathing bandages, went again to the vase of flowers, finding propped against its base a curious star-shaped stone like some fossil starfish from Silurian coral beds, a stone that went far to calming my abruptly whirling mind and fluttering heart.

And suddenly I remembered. I remembered it all! And with the memory a name sprang spontaneously to my lips.

'Crow!' I cried, 'Titus Crow! *Where are you?*'

His name, and my question, seemed to echo hollowly in the white room about me, hanging in the air. Particularly the question.

Where indeed . . .?

I must have slept then, for when I opened my eyes next it was night, or rather late evening. The shadows were long in my room and beyond the windows the first tendrils of a gray mist were rising. There was the smell of the country in the less than antiseptic air flowing into the room from a ventilator fan in the opposite wall. The room was pleasantly cool. I guessed that I was not in London, but wherever I was I knew that Peaslee was not far away, and that therefore I was safe from . . . *them!*

Them – the burrowers beneath and all the other horrors of the Cthulhu Cycle – I shuddered at the thought of them, then made a conscious effort to thrust them out of my mind. First I must think about myself.

At least I was feeling much better. That is, my pains were noticeably less and the bandages had been removed from my head and neck, allowing me at least sufficient freedom of movement to peer about my room. Above my bed, on the wall, I saw a button with the – from my position – inverted legend RING. How I was supposed to comply, even if I had wanted to, was quite beyond me. My arms were still in plaster. No matter, for the moment I desired no company.

At least this time I seemed wide awake, capable of thinking clearly and reasonably. And indeed I had a lot to think about. I cast a few cursory glances about the room, sufficient to assure myself that I was definitely in a hospital, probably a private institute, if the impeccably delicate decor and my clinically immaculate immediate surroundings were anything to go by. Then I settled down to the more serious business of getting my thoughts – my memories of what had gone before, leading up to this present as yet unexplained confinement – sorted out in my mind into some sort of recognizable order.

Those memories still had many nightmarish aspects. Indeed, they were unbelievable to a point which might only suggest – to anybody mercifully less well informed – an incredible degree of gullibility, even insanity in any believer. And yet I knew that I believed, and that I was certainly not mad . . .

No, I was alive, sane and safe – but what of Titus Crow?

The last time I'd seen him had been at Blowne House, his sprawling bungalow retreat on Leonard's-Walk Heath; that had been on the 4th Oct. 1969, when Ithaqua's elementals of the air had attacked us in all their massed might. We had been trapped there, and no way out; we faced certain death; Crow's home was being reduced to rubble around us! At the last we were left with no other alternative but to put our faith in the grandfather clock: that old (*how* old?) coffin-shaped device, yes, which had once belonged to my father, for which Crow had named it 'De Marigny's Clock'.

19

But 'clock'? A misnomer that, if ever there was one. No timepiece at all but a device come down from pre-dawn days of extradimensional magic – literally a toy of the Elder Gods themselves! As for its history:

First, tracing the clock's line as far back as possible in the light of my limited knowledge, it had belonged to one Yogi Hiamaldi, a friend of the ill-fated Carolina mystic Harley Warren. Hiamaldi had been a member, along with Warren, of a psychic-phenomenalist group in Boston about 1916–18. He had sworn that he alone of living men had been to Yian-Ho, that crumbling revenant of aeon-shrouded Leng, and that he had borne away certain things from that lost and leering necropolis. For a reason unknown, the Yogi had made a gift of the clock to my father, though I am unable to recall ever seeing the thing as a child before I was sent out of America. I can only suppose that my father kept it at his New Orleans retreat, a place that had always fascinated me but that my poor nervous mother had always done her best to keep me away from. After my father died the clock was sold, along with many of his other curiosities, to a French collector. Titus Crow had been unable to discover how the thing had suddenly turned up so many years later at an auction of antique furniture in England, but his subsequent attempts to trace the previous French owner had failed miserably; it was as though he had simply vanished off the face of the Earth!

I remembered, too, a curious affair involving an East Indian mystic, one Swami Chandraputra, I believe he called himself, who had also allegedly 'disappeared' in strange circumstances connected somehow with the clock. At the time, though, I was only a lad living largely away from my father. Crow knew the story more fully, for he had researched all of these things. Even with all his research my friend had been unable to discover where or when or by whom the peculiarly ominous thing had been made, or even why. Plainly its weirdly meandering hands moved in sequences completely alien to any earthly chronological system, and at best its ungovernably aberrant ticking must drive anyone of less than iron fortitude and unbending resolution to distraction.

In Crow's case, however, it was this very lack of an easily discernible purpose, and similarly the unfathomable mystery of its origin, which had served to endear the clock to him; and he had spent many years in intermittent, frustrated and invariably vain study of the thing. Then, as a guest of Professor Peaslee at Miskatonic University, Crow had finally recognized in one of the library's great old occult volumes a curious sequence of odd glyphs which he had been delighted to note bore a striking resemblance to the figures on the dial of his huge clock. Moreover, the book bore a translation of its own hieroglyphed passage in Latin!

Armed with this Rosetta Stone knowledge, my friend had returned to London where he was soon at work again uncovering many of the strange machine's previous mysteries. And he had been right, for it was indeed a vehicle – a space-time machine of sorts with principles more alien than the center of a star, whose like we can at least conjecture upon. Titus Crow, however, was never a man to be denied anything once he set his mind after it. And so he had persevered. Once he had written to me to say of his work on the clock: 'I am in the position of a Neanderthal studying the operational handbook of a passenger-carrying aircraft – except I have no handbook!' Though of course he was exaggerating, the weird device's functions were certainly obscure enough to baffle anyone.

And yet when the final choice presented itself – between the clock and those hellish winds of darkness sent by Ithaqua to destroy us – full of trepidation and dread though we were, nevertheless we entered into the vehicle's strangely huge, greenly illumined interior . . . and then everything seemed to turn upside down and inside out! Amid the whirling, rushing, dizzying motion of that experience I had yet been somehow aware of the final destruction of Blowne House; while from the depths of a shrieking purple mist that rushed ever faster into a gaping hole in the fabric of the universe itself, I heard Titus Crow's distant, fading voice:

'Follow me, de Marigny – with your *mind*, man – with your mind!'

Then he was gone and a Stygian darkness closed about me, buffeting, crushing, squeezing me like toothpaste from a tube out of that . . . that place . . . where I had no right to be. And finally, after an eternity of torture and tissue-rending pressures, there had been those sensations of falling, of water and then of strange hands tugging at me . . .

Then the white sheets of the hospital bed. And the flowers. And the comforting star-stone, left no doubt by Wingate Peaslee to guard me from the anciently malign horror of the CCD. Something about the professor's card bothered me, however. What had he meant by 'long lost but found again'? Didn't that imply the passing of a considerable amount of time? Well, I could always ask him when I saw him.

Until then, while far from sound in body, I was at least sane . . . and safe.

But what of Titus Crow?

2

Of Dreams and Ten Years Lost

(From de Marigny's notebooks)

It must have been early morning before I managed to get to sleep, but even then my slumbers were not peaceful. Everything that I had chewed over in my mind before finally sleeping kept rising to the surface of my subconscious, and the result could only be called nightmarish!

I dreamed – or nightmared – about the Cthonians, those monstrous subterraneans alive even now and burrowing in the Earth's secret places, threatening the very sanity of the world with a resurgence of hellish magic and mayhem and plotting the release of worse horrors yet, such as loathsome Lord Cthulhu and others of his Cycle.

I read again, or at least was allowed shuddering glimpses of, the books and documents of an unthinkably ancient 'mythology': works such as the *Pnakotic Manuscripts*, supposedly a fragmentary record of a race lost before history began; and the *R'lyeh Text*, purporting to have been written by certain minions of Great Cthulhu himself. And dreaming still, I averted my eyes from the pages of such tomes as the *Unaussprechlichen Kulten* of Von Junzt, and Ludwig Prinn's 'cornerstone' *De Vermis Mysteriis*. All of these books, or copies of them, I handled again as I had in reality handled them: the Comte d'Erlette's *Cultes des Goules*, Joachim Feery's *Notes on the Necronomicon*, even Titus Crow's own priceless copy of the anonymous *Cthäat Aquadingen* . . .

In books such as these, under Crow's guidance, I had first studied the legend of the Cthulhu Mythos: of Beings seeped down from the stars in Earth's youth, and prisoned here by greater Beings yet for blasphemies of cosmic enormity. The alien names of these forces rang again in my sleeping brain – Cthulhu, Yog-Sothoth, Ithaqua, Shub-Niggurath – and I felt a fever's heat grip me as if I had uttered some demoniac invocation to open the gates of hell!

Then for a moment I was back in Crow's study – in the reeling, tottering shell of Blowne House – with that ancient, madly ticking clock standing there, its door open, issuing a swirling, throbbing green and purple light – and my friend's face wax as he held me by the shoulders and shouted some instruction which was drowned in the tumult of winds!

'Titus!' I shouted back. 'For God's sake – *Titus*!' . . .

. . . But it was *not* Titus Crow's face, and it was not waxen. It was instead Peaslee's face, worried and drawn; Peaslee's arms reaching down to me, his veined old hands holding me firm; Peaslee's voice, calming, soothing me.

'Easy now, Henri! Easy! You're safe now. Nothing can harm you here. Easy, de Marigny.'

'Wingate! Professor!' I was barely awake, drenched in sweat, my whole body trembling and shuddering in reaction. Wildly, despite the restrictions of my various dressings, I tore loose from his restraining hands to peer fearfully about the room.

'It's all right, Henri,' he repeated. 'You're safe now.'

'Safe?' The nightmare was quickly fading; relief abruptly flooded my whole being. I let my head fall back against the damp pillows. 'Peaslee, what happened?' I stupidly asked.

The frown on his face turned to a wry, wrinkled grin. 'I was hoping you could tell me that, de Marigny!' he replied. 'The last I heard of you was in Crow's letter, retrieved from the ruins of Blowne House. Of course, I've never given up hope, but ten years is a long time, and – '

24

'What?' I cut him off. 'Did you say *ten years*?' I blinked the blurred edges of sleep from my eyes and at last saw Peaslee clearly where he bent over my bed, the smile fading again on his old face. And it was an *old* face, older by far than I remembered it and by my reckoning certainly older than it ought to have been.

'Yes, Henri, it's been ten long years since I last heard of you.' He frowned. 'But surely you know that? You *must* know it! Where have you been, Henri? And where is Titus Crow?'

'Ten years!' I slowly repeated it, suddenly exhausted, utterly washed out. 'My God! I remember . . . nothing. The last thing I recall is seeing – '

'Yes?'

'The clock, Crow's great clock. We went inside the thing, Crow and I, him first, myself following immediately behind him. We were somehow separated then. I remember Crow calling to me to follow him, and then . . . nothing. But ten years! How could such a thing be?'

For the first time then, I saw that my visitor was holding someone back from my bed. Finally this stranger exclaimed, 'Really, Professor, I must protest. Mr de Marigny is your friend, I understand that, but he's also my patient!'

The voice was female, but so aloof as to be almost harsh; the face atop the tall figure that finally pushed itself past Peaslee was hawklike and severe. It came as a shock, then, to find that the hand whose fingers searched for my pulse was surprisingly warm and gentle.

'Madam,' Peaslee replied, his New England accent barely showing, 'my friend is here at my request, and I am paying for his treatment. You must understand that his mind is the only key to certain very important problems – problems I have waited ten years to solve.'

'All that is as it may be,' the matron answered, quite

25

unperturbed, 'but no amount of money or pressure over-rules my authority here, Professor. The only way you may do that is to take Mr de Marigny out of my nursing home, which would not be in his best interests. In the meantime his welfare is my concern, and until he is well, or until you decide to terminate his stay here, I will care for him as I see best.' She paused, then acidly added, 'You are not, I believe, a professor of medicine?'

'No, madam, I am not, but – '

'No "buts", Professor, I'm quite sure that Mr de Marigny has had enough excitement for one day. You may see him again the day after tomorrow. Now I'm afraid you must leave.'

'But – '

'No, no, *no!*' she insisted.

Peaslee turned his seamed, angry face to me. His vastly intelligent eyes flashed furiously for a moment, but then he grinned a moment later, his natural good nature showing through all his impatience.

'Very well,' he finally agreed; and then to me: 'It will all have to wait until later, Henri. But she's right, you'd better rest now. And try not to worry. You'll be perfectly safe here.' He grinned again, wickedly casting a quick glance at the matron where she stood now at the foot of my bed penciling a line on a graph, before bending over me to whisper, 'I doubt if even Cthulhu himself would dare to brave this place!'

After Peaslee had gone I slept again, this time peacefully enough, until about midafternoon. When I awakened it was to find a young doctor at work removing the splints and casts from my arms. Matron Emily, as she insisted I call her, was assisting him, and she seemed genuinely delighted when at last my arms lay bare over the sheets.

26

'You wouldn't believe it,' she told me, 'if you had seen how badly mangled your arms were. But now . . .'

Now there were one or two minor scars, nothing much to show that my arms had suffered anything but superficial cuts and abrasions. 'Your friend the professor,' she continued, 'brought in the world's finest surgeons and specialists.'

She allowed me to sit up then, making me comfortable with pillows for my back. I was given a mirror, too, and allowed to shave myself. I soon learned not to move my arms too quickly; the bones were still very sore. By the growth of hair on my face I judged that it must have been all of a week since last I had seen a razor. Matron Emily confirmed this, moreover informing me that she had shaved me twice herself at similar intervals. I had been in her nursing home for three weeks.

I asked for the day's newspapers then, but before I could settle to read them a second doctor came in to see me. He was a bespectacled, bald little man with a busy, bustling attitude. He gave me a thorough going over: chest, ears, eyes, nose – everything. He *harrumphed* and grunted once or twice during his examination, made copious notes in a little black book, had me clench my hands and bend my elbows repeatedly, painfully, then *harrumph* some more before finally asking me my age.

'I'm forty-six,' I answered without thinking; then, remembering that ten years had inexplicably elapsed since the world had last seen me, I corrected myself. 'No, better make that fifty-six.'

'*Harrumph!* Hmm, well, I prefer to believe your first statement, Mr de Marigny. Despite your injuries you're in a remarkably good state of preservation. I would have said forty-two, perhaps forty-three at the outside. Certainly not fifty-six.'

'Doctor,' I eagerly cried, grasping at his arms (and at a

27

straw at the same time) as I sought his eyes with mine. 'Tell me – what year is this?'

'Hmm?' He peered at me through the thick lenses of his glasses. 'Eh? The year? Ah, yes, you're having some trouble with your memory, aren't you? Yes, Peaslee mentioned that. Hmm, well, the year is 1979. Does that help any?'

'No, that doesn't help,' I slowly answered, dismayed to discover Peaslee's statement with regard to my lost ten years corroborated, even though I had known it would be. I shook my head glumly. 'It's strange, I know, but somewhere I seem to have mislaid ten years. Only I'm pretty damned sure I haven't *aged* ten years!'

He looked at me steadily for a moment, seriously, then grinned. 'Oh? Then you must count yourself lucky, er, *harrumph*!' He started to pack his instruments away. 'Years seem to hang like lumps of lead on me. Each one weighs that much heavier and drags me down that much faster!'

I spent the rest of the afternoon vainly attempting to formulate some sort of answer to this problem of the time lapse, giving it up in the end when I remembered the daily newspapers. They lay on a low chair to the right of my bed, within reach but out of sight, which was why I had forgotten them. But no sooner had I picked up the first newspaper than the enigma presented itself yet again – in the date at the top of the first page. Ten years . . .

Deliberately then, and with a genuine effort at concentration – something which should have come far easier to me – I forced the recurring problem from my mind and began to read. What I expected to find, what modern wonders had been wrought in this 'future' world, I really do not know. And so it was with a definite sense of relief that I discovered very little to have changed. The Big Names of the day were different, certainly, but they featured in the same old headlines.

Then I came upon an article about the Mars program in an illustrated scientific journal of recent date, noting that space probes had already been sent around Mars and recovered, and that they had been brought down under their own power on dry land. Progress! The title, by no means purely speculative, was 'The Exploration of Space – Men on Mars by '85.' But no sooner had I come across this article than I remembered what the Foundation had found on the moon: the secret that not even the American astronauts themselves had known. Nevertheless, certain of their instruments had transmitted back to Earth the fact that life did exist beneath that stark, cruel surface, a life even more cruel and stark. The octopoid spawn of Cthulhu was there, imprisoned on Earth by the Elder Gods *before* the moon had been hurled into orbit from the Azoic Pacific, molten again following that terrific battle which the forces of evil had lost. Little wonder that the full moon has driven men to madness and caused dogs to howl down the centuries . . . And then I wondered just what new horrors the first men might find on Mars . . .

Just how widespread throughout the universe were the prisons of the Elder Gods, wherein they had chained the malignant powers of the CCD? The great occult books had it that Hastur was imprisoned near Aldebaran in the Hyades, and that the Elder Gods themselves were palaced in Orion. So very far away! I was no mathematician, but I still knew the definition of a light-year, and while no man could ever hope to visualize such a distance, nevertheless I could at least conceive of thousands of such units. So very far . . . What hope then for little Mars, mere millions of miles away, in the selfsame star system as the home planet of Man, a system which had actually formed part of the inconceivably ancient battleground?

Puzzling just such disturbing questions as these, with that scientific journal still in my hands, I eventually felt myself nodding. In fact it had been growing dark in my room for some time. Matron Emily had looked in once or twice but had steadfastly refused to put my light on, saying that it was best I should get some sleep. Perhaps it was simply the added psychological effect of her words, or it just could have been the result of too much eyestrain in the steadily darkening room, but whichever way it was I soon succumbed to sleep, and it seemed that I began to dream almost immediately.

Now I have never been what you might call a great dreamer. In fact those dreams from which Peaslee had so mercifully rescued me were as strong and stronger than any I had ever previously known. By this I mean to say that it was extremely rare for me to dream so vividly; and yet no sooner had I closed my eyes when, for the second time in one day, I found myself assailed by strange nightmares and fantasies.

I floated in a region of weird forces outside yet forming a part of space and time; and I saw the great, coffin-shaped clock hurtling toward me out of even weirder nether regions while Crow's voice called out to me. But this time it was no exhortation to follow him that I heard but more a cry for help – an urgent request for assistance which I could not quite make out in its entirety before the clock drove on along paths unknown in nature into the distance of lost temporal wildernesses. And though the clock – or space-time ship, or whatever the thing was – had gone, still there sounded in my ears the eerie echo of Crow's lost cry for help, the tormented SOS of a soul in distress. That, at least, is the way it seemed to me, and I was later to learn that this interpretation of my friend's telepathic communication was not far short of correct.

Again and again, recurrently, this vision of the clock driving through hyperspace-time came to me; and over and over again I threw myself in its path only to be flung aside, left to swim frantically in its wake, vainly attempting to rescue my friend from whatever horrors threatened him. But who may swim against the tides of time?

Finally I woke up, and it was night; the room was still and quiet; my star-stone gleamed whitely against the flower vase in a stray beam of moonlight.

For a long time I simply lay there, feeling the cool of the sheet against my hot, naked arms, and the rapid beat of my heart within my chest. And in a short while my thoughts turned again to wondering about the plight of my poor friend, lost from men for ten long years. . . . And I admit that I despaired.

3

Of Peaslee and the Wilmarth Foundation

(From de Marigny's notebooks)

Two mornings later, bright and early and just as he had promised, Peaslee came to see me. It seemed that I was no sooner awake and shaved, just starting in on a very ample breakfast brought in by Matron Emily (my meals had been growing progressively larger and more regular over the past two days) when he opened the door to walk in unannounced.

'De Marigny, you look well!' He came and sat by my bed. 'God, man, do you intend to eat *all* of that? Still, I suppose it's more substantial than all that muck they've had to pump into you over these last weeks. How do you feel?'

'Fine,' I mumbled around a mouthful of bacon and egg, 'and I'll feel even better after they get my legs out of this concrete tomorrow. Listen, you talk and I'll eat, then I'll talk. Not that you'll get much out of me, I'm afraid, for I've nothing really to tell. But how about you? What of the Wilmarth Foundation?'

'The Foundation?' Peaslee smiled broadly, deep wrinkles forming in his aged face. 'All's well within the Foundation, Henri, in fact things could hardly be better. We haven't got them all yet, the minions of the CCD, not by any means – but their numbers decrease every year, and that's the important thing. Oh, there are still certain problems, many of them in the USSR, but even the Soviets are starting to come around to our way of thinking.'

'And the organization retains its cloak of secrecy?'

'Certainly. More people in high places know of the Foundation's work now, yes – that was necessary for our expansion and continuation – but mundane mankind strolls blindly by. It has to be that way. To let people know what has been going on, what still goes on, would be to invite disaster. There are still . . . beings . . . that could be called up. The last thing we want is an upsurge of interest in such matters. The fear of large-scale panic is not so great these days; there are too many wonders to see, too many marvels to behold. A handful of ghosts and nightmares from a time already lost when the Cambrian was the veriest baby of an age would no longer drive the world to madness, but to have people *alerted* to these things, to have them seeking out and reading the great old books again, and perhaps dabbling . . . Oh, no. We can't have that, de Marigny. And so the Foundation remains secret, and its work carries on as before.'

I nodded, then inclined my head toward the vase of flowers and the curiously shaped stone at its base. 'For all your reassuring words,' I said, 'I see you're not about to take any chances with my life!'

'Indeed we're not!' he declared. 'For we've already lost you once too often. And you're honoured, de Marigny, for that's a very special stone. It is one of the originals, excavated with a handful of others when the Foundation killed a Cthonian recently, one of the biggest and worst yet. That was during a supposed archeological expedition to the region of Sarnath the Doomed in what was once the Land of Mnar, Saudi Arabia to you. That stone was manufactured by the Elder Gods themselves, whoever or whatever they were.'

I leaned across to take the object of our conversation in my hand, peering at it intently. There appeared to be fine lines drawn on its surface, whorls and squiggles, curious glyphs that seemed to defy my eye to follow their intricacies. 'There are . . . markings!'

'Do you recognize them?' the professor asked at once, vastly interested.

'Yes, I think I do,' I answered. 'They're very similar to the hieroglyphs on Crow's clock, his space-time machine. Do you think there could be some connection?'

'It would certainly seem that there is,' he answered wryly. 'I've kicked myself a thousand times since I first saw that clock at Crow's place when I stayed there. I knew then that it was a very important thing, but who could have guessed just how important? I should have taken notes, photographs. Why, Crow even told me he believed the thing to be – '

'A toy of the Elder Gods themselves?' I finished it for him.

'Yes, exactly. Of course, all is not quite lost: we have the books at Miskatonic which supplied Crow with his first really important clue to, well, how to drive the damned thing! But I dearly wish now that I had photographed the clock itself. Every fragment of information is of value in the overall picture, like a piece in a jigsaw puzzle, and this must surely be one of the basic puzzles of the universe itself.'

'But what else of the Foundation?' I impatiently asked when he was done. 'How far have you gone in ten years? What successes, what failures? What new knowledge? Have you found R'lyeh in the Pacific? And Shudde-M'ell – what of the Prime Burrower now? God, Peaslee, but I'm dying to know everything. Ten years – I've lost ten years!'

'Whoa!' The professor held up his hands. 'Slow down. I'll tell you everything, of course, but it's best if I start with what we have *not* done. For instance, we have not found

R'lyeh, no, and that in turn leads us to believe that the Johansen Narrative is at fault – not in its premise that a fantastic city of alien dimensions, angles and proportions exists beneath the Pacific – but that the specific island which rose up from the ocean floor in 1925 was R'lyeh, and that its hellish denizen was Cthulhu. That it was *one* of the Cthulhu spawn seems a certainty, but Great Cthulhu himself? We doubt it. You may research it for yourself, Henri. The Foundation did long ago. Basically Johansen's story is this:

'On March 23rd, 1925, at latitude 47°9' south, longitude 126°43', the *Alert*, under Johansen's command and in those waters following a series of complicated misadventures that had left her wildly off course, landed on a small island where an island had never been sighted before. Now the sea in that area is two thousand fathoms deep. It is on the very edge of the Pacific-Antarctic Ridge, which falls away to three thousand fathoms and even deeper. The area is not noticeably volcanic, and in any case a cataclysm of sufficient force to bring even a small area of the ocean floor to the surface would without a shadow of a doubt have been recorded. So it would seem we might throw out the fanciful Johansen Narrative forthwith, except that the Foundation, like Charles Fort, prefers to make its own decisions!

'The buckling of the Pacific floor, in places more a stretching, as Australia tends northward in the continental drift, has been very pronounced in the area of the Pacific-Antarctic Ridge since early Miocene times. The island that rose in March, 1925, was in fact a phenomenon of this geologically prolonged buckling, and its disappearance again shortly thereafter may be put down to similar seismic forces.'

'I've read Fort too,' I remarked dryly, 'and I think he'd have taken exception to what you just said, Wingate.'

'Eh? Oh, of course, so he would – if we hadn't sent

35

down bathyspheres at that precise point just three years ago, and if we hadn't discovered what we did.'

'Go on,' I said, putting my plate aside at last. 'What did you find?'

'Our first bell was simply, well, a diving-bell, nothing more. A device lowered into the sea to record with cameras whatever it saw. It hit bottom at only two hundred fathoms, at the very peak of the submarine range, which is now, incidentally, quickly sinking back into the deeps. But before we lost it we were afforded fantastic glimpses the like of which – '

'Lost it?' I interrupted.

'Yes.' He nodded grimly. 'We lost it. Cables wrenched loose, bell smashed to smithereens – and a structure capable of withstanding thousands of tons of pressure at that! We recovered fragments later, fantastically dented, gnawed and crushed. A sea-shoggoth, we're inclined to believe, perhaps a number of them, about their immemorial task of protecting and worshiping their dreaming masters, the spawn of Cthulhu.

'I went down in the second bell myself – '

'You did *what?*' Again I cut him off, marveling that he could so blandly admit what seemed like the most colossal lunacy.

He offered me an ancient, wrinkled grin and leaned over to tap a fingernail on the surface of the star-stone where I had replaced it by the flower vase. 'Aren't you forgetting something, Henri? Yes? Well, then, as I was saying . . .

'It was three months later. We were ostensibly charting the Pacific-Antarctic Ridge. I went down with two younger men from Miskatonic in a powered bathysphere that was really more of a submarine. We had the protection of a number of star-stones, of course, but nevertheless the weather was bad and we'd been dogged by troubles all the way out from Boston: storms, mists, accidents, etc. Mind you, we were not so naïve as to believe that such troubles were merely coincidental. We've learned a lot since the old *Sea-Maid* days . . .

'There was a particularly heavy swell on the sea and an ominous mist that morning, but our telepaths on board the mother ship were all alert. Besides, we had massed what protective devices we could against any possible interference by the dark forces. Our little vessel fell away from the *Surveyor*, on loan to Miskatonic University from the American Oceanographic Society, and sank slowly down in a controlled, spiraling dive to the bottom. That bottom was in fact a top, the top of a range which may one day rise again, and permanently. If so, it will stretch from somewhere about three thousand miles west of Freemantle – or where Freemantle is now – to Easter Island, over ten thousand miles away. Indeed Easter Island, New Zealand, the Pitcairns and certain other island groups may well form its highest peaks. Somewhere in that vast range R'lyeh may rise too, and other cities of the Cthulhu spawn, like the one we found there two hundred and fifty fathoms down beneath the *Surveyor*.

'The place was . . . fantastic! We saw it in the beams of our powerful searchlights almost as it must have been in its Azoic heyday over a billion years ago. It was crusted, certainly, with millions of centuries of oceanic growths, but its sheer unthinkable size had defied all but a minimal obliteration of outline through the aeons.

'We saw the immense carved doors with their symbols of the Cthulhu spawn, the great squid-dragon bas-reliefs mentioned in Johansen; we noted and grew sick and dizzy at the madness of elusive angles that refused to stay either convex or concave but seemed to alter of their own accord, as in optical illusions. Despite our protective star-stones, we shuddered at the lurking menace, the morbidly insane horror still inherent in these colossal, monolithic structures of non-Euclidean architecture.

'The extent of these upper ramparts of the city – for want of a better word – was perhaps nine or ten acres, and this was without doubt that same shockingly alien buttress which had formed Johansen's island. But the crazy staircases and mammoth monoliths falling away on all sides, swimming down in seemingly endless tiers . . . Without descending to greater depths yet, even our powerful searchlights could only hint at the outlines of these leviathan levels. That city – if I may still apply a word which smacks of teeming, mundane life to such a nighted necropolis of the undead – must have been immense beyond words, reaching down into the roots of the Pacific-Antarctic Ridge itself.

'Myself, I believe I might have stayed longer, explored further and deeper, but the third member of my crew, young Ridgeway, had worked himself into such a state that to extend our visit was plainly out of the question. Ridgeway is a telepath, you see, which helps considerably in his work at Miskatonic, where he's a professor of psychology. Down there in the depths, however, with God-only-knows-what lurking behind those colossal stone blocks and hideously carved doors, well, he just couldn't take it. Without the star-stones there can be little doubt that he'd have been a mindless jelly in a matter of minutes. As it was he was hard enough put to keep from screaming. You remember what happened to poor Finch when he deliberately went deep into the mind of that horror beneath the Yorkshire Dales? This would have been just as bad, except Ridgeway was doing his best to keep the telepathic sendings of the Cthulhu spawn out of his mind, while yet trying to gauge their mood. And their mood was ugly, you may depend upon it.

'So finally we set out for the surface and poor Ridge-way, his face horribly screwed up, unable to speak coherently, sank into a corner of our craft. And then we saw them. The guardians of the tombs, the watchers through the immemorial night of the Cthulhu spawn, the most blasphemous shapes you could ever imagine! Sea-shoggoths, dozens of them, held back by our star-stones just as we once held off that smaller specimen from your boat *Seafree* at Henley. But these were giants of their type, de Marigny, the royal guards of the kings of evil. Mountains of protoplasmic filth floundered and wallowed in the depths like cosmic corks in the whirlpool of Andromeda! And even knowing that we were safe, still I was relieved that they kept their distance, and even more relieved when at last the keel of the *Surveyor* opened to receive us.

'Our excursion into the deeps had been brief, but we had seen enough. Since then, of course, the Foundation has – '

'Let me guess,' I quickly interrupted. 'A further series of atomic tests in the Pacific, particularly in that region?'

'No, no, out of the question. We're no longer allowed to toss atomics around willy-nilly, Henri. No, but there's more than one way to skin a cat. We simply peppered the entire submarine range with radioactives of a very short half-life, quite definitely sufficient to destroy most of the shoggoth cultures, but not of a duration to permanently damage other marine life. We couldn't hope to get all of the shoggoths, of course – there are too many millions of square miles of ocean. And it's very likely that we didn't get a single one of the Cthulhi within their incredible vaults and sepulchers, but certainly we must at the very least have raised all hell down there. Cthulhi, by the way, is our most recent name for the Cthulhu species itself, as opposed to the CCD in general. No, there was little chance of getting them all, and of course our actions were governed considerably by the laws of ecology; that is, we had no desire to sterilize the entire Pacific! And so, as I've said, we simply peppered that known range and other suspect places, doing our best at the same time to avoid harming areas of exotic marine life. But, in any case, there's not a great deal of life as we normally think of it at that depth.'

'Oh?' I showed my surprise. 'Three hundred fathoms?'

'Very little lives down there, de Marigny,' he insisted, 'and there's less the deeper you go. You have to remember that Johansen's island was only the veriest tip of a great peak. The rest of that particular city just went down and down and down, to regions where there could not possibly be any other life but . . . theirs. We calculate that there could be anything up to half a million square miles of city under the Pacific, and maybe as much again in other oceans! While we still don't dare let our telepaths play about too much with the Cthulhi, nevertheless we have reason to believe that there could be as many as five hundred individuals of that species imprisoned in the great deeps. Cthulhu, the prime member himself, the race-father of course, is only one of them, though in all probability he's the oldest, the most powerful and the nastiest. Possibly he was the very first of them to arrive on Earth when they seeped down from the stars, long before the soup of terrene life felt the first stab of generative sunlight.'

I heard the professor out, but in effect he had left me behind over a hundred words earlier. 'Half a million square miles.' I eventually repeated the statement that held me in so much awe. 'A whole damn continent of sunken tombs. But that's' – I made rough, rapid calculations – 'some five times the size of Great Britain!'

'My dear Henri,' the professor sighed, inclining his

head at me, 'much as it pains me to belittle your Great Britain, in the so much vaster scheme of things she's a tiny pebble in a very large pond. Any one of a hundred trenches in the floor of the Pacific could swallow her whole, without raising the merest ripple on the surface. We are talking about an ocean that covers tens of millions of square miles – hundreds of millions of cubic miles of water!'

I knew that he was right, of course, but nevertheless my mind boggled at the figures. I whistled softly and echoed him yet again: 'A pebble in a pond – Great Britain!'

4

Of the CCD in England

(From de Marigny's notebooks)

Then I turned my mind to other questions. 'While we're on the subject of Britain, what about Crow's warning that you'd need to take another look there? I remember he mentioned Silbury Hill, Stonehenge, Avebury, Hadrian's Wall and certain other places in the Severn Valley and the Cotswolds. Did you ever get around to them?'

Peaslee frowned. 'Yes, we did take another look at the British Isles, and we found various trouble spots that we'd somehow overlooked before. In the vicinity of Hadrian's Wall, for instance, not all that far out of Newcastle, there is a gate to an outer dimension, to one of the more remote prisons of the Elder Gods. This gate is, well, locked, I suppose you'd say. Lollius Urbicus in his *Frontier Garrison* tells us that it was opened at least once in his time, probably on a number of occasions. Urbicus wrote that circa 183 A.D., "the barbarians were wont to call out devils which they sent against us; they called them out from the air and beneath the ground, and one such which they sent killed half a centuria of soldiers before falling to their swords."

'Now what do you make of that? Plainly these barbarians Urbicus mentions must have been early British – Scottish? – dupes of the CCD. Not so rare or strange, really. There are records to show that the Ptetholites were similarly employed by the CCD thousands of years before Urbicus. They, too, were adept at calling up dark forces. Oh, yes, your witches and warlocks were real enough, Henri, but their magic was simply a vastly alien science.

'Titus Crow had a copy of *Frontier Garrison*, to say

nothing of certain far more conclusive and damnable *reliquiae* of those times; it surprises me he never mentioned the subject to you.'

'He did, come to think of it,' I answered with a frown. 'In fact I believe he wrote a short piece of macabre fiction around just such a creature as Urbicus mentions. Now what was the story called . . .?'

'*Yegg-ha's Realm*,' Peaslee promptly answered.

'Yegg-ha!' I snapped my fingers. 'Of course, I remember now. Titus once told me about a skeleton he'd dug up near Hadrian's Wall between Housesteads and Briddock – he was something of an archeologist on the quiet, you know – and he hinted that its owner must have been other than human. Yes, and I remember that he tied his discovery in with Lollius Urbicus, too.'

'Right,' Peaslee agreed, 'and he wrote his story pretty much as it must have happened, though of course he presented it as fiction. Even so it was pretty realistic. I've read it since and I can quite understand the stir it caused when it was first published in *Grotesque*. As for the bones he dug up, they were, as you say, other than human. Indeed, they were monstrous! Mind you, I never saw the actual remains, the great featureless skull or the *archaeopteryx*-like wing fragments. For some reason Crow destroyed them not too long after he found them, but he showed me photographs. Those pictures were definitely of something from . . . outside.'

'From what I know of Titus Crow,' I put in as Peaslee paused, 'it rather surprises me that he didn't go looking for this gate himself.'

'Ah, but he was much less well informed in those days, Henri. We all were. No matter, he had the right idea in the end. As I've said, it was because of what Crow told me that we did finally track this gate down. We actually found it, a door to an imperfect, synthetic universe, manufactured by the Elder Gods to imprison beings the Earth couldn't bear to harbor! We found it, and now we've locked it once and for all.

'Of course the thing was not physically a gate or a door; it was, rather, a place where our space-time continuum occasionally overlaps with another. The CCD knew this and telepathically fed the barbarians sufficient knowledge to allow them to open the way for the beings beyond. But the prisons of the Elder Gods are not so easily broken open. Only the minions, the underlings of those imprisoned powers of evil managed to break out, hideous but nevertheless flesh-and-blood creatures like Yegg-ha, while the actual inmates of the prison-dimension were obliged to remain in their timeless bondage. And that in turn leads us to the following questions: which of the Great Old Ones did Yegg-ha and his sort serve? And would it be possible for modern, rather more sophisticated dupes of the CCD to call them out?

'Of the latter question, there's little to fear of that now. We've put the most powerful locks we know of on that gate; we have literally welded it shut with our developing science, which was once the magic of the Elder Gods. If ever the gate is tampered with again, it will have to be by men who know as much as we do, and you may only find such men within the Foundation.'

'Don't forget, Wingate,' I reminded him, 'that there was once a so-called mad Arab, one Abdul Alhazred. *He* knew as much as we do, probably more.'

'Alhazred,' the professor answered, 'was the greatest dreamer, seer and mystic of all time. Aleister Crowley was a nobody by comparison, Dee a pewling babe, Eliphas Levi a mere dabbler and Merlin, if he ever existed, a first-year apprentice. Certainly there was an Alhazred; there was also a da Vinci, a Van Gogh and an Einstein. Such men occur once, and in the case of

Alhazred we may thank all that's merciful for that! And I think, too, that he really was more than a little mad. That way he would have been an ideal receiver for the telepathic sendings of the CCD. Did it ever occur to you to ask yourself just *where* Alhazred came by all of his occult knowledge in the first place?'

'No,' I answered truthfully, 'that's something I never thought about.'

'Hmm! Well, don't worry, there are thousands of questions that no man has yet thought to ask; questions are meaningless anyway until the answers are at least half known.'

'And have you decided or discovered which of the Great Old Ones Yegg-ha served?' I asked.

'Not for certain, but we have our ideas.

'One proposal is that this outer dimension is compartmented, that is, it is divided between various imprisoned beings. For example, we know that Yog-Sothoth is conterminous with all space and coexistent in all time, or at least we are told this in the old books and documents. But how can this be? And if it is so, why isn't he here now and ravaging? Well, we believe that he is only omnipresent insofar as his universe borders on both the time and space fabrics of our own continuum. The concept is that one edge of his place lies parallel with our time while another impinges upon our space. At that point near Hadrian's Wall the two universes overlap, and with a little help it is possible for certain of these lurkers at the threshold to step over to this side. You'll recall, of course, that Yog-Sothoth is actually known in the Cthulhu Cycle as the Lurker at the Threshold?'

'Yes, of course. Then it's Yog-Sothoth who bides his time behind the barriers of this synthetic universe?'

'Compartmented, I said, de Marigny. We believe that Yog-Sothoth is imprisoned in one compartment – but there are many others! What of Yibb-Tstll and Bugg-Shash, for example? They, too, are supposed to inhabit prisons in other dimensions. And Azathoth, before we discovered him to be simply the definition of a nuclear explosion, was also supposed to be omnipresent. Nor can we say that he is not, for certain nuclear theorists have it that the fabric of space-time is momentarily ruptured at the center of an atomic explosion. Who can say what horrors and nightmares man himself has visited upon the dwellers in yet more distant dimensions with his use of that lunatic weapon? This is one of the reasons why the Foundation supports the ban on all nuclear tests.

'However, I seem to have sidetracked a bit. I was answering your questions about the remaining CCD-inspired problems in Great Britain, wasn't I? Yes, well, after Hadrian's Wall we moved on to Salisbury Plain. With the permission of the British Archeological Society we checked Stonehenge out, as Crow had hinted we should. Nothing was there now, but there certainly was at one time in the remote past. We found star-stones there, deep in the earth, as old as any we've ever seen; in fact Schneider of archeology at Miskatonic believes that the monument itself was once in the shape of a great five-pointed star. Moreover, the *G'harne* Fragments bear him out. The outer points are long gone, but the hub of the thing remains. God only knows what horror the Elder Gods incarcerated down there that they required such a monumental tombstone to keep it down! The *G'harne* Fragments have it that when the early Cimmerians invaded Gunderland, some twenty thousand years ago, they destroyed the Great Elder Sign's pointed outer ramparts and thus set free the Being of the Great Star, and of course Gunderland covered that southern part of England in which Salisbury Plain lies. As to what became of the monster after that . . .' He shrugged.

'It may seem fantastic, but as for Stonehenge itself . . . well, despite what all your so-called experts may say to the contrary, the pyramids are the veriest babes of buildings when compared with Stonehenge!'

'You mentioned the *G'harne* Fragments,' I said, choosing that focal point from the mass of information the professor had presented. 'Poor Wendy-Smith once worked on those shards, didn't he? And Professor Gordon Walmsley of Goole, too. Do you mean to say that we finally have a translation? I thought the fragments were supposed to be unfathomable, that their ciphers and glyphs were quite beyond understanding?'

'Oh, yes!' he exclaimed. 'We have a translation, all right. In fact we know almost all there is to know about the fragments now, except perhaps how they survived the centuries. Mind you, the Foundation can't claim the first translation or even the second, not by any means. Wendy-Smith must have translated quite a bit – and all power to him for that – but we took our lead mainly from Walmsley. I don't know if you're familiar with his book, *Notes on Deciphering Codes, Cryptograms and Ancient Inscriptions*, but if you are you'll recognize Gordon Walmsley of Goole as the greatest ever in his field. Little good his knowledge did him in the end, though.'

'So Wendy-Smith and Titus Crow were wrong about Stonehenge, were they? The monument is safe then?'

'Yes, but we can't say the same for certain other parts of Great Britain, Silbury Hill, for example, and Avebury. These places harbor an ethereal taint going back untold centuries. You must understand, there is little physical about this rare brand of evil. It is as vague and ill-defined as a picture drawn on quicksilver, transient as the phases of the moon, but just as surely recurrent. There were days, weeks even, when our telepaths and mediums gave these places spotless certificates of safety, as it were. And there were other times when the telepathic and parapsychological ethers were crammed with presences that simply brooked no interference. It's no mere coincidence, I may tell you, that the Society of Metaphysics now has its headquarters in Tidworth; we intend to keep a close watch on the whole Salisbury Plain area.

'Similarly, we have agents permanently stationed in such towns as Marshfield, Nailsworth and Stow-on-the-Wold in the Cotswolds; and we are particularly interested in certain backwaters and centers of malign influence such as the decaying hamlets of Temphill and Goatswood along the Severn Valley.'

'The Cotswolds,' I repeated him, 'and Marshfield! Don't tell me that you've found something in Marshfield? Why, Crow's old confidante, Mother Quarry, used to live there. It was her letter which warned Crow of the danger when he and I had fallen into that last trap of the CCD. She had had one of her visions, I remember. The way Crow used to talk of her, I always saw her as some old charlatan.'

'Then you wronged her, Henri,' Peaslee said. 'Mother Eleanor Quarry is one of the best mediums we've yet discovered. We employ such people now as frequently as we used to employ our telepaths in your day. Often the two talents complement each other; they go hand in hand. Mother Quarry heads a very effective group in the Cotswolds, and she still lives in Marshfield at her old home, which is now the group headquarters.'

'You employ mediums,' I mused. 'Isn't that carrying things a bit far? I mean, the Foundation's operational center at Miskatonic is a world-renowned seat of learning and science. Surely metaphysics and the like has little in common with – '

'De Marigny, you've much to catch up with, I fear,' he said, cutting me off, 'and there seems to be a lot you've forgotten, too. Metaphysics has *everything* to do with our work! Why, didn't the Elder Gods themselves use the occult arts, and weren't those same occult arts their sciences? We're looking at all such sciences today, Henri, in as enlightened a way as our bigoted human minds will allow. At Miskatonic right now there are groups of specially talented people seriously studying such subjects as telekinesis and levitation . . . to say nothing of mere crystal-gazing, divination and necromancy. Why, certain of our seminars read like a shaman's thesaurus! Oh, yes, you've much to catch up on.'

'Well,' I answered, 'that's what you're here for, Wingate. You may as well tell me as much as you can, for I've damn little to tell you.'

'You remember nothing at all of your lost ten years, then?'

'Nothing.' I shook my head. 'Except . . .'

I made myself a little more comfortable on my pillows before continuing. 'Oh, it's nothing really, just that I have an idea.'

'Oh? Well, go on, Henri.'

'Yes, I have this . . . idea. You see, Wingate, I don't seem to have aged at all in ten years, not by a single day, and I can't help wondering if . . .'

'Yes?'

'Well, when Titus and I entered that great old clock, when we fled Blowne House before Ithaqua's air elementals could get in at us, I remember Crow saying something about a trip into time, a journey into the future.' I paused.

'That is very interesting, Henri,' Peaslee said, his old eyes wide and staring at me intently. 'Go on.'

'I was wondering if . . . if perhaps Crow had indeed managed to pilot his craft into time, into the future, and if I – '

49

'If you had fallen overboard, as it were, before he got his ship properly out of port?'

'Yes, something like that,' I answered.

'Of course it's possible,' the professor told me after a moment's silence, 'and it would certainly explain why you haven't aged, to say nothing of your amnesia. How might a man remember ten years that never happened?'

'And you don't find the concept of time-travel too fantastic?'

'Not at all, Henri. I've seen far too much of the so-called fantastic to be awed by mere concepts. And after all, we're all time-travelers when you think about it.'

'Eh? How do you mean?'

'Why, aren't we all traveling into the future right now? Of course we are, except that we're traveling at a speed of only one second per second. From what you've told me, I'm beginning to believe that Titus Crow found a way to travel faster, that's all.'

After a while I said, 'Matron Emily tells me that when I was taken off the buoy at Purfleet I didn't even need a shave. Titus and I, we must have journeyed those ten years overnight! And since then, since my return, it's been almost two months. How far into tomorrow, then, is Titus Crow right now?'

Peaslee turned his suddenly troubled face away. 'That's something we may never know, Henri. There's still hope, of course. There will always be hope, but – '

'I know,' I said, and abruptly there passed before my mind's eye a scene remembered from a dream, of a coffin-shaped meteor plunging endlessly through nightmare vastnesses of space and time. 'I know . . .'

5

Cthulhu's Cosmic Miscegenation

(From de Marigny's notebooks)

For a long while we were silent. Then, deliberately changing the subject and entering into a long, informative narrative, Peaslee rapidly brought me up to date on all of the more recent successes of the Wilmarth Foundation – its successes, and a few of its failures. It would take too long to detail the professor's complete discourse, and in any case I doubt if my memory is up to it, but I can at least outline a few of the things that he revealed to me.

For instance, he talked about the translation of the *G'harne* Fragments and the great boost that those ancient, decaying shards had provided to the impetus of the Wilmarth Foundation. He talked about the submarine destruction of Deep Gell-Ho and its shoggoth inhabitants, of the collapse of rotting Kingsport on the New England coast and the fact that the gray sea was now eating away at certain previously unsuspected caverns of maggoty loathsomeness and ages-old decay. He talked of Lh'yib, mentioning what men had done to Ib's sister city beneath the Yorkshire Moors in lowered tones; then he brightened as he related the advances made against blue-lighted K'n-Yan, red-lighted Yoth, and Black N'kai. I remember, too, that he mentioned a certain Moon Bog of Irish myth and legend, in dark connection with the so-called nameless city of olden Turkistan.

Much of what I heard was completely new to me, only recently fathomed or discovered by the Foundation, so that I thrilled to such *outré* names as Sunken Yatta-Uc, a city drowned in the forgotten inner cone of Titicaca's volcano; Doomed Arkan Tengri, a derelict aerie of mist-obscured peaks and icy pinnacles in the white wastes south of the Kunlun Mountains; and the Jidhauas, savage nomads of Mongolia's Gobi Desert and worshipers of Shudde-M'ell.

All of these things were fascinating to me, but one subject in particular that Peaslee touched upon toward the end of his long narrative completely absorbed me. It was in connection with Shub-Niggurath, yet another weird name from the Cthulhu Cycle of myth. Yes, Shub-Niggurath, 'the black goat of the woods with a thousand young', occasionally called the Ram with a Thousand Ewes or, as Peaslee preferred to refer to the mythological figure, Cthulhu's Cosmic Miscegenation!

I knew that previously Shub-Niggurath had been looked upon as a symbol of fertility, a being locked away with the CCD by the Elder Gods, and that in the *Necronomicon* it was recorded that 'he shall come forth in all his (her?) hideousness when again the Great Old Ones are freed to walk the world as once they walked long ago.' Recently, however, the Wilmarth Foundation had interpreted all of this somewhat differently. Students of the Cthulhu Cycle pantheon had finally explained away certain conflicting statements as to Shub-Niggurath's sexual characteristics. For an example of the latter ambiguities, the Ram with a Thousand Ewes was often mentioned as being the *wife* of Hastur; and, even more confusingly, in the *Cthaat Aquadingen* Shub-Niggurath is referred to as 'Father & Mother of all Abominations, & of Others worse yet which will not be until ye Latter Times.'

Father *and* mother . . .?

The answer, Peaslee told me, is simply that Shub-Niggurath is the greatest fertility symbol of all, and in fact much more than a mere symbol. He/she is nothing less

52

than the power of miscegenation itself, amazingly inherent in the majority of the CCD. He/she is their ability to mate with the daughters of Adam and the sons of Eve, and with others of this wide universe somewhat less human.

Thus, along with Azathoth and Nyarlathotep, Peaslee had relegated Shub-Niggurath, too, to a symbol of power proper as opposed to a physical, alien being. And of that monstrous cosmic miscegenation of the CCD the professor had much to say. He talked of the unthinkable consequences and results of the matings of them with human beings, mentioning that such vague reports as are occasionally heard of blasphemous offspring are often known to have direct links with the CCD. The Foundation, he went on, had collected and collated many valuable and damning data, but he feared that only the surface had been scratched.

From a host of hideous cases he quoted a few facts. He mentioned the twins born to an unmarried illiterate albino woman at Dunwich in north-central Massachusetts; the loathsome *serpentes* children whose mother hacked her husband to death in a lunatic fit nine months before her family was – spawned? – in Caddo County, Oklahoma; the Irish half-wit woman who gave birth to a boy with stubby, vestigial wings after her medium mother had been plagued with nightmares of a flying demon, and so on. The cases were seemingly endless.

I remember having stopped Peaslee at about that point in his narrative to question him with regard to his term Cthulhu's Cosmic Miscegenation: wasn't 'cosmic' just a trifle ambiguous or superfluous? It was then that he told me what little he knew of a certain shadowy intelligence deep in the sub-oceanic vaults of Y'ha-nthlei beyond Devil Reef. Basically what he said was that man was not alone in intelligence in the universe, and that the CCD had not confined their spawnings to human flesh and blood alone.

He had said more or less the same thing before, but now he was more explicit.

Before the Great Uprising, Peaslee told me, Cthulhu himself fathered three sons 'upon a female sentience from remote, ultra-telluric Xoth, the dim green double sun that glitters like a dæmonic eye in the blacknesses beyond Abbith . . .' This quote is taken from the *Ponape Scripture* which, according to Peaslee, is a primal document brought back from the Isle of Ponape by an Arkham merchant-skipper, Captain Abner Ezekiel Hoag, in about 1734. Circulated privately, the manuscript finally ended up in the Kester Library in Salem, where the Wilmarth Foundation first became interested in it.

From that book and one or two others, particularly the *Zanthu Tablets*, the Foundation had culled most of its knowledge with regard to Cthulhu's progeny, before setting themselves to the task of verifying or condemning such accounts. Considering the history of the *Zanthu Tablets*, it is not really surprising that the Foundation had only looked at that source seriously in comparatively recent years. Purported to be the work of a prehistoric Asian shaman or wizard, the tablets were allegedly discovered by Professor Harold Hadley Copeland in Zanthu's stone tomb in 1913, and a translation was published by Copeland three years later in a quickly suppressed brochure of 'fragmentary and conjectural content, seeming deliberately contrived to undermine all recognized authorities, especially science and theology.'

Well, people had called Sir Amery Wendy-Smith a madman, and they had scorned Gordon Walmsley of Goole and many others whose work was later to prove invaluable to the Wilmarth Foundation, and the Foundation had learned a lesson from such examples. After a number of years of hard work, Peaslee's researchers had been able to state quite conclusively that both the *Ponape Scripture* and the *Zanthu Tablets* were works which, along with those other monstrous books passed down the ages, had a firm foundation in fact and unthinkably distant prehistory.

This is what was finally brought to light: that until such evidence was discovered to suggest otherwise, it must be accepted that Cthulhu *had* fathered three miscegenetic sons upon an extraterrestrial being, and that these creatures were still mercifully imprisoned in black and shrieking abysses of earth.

The three sons were: Ghatanothoa, 'the monster on the mount', interred in crypts beneath a primal mountain, now lost in depths of ocean at the southern edge of the southeastern Pacific Plateau, about a thousand miles south of Easter Island; Ythogtha, 'the abomination in the abyss', lying chained by the Elder Sign in Yhe, which location the Foundation has not yet pinpointed; and Zoth-Ommog, 'the dweller in the deep', dreaming insanely in unfathomed gulfs off Ponape. There were three sons . . . *and a daughter*!

Cthylla was her name, the Secret Seed of Cthulhu. Her presence had been carefully edited from all the ancient texts except in the most oblique references; the minions of the CCD had even removed her likeness from the Columns of Geph in the coastal jungles of Liberia before attempting to destroy the columns themselves, to keep word of the Secret One safe. Cthylla, a name Von Junzt was heard to scream out in supplication just once, before dying in 1840 in a locked and bolted Dusseldorf chamber with the marks of taloned fingers upon his throat; a name Alexis Ladeau, Von Junzt's closest friend, wrote upon a stone floor in tottering letters of his own life's blood after

55

reading certain sections of his friend's insane *Unaussprechlichen Kulten*. He had burned the book to ashes before slicing his throat through with a razor. Cthylla, of whose existence no other trace, no single clue remains extant in any form recognizable to mundane mankind, Cthylla *nevertheless exists and is worshiped in the world today*!

Knowing in the end that he was beaten by the Elder Gods, and seeing that his lore would be handed down through the æons by his worshipers and that eventually other rulers of Earth and the universe might try to seek him out and destroy him, Cthulhu was determined not to let his daughter, his secret spawn, fall into any such peril. Whatever Cthulhu's own future fate, his seed must be protected. The existence of his sons, too, he had tried to obscure; but his daughter, who would be the spawn-mother of distantly future generations, her concealment *must* be complete . . .

This was no mere fatherly concern for his child, as one might expect in a human being; Cthulhu was in no way human, knowing nothing of emotions as man might understand such. So where, then, did he get this desire to provide safety in obscurity for his daughter? Certain rites telepathically received and recorded by Foundation telepaths in Innsmouth held the abominable answer.

In 1975, in fact during the last week of October of that year, particularly Halloween itself, a hideous mental babble, emanating from tremendous depths beneath the bed of the gulf beyond Devil Reef, was picked up by a special team 'vacationing' in Innsmouth. Unaware that they were listening in on rites lost in every other instance in unbelievable antiquity, the Foundation people recorded the oft-repeated liturgies, discovering them to be the bicentennial incantations of Mother Hydra and Father Dagon to Cthylla, daughter of Cthulhu. They perceived that these ancient rituals had last been practiced in 1775; then, to mark the occasion, Dagon and his Deep Ones had taken hold on the minds of certain Innsmouth seafarers, thus influencing their participation in dark Polynesian religions and the eventual reunion of an alliance lost before the first coelacanth swam in Earth's seas – the liaison between the tomb-guarding Deep Ones of the Pacific and their kin in Y'ha-nthlei, whose nether vaults held dreaming Cthylla!

The Deep Ones were dead and gone now, those semi-human hosts of Y'ha-nthlei, and all the shoggoths of that sunken city with them, wiped out to the last by the Wilmarth Foundation during a second purging of Innsmouth in 1974; but deeper still beneath the bed of the gulf, in vaults which man might never have hoped to guess at, there, tended by faithful Hydra and ministered by Dagon, there Cthylla slumbers yet, awaiting . . . what?

Yet again, relying upon their telepathic and psychic fraternities, the Foundation's researchers think they have discovered the answer.

It all has to do with Cthulhu's enigmatic symbol-statement: '*Ph'nglui mglw'nafh Cthulhu R'lyeh wgah'nagl*,' which, translated from the R'lyehan, reads: 'In his house at R'lyeh dead Cthulhu waits dreaming,' and in that conjectural couplet from Alhazred's *Necronomicon:*

That is not dead which can eternal lie,
And with strange æons even death may die.

That Alhazred, that great dreamer and mystic, plucked the latter lines direct from the minds of the Cthulhi can no longer be doubted, for it is known now that there is a second couplet, used in conjunction with the first in

Cthylla's rites; and these further lines may be interpreted as follows:

> The dreamer dying faces death with scorn,
> And in his seed will rise again reborn!

Cthulhu the phoenix, rising up from the ashes of his own destruction in the spawn of his daughter's darkling womb . . . *reincarnation*!

To bear out this chilling concept, by no means far-fetched in the light of what is already known of the CCD and particularly of Cthulhu, the Foundation's researchers have returned again to Alhazred in yet another cryptic passage from the rarest *Al Azif* of all:

'Tis a veritable & attestable Fact, that between certain related Persons there exists a Bond more powerful than the strongest Ties of Flesh & Family, whereby one such Person may be *aware* of all the Trials & Pleasures of the other, yea, even to experiencing the Pains or Passions of one far distant; & further, there are those whose Skills in such Matters are aided by forbidden Knowledge or Intercourse through dark Magic with Spirits & Beings of outside Spheres. Of the latter, I have sought them out, both Men & Women, & upon Examination have in all Cases discovered them to be Users of Divination, Observers of Times, Enchanters, Witches, Charmers or Necromancers. All claimed to work their Wonders through Intercourse with dead & departed Spirits, but I fear that often such Spirits were evil Angels, the Messengers of the Dark One & yet more ancient Evils. Indeed, among them were some whose Powers were prodigious, who might at Will *inhabit* the Body of another, even at a great Distance & against the Will & often unbeknown to the Sufferer of such Outrage.

Moreover, I have dreamed it that of the aforementioned most ancient of Evils, there is *One* which slumbers in Deeps unsounded so nearly Immortal that Life & Death are one to *Him*. Being ultimately corrupt, *He* fears Death's Corruption not, but when true Death draws nigh will prepare Himself until, fleeing *His* ancient Flesh, *His* Spirit will plumb Times-to-come

& there cleave unto Flesh of *His* Flesh, & all the Sins of this Great Father shall be visited upon *His* Child's Child. I have dreamed it, & my Dreams have been *His* Dreams who is the greatest Dreamer of all . . .

Cthulhu, then would be reincarnated in the womb of his daughter, to be reborn as her child. To Dagon would go the honor of fathering this blasphemy, Hydra would be nurse and handmaiden, Cthylla herself would raise the hybrid horror with Cthulhu's monstrous mind and psyche. Then in the waxing strength of a young adult – pointless, horrible even to conjecture what *characteristics* this thing might have! – he could again commence the influencing of men's minds, and this time from a location very close indeed to vast centers of human life.

Cthulhu, alert again, powerful, would be sending out his hellish dreams from the deeps beneath Devil Reef, *unsuspected* – for of course officially he would be dead!

Having told me so much, even though I pressed him for further details, Peaslee would say no more on the subject of Cthulhu's reincarnation. It seemed to me that there was more he could have told me, certainly, but that it was of such importance and of so ultimately secret a nature that he simply dared not mention it, not even to me. Furthermore I could see that he was biting his tongue, presumably for having said too much already. In any case, the lateness of the hour saved him from any further embarrassment: he used it as an excuse to take his departure.

59

Part Two

1

Of Visions and Visits

(From de Marigny's notebooks)

Less than a week later Peaslee visited me again, this time to wish me luck for the future and to say farewell for the time being. There was work waiting for him in America. Before he left we talked of Titus Crow once more and then, finally, the old man asked me if I had any plans with regard to the Wilmarth Foundation. Did I want to come back into the organization? If so, there would always be a place for me. I thanked him but turned his offer down. I had my own interests, my own discoveries to make in this 'new world'.

It was only after a further period of six weeks in the hospital, with at least half of that time taken up with physiotherapy, the retraining of my poor, unaccustomed muscles, that I was finally allowed to sign myself out and go my way as a free man. In fact the last few weeks had seemed like a sort of imprisonment, and I was very glad when I was at last able to get back into the world, albeit a world with which I was greatly out of touch.

During those frustrating weeks there had been one regular visitor at the hospital, however, a lady whose presence helped combat the tedium of waiting out my time until the doctors would give me a clean bill of health: my dear old part-time housekeeper, Mrs Adams, who could only ever speak of Titus Crow as 'that dreadful Crow person', for in her eyes Titus had always been to blame for dragging me into whatever adventures overtook us. My hospital, I had discovered, was on the outskirts of

Aylesbury; Mrs Adams, when she finally knew my where-abouts, traveled up daily from London just to spend an hour or so with me. She had kept my place going all this time, visiting the house twice a week for ten long years in my absence. As she herself put it: 'I knowed you'd be back sooners-laters, Mr 'Enri, sir.' And now, though I was still using a walking stick, now I *was* back.

Fortunately I had all but dissolved my small but lucrative antique business some time after joining the Foundation, and so very little had wanted or wasted for my absence. I intended now to revive my lifetime interest in beautiful old books, pottery and furniture, but first I would spend a few days simply getting used to the feel and atmosphere of my old home again.

While the house itself was the same as ever, the district had seemed to change enormously. 'Progress', as they call it, waits for no man – not even a time-traveler. Indeed, *especially* not a time-traveler! Out walking in a neck of the city I'd once considered my own, it was as if I trod the streets of some strange, foreign place. New buildings, alleys, posters; a well-remembered old cinema had been replaced by a shopping arcade; even the faces were different, where shops I'd once used had now passed into new hands or disappeared completely, demolished. The underground was the same, and yet was not the same, but that didn't bother me much: its system had always been beyond my comprehension. And in all truth I had not used the tube since first learning of the existence of the burrowers beneath; and because of them, despite all Peaslee's assurances, I did not intend to use it again . . .

Not that I ventured far from my house during those first few weeks out of the hospital. I did not, except to make one very special trip to Leonard's-Walk Heath late in November. Blowne House, Crow's strange, foreboding bungalow retreat, had once sprawled on the heath. All I could find now was a shattered ruin, a drab and desolate skeleton of a house. The bricks of the old chimney were crumbling onto rotten floorboards; the creepers of wild brambles made slow but steady incursions throughout the surrounding gardens; nettles grew in threatening clumps along the drive. In another five or six years it would almost seem as if the place had never been . . .

And it was there, standing in those ruins with my nostrils pricking in painful nostalgia, lost in memories of days spent with Crow in arcane study and esoteric discussion, it was there that I experienced for the first time during waking hours a dizzying assault on my senses which was to occur ever more frequently during the following weeks. As the world started to spin around me and the gray November sky turned black, I hastily sat down on the old, bare floorboards with my back to the base of the crumbling chimney. No sooner was I seated than I experienced a wild rushing sensation, a dizzy tumbling as if I had fallen from some primal cliff into the blackness of a pit that reached down to the Earth's very core. I seemed to fall for ages, until I began to think that the sickening descent would never end. It was altogether a nauseating, stomach-wrenching, mind-numbing experience; and yet, as I sensed the approaching end or climax of this nightmare fall, even as my senses began to right themselves, I knew that what was occurring was nothing new to me. I had known this before, but only in dreams.

Well, dream or developing psychosis or whatever it was, I finally recognized my surroundings. Whereas a moment before I had seemed to whirl and plummet in blackest depths, now in a mere instant my numbed senses had become super-sensitive. I smelled the strange winds that roar between the worlds, bearing the odors of darkling planets and the souls of sundered stars; I felt about me the emptiness of remote and infinite vacuums of space, and their coldness; and I saw, blazing on a panoply of jet, unknown constellations and nameless nebulæ stretching out and away through the light-years into unthinkable abysses of space. Finally, winging through the nearer voids, I spied that enigmatic coffin shape recognized of old, and again, as in delirious dreams, I heard my lost friend's voice.

He made no new demands that I follow him, but as on a previous occasion simply called out to an empty void: 'Where are you, de Marigny? Where are you?'

'Here, Titus!' I yelled in spontaneous response, hearing nothing of my own voice above the roar of the wind blowing between the worlds. '*Here!*' I screamed again, at which the great clock seemed to swing a little, hesitantly turning toward me in its hurtling flight across the heavens. And I heard Crow's answering cry ringing out in amazed exultation:

'De Marigny! Where? *Where are you?*'

I would have answered again at once; but then, swelling out of the blackness in the wake of Crow's weird craft – bloating up in a green and rotten glow of corruption, filling my entire view in an instant and reaching with slimy tentacles – there came a shape . . . the shape of utmost lunacy!

Cthulhu! I knew him at once. Who could mistake him?

First the tentacles, seeming to reach back infinitely to the face from which they sprang; and that face itself, evil rampant, express and implied in a single glance; and to the rear, dwindling away in distant abysses of the void, the vast arched wings supporting an impossibly bloated body. Cthulhu, even now reaching to wrap fearsome face-tendrils about the toy coffin-ship!

'*Look out!*' I finally managed to scream, flinging my hands up before my eyes . . .

. . . And then I again felt the stomach-wrenching

sensation of falling as from a vast, immeasurable height, and all my senses fought for stability in the headlong rush of my psyche back to its home in material flesh.

Cold daylight rushed in upon my startled eyes. The dampness of rotting floorboards touched me through my clothes and my back felt the hard chimney bricks behind me.

Strangely fatigued by an experience which could hardly be called physical, I eventually forced myself to my feet and left the ruins of Blowne House. But I could not shut out of my mind that hideous vision of Cthulhu pursuing Crow's clock, a vastly loathsome bulk against a background of leering stars and nighted nebulæ. Thus I went my way oppressed by a gloom springing not alone of the bleak November skies, a gloom which seemed to weigh tangibly upon my shoulders.

Some few weeks later these terrible attacks had become so frequent – each one occurring without the slightest warning – that it was almost unbearable. I had just about made up my mind to see a doctor, a psychiatrist, frankly, about the problem. Then, just ten days before Christmas, I received a most disturbing, indeed an astounding communication. Having slept late on that particular morning, I found this letter waiting for me with my morning newspaper:

Marshfield

Dear Mr de Marigny –

Do please make yourself available at home on the afternoon of the 16th; I shall be traveling down to see you. I should get into London about 3 P.M. – and no need to meet me, I'll know where to find you. I may come by car. *And please, no mention of this to anyone from the Foundation*. As you know, I am just as much a member of that organization now as you yourself were ten years ago – I mention this simply to assure you that my visit goes in no way against our own and the Foundation's mutual interests – but I want to talk to you about Titus Crow, and I have reason to believe that he would not want what I have to tell you to go any further.

Until we meet then,
Sincerely,
Eleanor Quarry

P.S. Do not look for me in the telephone book. I have no telephone. I abhor the things.

EQ

Upon first reading this completely cryptic note my mind simply went blank; I frankly did not know how to react. Only after a second hurried reading did the implications begin to dawn on me, and then a whole host of suddenly galvanized emotions brought me quickly to what must have been a sort of mental hysteria.

Eleanor Quarry, 'Mother' Quarry, was the medium whose timely letter had warned Titus Crow of the CCD's insidious trap ten years earlier; it had sent us fleeing for our lives from stricken, doomed Blowne House in the doubtful confines of an alien time machine whose shape was that of a hideous grandfather clock. While I had never met her, I had always looked upon her peculiar psychic practices very dubiously, despite the fact that Titus Crow had seemed to have the utmost faith in her. Anyway, here she was, this woman, as good as telling me that Crow was alive, almost implying that she had been in communication with him, and that the substance of that communication was for my ears only!

Well, what was I to make of it? My mind flew in several directions at once, quite uselessly, completely out of control. Questions piled themselves up in my head, unanswered but demanding attention, whirling madly about in my mind until I had to force myself to sit down and think the problem out as calmly as possible.

If Crow *was* alive, where was he now, and why the secrecy? Could it be, perhaps, that he was in some terrible peril, maybe even a prisoner of the CCD? No, that last seemed out of the question. The CCD would never hold Titus Crow a prisoner; they would simply kill him out of hand as soon as the opportunity presented itself. He had been far too dangerous to their cause, a thorn in their sides. So had I, for that matter.

But just think of it – Titus Crow alive!

My mood leaped from one of worried tribulation to wild speculation. *Crow alive!* Could it really be? Had we indeed traveled into time, he and I, and was that really the reason behind my apparent loss of ten years? And had he then gone on into the future while, incapable of understanding the time-clock's principles, I had fallen overboard almost at the onset of our flight?

On the other hand, why was it important that he now remain incognito, as it were? Again my spirits tumbled. How much confidence could I place in this woman, this Eleanor Quarry? And could this possibly be yet another ploy of the CCD? I did not care at all for the woman's demand that I should not mention her proposed visit to anyone from the Foundation.

But the sixteenth! Why, that was tomorrow, and today was already well into the afternoon. In just twenty-four hours I would know as much as there was to know of this mystery. All my questions would be answered . . . but it would certainly be the longest twenty-four hours I had ever known in my life . . .

2

Mother Quarry

(From de Marigny's notebooks)

The knocking at my door brought me bolt upright in my chair, startling me from unquiet but mercifully unremembered dreams. A glance at my watch showed me that it was three P.M. exactly.

I realized what had happened: finally exhausted, having paced the floors of my house all through the previous evening and night, mentally juggling with the infinite possibilities in connection with Eleanor Quarry's visit, I must have fallen asleep right after an early lunch. And now, now here she was and I was still unshaved, blinking the sleep from my eyes, clutching my star-stone tightly in one hand for fear it was *not* Eleanor Quarry at the door at all but something else.

Not knowing what to expect, still half asleep, I went to the door. The knocking came again, more decisively, and a voice, not loud but penetrating the door quite clearly called, 'Mr de Marigny, I am *not* a shoggoth, I assure you, so do please open up and let me in!' That voice had the instant effect of dispelling most of my doubts and fears, so that I immediately threw open the door.

Eleanor Quarry was tiny and old, elegant in a smartly modern matching jacket and skirt; she was gray-haired, with gray unfaded eyes that twinkled despite their age through ancient pince-nez glasses. She took my hand firmly and pumped it as I stepped aside to let her in.

'I'm Eleanor Quarry,' she said, making the introduction formal, leading the way to my study as though she had lived in my house all her life, 'but please call me Mother. Everybody does. And do please stop thinking of me as an old charlatan. I am a perfectly respectable, quite genuinely psychic person.'

'I can assure you, er, Mother, that I – ' I began.

She cut me off. 'And don't lie, young man. You've always considered me to be a charlatan, I know you have. Doubtless it's due to the way that rascal Titus Crow has spoken of me. And yet he always had more than a fair share of the old sixth sense himself, you know.'

'Er, yes, indeed he had,' I answered, beginning to feel more at ease. In my study she turned to face me, smiling when she saw the star-stone in my hand.

'I wear mine around my neck,' she leaned forward to whisper, a mock frown drawing her eyebrows together.

'Oh! Er, I just – '

'No need to explain.' She smiled, drawing up a golden chain from her bosom. At the end of the chain a star-stone dangled. 'A damned uncomfortable thing,' she remarked, 'and yet very comforting, too, in its way.'

My last doubts were finally dispelled. I smiled at my visitor and rubbed ruefully at the stubble on my chin. 'I had intended to shave before you arrived,' I started to explain, 'but – '

'No, no, you were right to have a little nap,' she said, cutting me off yet again. 'No doubt your mind is all the fresher for it, and that's important over all, that your mind be fresh, I mean. Anyway, I like my men rugged!'

She began to laugh and I joined in, but I sobered quickly as I thought back over the preceding few minutes to some of the rather weird correct guesses this lady had made. She had been more or less right when she hinted that perhaps I pictured something other than a human knocking on my door; she had been right to accuse me of believing her an old fraud (though I was already changing my mind) and finally she had correctly – to my confusion and embarrassment – named me a liar, albeit a white one.

Perhaps she was a fraud even now, but if so then she was a very clever one.

'I *am* psychic, Mr de Marigny,' she said, breaking into my thoughts, 'though in the main my powers should really be relegated to the lower levels of ESP, and even there they are limited. Primarily I am telepathic, a one-way receiver, a mind reader. If I could only *project* as well . . . ah, but then Titus Crow wouldn't need you!'

So fascinated had I become with this remarkable old woman that I had almost forgotten the purpose of her visit. 'Titus!' I gasped, suddenly remembering. 'Titus Crow! But is he . . .?'

'Alive?' She raised her eyebrows. 'Oh, yes, he is alive. He is close, too, and yet far away. Frankly, I do not understand as much as I would like to understand. Although I have received his messages, I could not tell where they originated. I mean that, well, for one thing, I don't believe him to be here on this planet.'

She stared at me for a moment as if waiting for some reaction, then nodded. 'Good. You don't find what I just said strange, so obviously I must be on the right track. You know more of his situation than I. No, Titus Crow is not on Earth, and yet he is distant in more than one sense, almost as though – '

'As though,' I finished it for her, 'he were also remote in time?'

Her mouth fell open and her eyes widened even as I spoke the words. Obviously she had read my thought an instant before I voiced it. 'But that is exactly it!' she cried. 'It surprises me I didn't think of it that way myself.'

'Oh?' I said. 'I hardly find it surprising. Time-travel is something out of science fiction, surely? Not something for merely mundane speculation.'

'And what of telepathy?' she returned, smiling.

I had to allow her that. 'It's my belief, at any rate,' I

continued, 'that Titus is indeed lost in time. Peaslee and I have talked about it; the professor agrees with me. But I suppose I'd better tell you the whole story. That way perhaps – '

'No need,' she quickly answered, stretching out a trembling hand to touch my forehead, 'simply let yourself think back on it.'

Her eyes clouded over and she swayed. Belatedly remembering my manners I steadied her and sat her down in a chair, and all the while her cool, trembling hand rested upon my forehead. Finally her eyes brightened and she withdrew her hand.

'So that is how it was,' she said. 'That old clock of his. Until now I had not known . . .'

Now it was my turn to express surprise. I had been on the point of telling her about Crow's departure from Blowne House into time, but should that really have been necessary? Surely, as a member of the Foundation . . .? Her last statement, if she was all she made out to be, struck me as being more than peculiar. 'But that's strange,' I said. 'I should have thought that you, of all people, would be the very one to know such things?'

She looked at me searchingly, questioningly for a moment, and then her eyebrows knitted in a frown of displeasure. 'I said I can receive the thoughts of others, young man, not that I *steal* them. I would not dream of looking into the mind of another uninvited either by word or gesture. That would be a hideous curiosity. I would no sooner do that than enter another's house unbidden or read another's diary.'

'But when you first knocked at my door – ' I started to protest.

'Do you think you are the only one who fears the CCD?' she quickly asked. 'When I came to your house I instinctively checked that it was a man waiting for me behind the door. I merely brushed your mind, sufficiently to read your own fear.'

'But it's been ten years since we departed. Surely, as a member of the Foundation, and as a personal friend of Titus Crow you – '

'About the Wilmarth Foundation,' she answered. 'I accept what I'm told; I don't probe where I'm unwelcome. This is an unspoken rule among all telepaths who work for the Foundation. If Peaslee had wanted to tell me about you and Titus he would have done so. I respect his leadership and where work is concerned I only interest myself in those projects and experiments which he authorizes. This does not mean, however, that the Foundation governs me utterly; on the contrary, I retain my own private interests. I have my own friends and I am loyal to them, as I hope they are to me. Titus Crow has been a friend for many years.'

'And you say that he has . . . contacted you?'

'He has, yes, and now that I know his predicament I am sure that I was right to come and see you. You were correct, he is lost in space and time, trying to find his way home. He is like a sailor of the old times, lost on alien seas, compass gone and the stars unreadable. I think you have some link between you, you and Titus, some sense perhaps akin to ESP, by which you feel for each other without being truly telepathic. He needs to home in on you, Mr de Marigny. He wants you to hold out a light in the darkness, one that he can follow back to his own time and space.'

I thought about what she had said for a moment, trying hard to understand. 'Are there no others with better qualifications?' I finally asked. 'Surely there are telepaths within the Foundation who – '

'But he does not want the Foundation to know,' she answered. 'And in any case, this link between you two is not truly telepathic. It is something grown of long and close friendship, closer even than my own with Titus. Are you not aware of this psychic affinity? Have you not experienced anything of it before?'

I nodded. 'At the very start of all this, when Titus first discovered the burrowers, I was in Paris. Suddenly I had to get back to England. I came home and I knew as soon as I found Crow's letter waiting for me that somehow he had unconsciously called me back. Since then the occasion has not arisen when – '

'Well, now he is calling you again.' She nodded decisively. 'This time consciously, knowing what he is about. Has it not been apparent to you? Has there been no hint that he has tried to contact you? No phenomena, dreams perhaps, or – '

'*Dreams!*' I cried, snapping my fingers. 'There have been the most terrifying dreams, of Crow in his great coffin of a clock, hurtling through endless alien universes and crying out to me, searching for me, *wanting to know where I* – ' Finally the last piece of the puzzle had dropped into place. 'Good Lord! And I thought I needed a psychiatrist!'

I thought about it for a moment longer before slapping my thigh with an angry hand. 'But why the devil haven't I realized before just what the dreams meant?'

'The devil indeed,' she answered me, her eyes narrowing. 'It occurs to me that you may well, though perhaps inadvertently, have answered your own question. Perhaps Peaslee told you that for some time now there's been a decided slacking off of specific CCD interference? While the telepathic output of the CCD has not noticeably lessened, for some time they have not been directing their hatred at any recognizable target, neither at specific groups nor any individuals that we have been able to discover. It has been almost as though Cthulhu were shielding his damned dreams from the Foundation, as though he were intent upon matters very important to him and that he feared the Foundation's interference. Could it be, I wonder, that Cthulhu and the other prime members of the CCD are expending this awful mental energy of theirs in an attempt to – '

'To foul Crow's return to Earth?'

'I wonder,' she answered.

'And my failure to realize that Crow needed my help, you see that also as evidence of CCD interference?'

'It's possible, but I don't think that they're aiming at you in particular. If that were so the Foundation would soon know about it. On the other hand, one of our top psychics at Miskatonic has a theory that the CCD have effectively thrown a mental belt about the whole world, a belt so tenuous as to be telepathically undetectable! And if such is the case, well, there must be a purpose behind it.'

'Titus Crow is only one man,' I said. 'Would his attempting a return out of time and space warrant such furtive CCD activity? I know that he's provided them with a bit of a headache from time to time, but . . .'

'That would rather depend upon where he's been, I think,' she answered. 'And what he's seen and done. Who knows what knowledge he may be bringing back with him?'

After a moment's thought I shrugged my shoulders impatiently. 'This is all very well, but mere speculation will get us nowhere. The only way to make anything concrete out of all this is to get Crow back here. You said he needed me to . . . to "hold out a light" for him or some such. What did you mean by that?'

'Only that you must *think* of him,' she immediately answered. 'Never let him out of your thoughts, not even for a moment. We know that you are not truly telepathic,

76

Mr de Marigny, but obviously there is this . . . this *something* between you two, like the psychic link between Siamese twins. He seeks the way home, into safe harbor, and you must be the lighthouse by which he pilots his ship.'

I nodded. 'Come to think of it, the dreams only come to me when he is on my mind, when I am suddenly reminded of him or when he is strong in my thoughts.'

'Yes,' she answered. 'That would be when your psychic contact with him is at its most powerful.'

I turned to her in consternation. 'But Cthulhu himself often features in these dreams of mine. I see the monster, reaching out for Crow's plummeting coffin-clock, face-tentacles lashing through black light-years of space and infinite abysses of time to fasten upon the vessel, reaching back to a bloated body that fills the cosmos with its evil . . . Would Titus Crow send me dreams such as these?'

'No, I don't suppose he would, but don't forget that he is not alone in his ability to send dreams! Cthulhu might certainly superimpose his own sendings on top of those of Titus. Why, for all we know that may well be the reason for Cthulhu's planet-encircling mental blanket: a jamming device to confuse Crow's calls for assistance!'

For a second or two I considered her answer, then said, 'I'll do as you suggest; I'll not let Crow out of my thoughts for a second. If he wants my mind to be a beacon, then I'll make it one. I'll recall to mind the adventures we've known together, deliberately dwell upon the horrors and perils we faced together as members of the Wilmarth Foundation. If that's the way to get him back, then I'll get him back.' I looked at her. 'Suppose I succeed. Should I contact you?'

She shook her head. 'No, that won't be necessary, I shall know. But until then, from this moment on, I'll have my crowd keep a watch on you, on this place.' She indicated with a movement of her head the room, the house about us. 'If the CCD are trying to stop Titus from returning, then you never can tell when – '

'When they'll turn from purely mental methods to more direct ones, you mean?' I finished it for her. 'Perhaps physical ones?'

She nodded gravely, then smiled. 'But that's looking on the black side. Somehow I don't feel in the least pessimistic. But anyway, come on, young man.' She stood up and held out her hand to me. 'Show me where your kitchen is. We've a lot to talk about yet, and already I'm dry as a bone! What do you say to a cup of coffee?'

3

Of the Return of Titus Crow

(From de Marigny's notebooks)

Some three hours later Mother Quarry told me that it was time she left; transport was already arranged. I took her to the door but she insisted on walking down the garden path on her own. As she reached the gate a car drove up and pulled to a halt. She waved as she climbed in beside the unseen driver and then the car whisked her away. I was left alone to consider the things she had said.

Earlier, over our coffee and cake – a delightful home-made confection left for me by Mrs Adams – our conversation had covered a number of facets of the Foundation's work, reiterating much of what Peaslee had told me. At the time the incongruity of the situation struck neither of us, but now I smiled grimly at the thought of it: the two of us sitting there in my living room, carrying on a conversation whose tone was in direct contrast to the 'Olde Worlde' atmosphere of the beautiful eighteenth-century table at which we sat, the Irish silver we used, the simple meal itself.

Of our entire conversation, however, the part which had proved of greatest interest to me was the lady's description of the manner in which Titus Crow had 'spoken' to her, how awareness of him had first come to her during a self-induced psychic trance. She had not been sure of his identity at first but had guessed that it might be Titus. He had said simply this, 'Find de Marigny . . . tell him I'm coming back . . . I need his help . . . Can't manage on my own . . . Tell him I'm coming, and tell him – ' But that was all. Somehow Crow's psychic or telepathic sending had been cut off short.

A few days later she had received a second message, differing only very slightly from the first. It was then, in her own words, that she finally recognized Titus Crow's psychic aura and knew for certain that the two messages had been from him. However cryptic the substance of those messages, nevertheless they conveyed more than enough meaning to Eleanor Quarry. She had wasted no more time but determined to look me up immediately.

She was already aware of the circumstances of my own rather spectacular return – it had been amply chronicled in the newspapers, and further details had reached her through the machinery of the Wilmarth Foundation – and so, allowing no time for an answer, knowing in her way that I would be there to receive her, she simply dropped me that vague note of hers and then visited me in accordance with its perfunctory arrangements.

And now the rest was up to me.

I showered, put on my robe, returned to my study and got out certain documents, photographs and manuscripts of special relevance to any attempted – evocation? – of Titus Crow. Night had already settled when, comfortably in my chair and puffing at a fragrant cigar, I deliberately set upon a more than merely nostalgic trip along the often dim and elusive, occasionally exceedingly dark, byways of memory.

At first it was hard work. I was making a very physical business of what should have been a purely psychical task, and in less than an hour I had developed a splitting headache. Once, as a boy, greatly interested in certain of my father's parapsychological experiments, I had tried to move a tiny feather with my mind. Telekinesis, I believe he termed this purely hypothetical ability. In the end, having developed just such a headache as I now suffered, I had blown the feather away with the merest exhalation of breath. And here I was after all these years still doing it the wrong way, attempting to fit a physical solution to a wholly psychic problem, forcing my mind where it simply would not go, not under stress, at any rate.

Pushing aside Crow's photograph, I stacked his letters and the remaining memorabilia neatly to one side of my desk. Then I took a deep breath, leaned back in my chair and closed my eyes . . .

. . . And my soul was immediately sucked into that whirlpool between the worlds for a single instant that yet seemed to last a thousand years. The howling, tearing winds of the void, winds no waking man should ever hear or feel, carried to me the dying screams of mortally wounded worlds and the waking cries of newborn nebulae. Stars rose like bubbles as I descended into the seas of space, time itself caressing me as I drifted with its tides. The alien energies of darkling dimensions washed my being with sensations experienced by no other man before me, except perhaps Titus Crow!

And I heard then that well-remembered voice, bringing with it a steadying, a slowing of pace, a return to slightly less ethereal awareness. That voice echoing desperately out of limitless, unthinkable vastnesses:

'De Marigny – where are you?'

'I'm here, Titus!' I cried in answer, and the sickening spinning of my psyche lessened further, as if my answer to Crow's mental cry for assistance had helped anchor me and orient my being amidst the hell of this extrasensory chaos. And my being, my Id, whichever part of myself it was undergoing this experience, now indeed seemed to rock briefly before jarring finally to a halt.

Spread all about me then, so intensely bright as to be painful, I perceived a panorama of hurtling stars, rocketing spheres as colorful as precious stones thrown on a vast satin cushion. At first they appeared almost as coruscating bubbles, then they rapidly expanded to flare past me, finally disappearing in a distant haze of light. And I thought I had reached a halt! Why, if the universe itself were not mad, then in fact it was I who hurtled headlong down these alien starlanes, for surely these stars must in reality be hanging comparatively steady in the void?

Bodiless though I was, nevertheless the chill of outer space and the loneliness of infinity gripped me, but could I really be alone? 'Titus!' I shouted again, shrinking instinctively as certain stars swelled far too quickly and much too close, blooming fantastically to roar by with furnace breath. 'Where – ?'

'Here, de Marigny!' The answer came from close at hand, but where . . .?

There! Directly behind me, driving me before it along its path like an insect pinned to the windshield of a car, was the coffin-shaped clock, Crow's time machine!

In times of stress, in fearfully dangerous situations or when faced with wonders or evils of apparently insurmountable magnitude, moments of utter import, the human being is likely to say the most ludicrously inept things.

I felt in no way inept when I asked Titus Crow, 'Where . . . where are you taking me?'

'I'm not taking you anywhere, Henri,' came his answer. 'You're taking me! We're following a direct course between you and your body.'

How to answer that? In my bewilderment I felt a wave of returning dizziness; the rushing stars began to blur.

Crow sensed my difficulty immediately and cried; 'Just keep talking, Henri! You're doing fine!'

'I . . . I didn't understand what you said,' I finally managed, steadying up, fighting a lunatic urge to duck as the solid-seeming whirls of a great spiral nebula loomed ahead. In another instant we were into the expanding mass of stars that comprised one of the nebula's arms –

and out the other side – and in the next instant the whole magnificent catherine wheel had dwindled in our wake.

'You are returning to your body,' Crow answered, 'doing it at a speed I can match.'

'What?' Still he was not getting through to me.

'It's like this: by an effort of will, using the sympathetic psychic link between us, we got you out here; I pulled and you pushed. The rest is automatic. At the moment you're heading back to Earth, back to your own space and time, back to your body where you belong. But you are also maintaining your contact with me, something you've never managed to do before, and so I'm able to follow you.'

'You're not shoving me along?' Crow's concept still eluded me.

'No, *you* are pulling *me*! But don't stop talking to me. The moment your attention wavers you're liable to snap straight back to your body and I'll lose you. This must be the twentieth time I've picked you up, and it's by far the most successful connection yet. Just keep it up, Henri!'

'But those other times there was . . . Cthulhu!'

'A mental projection, that's all,' he answered, confirming Mother Quarry's excellent guess. 'The CCD are doing all they can to stop me from getting back.'

'And yet they haven't gone for me,' I told him. 'Not directly, at any rate.'

'There may well be good reasons,' he answered. 'I think you'll find that they've erected some sort of mental barrier about the Earth, an almost impenetrable barrier. Also, I know that they're keeping a pretty close watch on me. And of course they must still be under pressure from the Wilmarth Foundation. I don't suppose this leaves them with a great deal of power to play with. They haven't caught on that I've managed to contact Mother Quarry and yourself because I've kept my sendings brief. If they try hard enough they can still get into my mind with their hellish dreams, but as for anything else – well, that's a different story. Briefly, they no longer *dare* interfere with me, not directly. I have a weapon, one that – '

'Yes?' I waited for him to continue.

'De Marigny, we're very close now! I think that perhaps this time . . .' I could feel his excitement, and was about to answer that I, too, sensed an early end to our fantastic flight, when I saw that one of the stars ahead was black . . . and that it was swelling and expanding as we closed with it in a manner altogether different from the others. In another instant the thing had assumed a shape, one which was not that of any star or planet.

'Titus!' I screamed. 'We have a visitor. And, my God! *I know him!*'

'I see it, de Marigny, but are we seeing the same thing?'

'How's that again?' I cried, astonished. 'What do you mean, are we seeing the same thing? It's Ithaqua, the Wind-Walker – and damn it, *he's close!*'

'Don't leave me now, Henri!' I heard Crow's frantic cry. 'We're almost home. It might take a very long time to pick you up again.'

I heard Crow's desperate argument and determined to stick it out with him come what may; but the living shape before me finally bloated into monstrous, definite being. It was huge, anthropomorphic, with carmine-star eyes glowing in Hell's own face, a shape of stark terror, striding splay-footed up the star winds, reaching with great taloned hands that visibly twitched in their eagerness to –

Again the universe seemed to spin and blur about me, but just as quickly Crow cried, 'Remember, Henri, it's just a mental projection! It's not really there, a telepathic image sent by the CCD. Don't let go now, man, we're almost home and dry!'

And then, even among all these fantastic events, came

yet another wonder. I heard a second voice, a *female* voice, one of such beauty and strength, rich and warming and yet delicate as finest crystal, that I knew its owner must be a most remarkable woman even before I realized just what her words meant. '*No, no, Titus. Not this time,*' that golden voice cried. '*This is Ithaqua; it is him and not one of Cthulhu's dreams. Take care, my love . . .*'

'*Look out, de Marigny!*' Crow yelled too late, as fingers of ice closed about me. '*Look out!*'

He need not have worried, for already his voice was fading and the stars were blurring again. In my terror I had lost my mental grip, stretching the thread of psychic contact too fine, until at last it had snapped! The hurtling clock and the man it carried, the monstrous beast-thing that but a moment before held me in its foul hands, these things and the very stars themselves now rushed away from me, receding in a twinkling. Yet still, over vast distances, I could somehow see that dreadful scene.

In a rage that his victim should so escape him the Wind-Walker turned from a short-lived, futile pursuit of myself to an awesome attack on Crow in his space-time machine. Moreover, before the scene dwindled away completely and the winds between the worlds once more claimed me, to whirl me off to my house of flesh on Earth, *I saw Crow fight back*!

He had said that the CCD dared not interfere with him directly, and now I saw what he meant. As the Wind-Walker reached for the coffin-clock, his burning carmine eyes full of blood lust and his whole attitude one of mad bestial fury, there shot out from the dial of that fantastic vehicle a pencil slim beam of purest light. The beam struck the striding god-thing square in his monstrous chest. Though I personally could never claim to be endowed with anything much greater than the usual sense perceptions, even I heard the telepathic shriek of most

85

terrible agony that Ithaqua uttered before turning and bounding away, seeming to stagger now as he fled for the farthest stars.

My last conscious act was an abortive attempt to hang on as there came from dark and rapidly receding deeps Crow's fading, aching cry: 'Wait for me, de Marigny. I'm trying to follow you . . . wait for me . . .'

Finding myself once again in my physical body was a painful affair, far more so than on any previous occasion. For though I had left my body sitting in an easy chair before my desk, (while my psyche had been busy dodging hurtling stars and nebulæ out in the farthest reaches of space,) that supposedly empty shell had apparently reacted to my psychical danger in a similar manner right here in my study! In fact, just as one often wakes up from a nightmare still fighting the horrors of the subconscious until the moment of total awakening and awareness, so I now found myself engaged in a desperate struggle with my Boukhara carpets. My chair lay on its side; a bookshelf and its contents had been brought down by my kicking, scrabbling feet.

Mercifully I had not knocked over my reading lamp; that still stood on my desk, holding the shadows back in my study. My robe was torn, drenched with cold sweat.

I got to my feet and crossed unsteadily to the bay window overlooking my garden. Night had fallen, black and cold, but the sky was clear and all the stars shone brightly down. Opening the windows, I looked up at those stars and shuddered, then instinctively shielded my eyes as, suddenly, the whole sky blazed with an incredibly brilliant flash of lightning!

I had time for one thought only – lightning? From a clear sky? – before feeling the effects of a tremendous rushing blast of air. The windows slammed in on me, throwing me to the floor; a rising wind howled wildly in the eaves; my reading lamp dimmed and almost went out, then burned bright again; and finally there came a clap of thunder to end all thunderclaps!

In another second the acrid reek of ozone filled the air of the room. My God! I thought. *It's hit the house!* But then, lifting my aching head up from the floor for the second time in the space of only a minute or so, I realized that nothing had hit the house, but perhaps something had *entered* it! For two sources of illumination now lit my study. My reading lamp was one of them, burning a steady electric yellow upon the desk; and the other . . .

The other was a purplish throbbing glow whose source lay in a corner of the room hidden from view by my desk. I climbed to my feet again, stumbling as I sought to recover from the combined effects of that blinding flash of lightning and its colossal accompanying thunderclap. And then, as I tottered forward, my jaw fell open in awed amazement and delight.

I had guessed what I would see, certainly, for I recognized that pulsing purplish glow of old. Nevertheless, there in the far corner of my study, charred, blackened, strangely steaming and peculiarly scarred, its frontal panel open to emit that eerie oscillating glow, stood the great coffin-shaped grandfather clock that once belonged to my father. And sprawled at its foot, his head even now lifting from the floor and his arms pushing his shoulders up and back, was Titus Crow, a grimace of pain upon his face as he tried vainly to rise.

'Titus!' I cried, starting forward. 'Is it you?' For indeed I had already noted strange inconsistencies. For one thing, this seemed a much younger man than the one I had known. But then, looking up at me and finally managing a grin – oh, yes, this was Titus all right, despite the fact that he looked young enough to be my brother!

'Any – *ah*! – coffee in the house, de Marigny?' he groaned painfully. 'Or perhaps – *oh*! – a spot of brandy?' Then his eyes rolled up and his shoulders sagged, and with a sigh he collapsed unconscious in my arms.

4

A Universe for the Taking!

(From de Marigny's notebooks)

Toward morning Crow came around briefly, long enough
to take a sip of coffee before lapsing again into deep
sleep. Fatigue was all that ailed him, and this much I was
sure of for I had called in a certain ecclesiastical doctor
immediately after Crow's collapse in my study. The doctor
was none other than the Reverend Harry Townley, a
friend, confidant and former neighbor of Crow's in the
old days. Now retired and having been out of the country
for some months, only recently returning, Harry had
known nothing of my own remarkable return until my
telephone call got him out of bed. The last he remembered of Crow and myself was in connection with a night
some ten years ago, when he had watched from his house
the so-called freak localized storm that ripped down
Blowne House brick by brick and, as far as Harry
Townley knew, destroyed the two of us utterly, leaving
no traces.

My call must therefore have been doubly shocking to
the old doctor. Not only was he receiving a call for
assistance from a man he had every right to believe dead,
but on behalf of a second dead man! And yet the urgency
in my voice had got through to him immediately, that and
the fact that I was not simply some rather grim hoaxer. It
was only after he had given the unconscious man a
thorough going over, when finally we left Crow sleeping
in a comfortable spare bed, that I noticed the doctor's
bemused expression. Of course I asked him what was
wrong.

'It's as well I've known Crow for so many years,' he

answered. 'I don't think there's much he could do now, or anything that could happen to him, to surprise me. And that's as well, too, for this time . . .' He shook his head.

'Go on then,' I prompted him.

'Well,' he slowly continued, 'first let me say that there can be no doubt about his identity. This *is* Titus Crow. And yet, there are places on his body where he should be marked but isn't, places where I remember small scars to have been, which now seem to have vanished. It would take the most brilliant plastic surgeon in the world half a lifetime to do such a beautiful job! And that's only the beginning. He is . . . younger!'

'I thought so, too,' I answered. 'But how can that be?'

'I have no idea.' He stared at me blankly. 'I don't see how it can be. I can only say that his is the body of a man of, say, thirty-eight years. Somewhere he's lost a quarter of a century. And even that is only part of it. The rest is completely . . .' He shook his head, at a loss for words.

'The rest?' I pressed him.

'Where have you been, you two, and what have you been up to?' he answered with questions of his own.

I shrugged. 'Myself, I've been . . . nowhen!'

'Eh?'

I shook my head negatively. 'Hard to explain. I just haven't been *here*, that's all. And as for Crow, don't ask me where he's been. If I told you what I believe you'd probably think I was a madman. I really think, though, that now that he's back he wants his presence here kept secret.'

He nodded. 'You can rely on me to say nothing about tonight. And I'm not the curious type. There's nothing you need tell me.'

'Fine,' I answered, 'but there's something I would like to know. What is it you've found out about Crow that's so fantastic?'

'It's his heart,' he answered after a moment.

'His heart? Why, what's wrong with his heart?'

'Oh, nothing much,' he answered, putting on his coat and starting for the door. 'Hadn't you noticed that there's no heartbeat?'

That good old English reserve indeed! 'No heartbeat?' I cried after him. 'My God! But if his heart's not working, then – '

'God?' he tossed over his shoulder, frowning as he cut me off. 'Yes, I suppose He must have had something to do with it, but who said anything about Crow's heart not working? It most certainly *is* working, and very efficiently at that, but it's not *beating*! It's humming, purring away like a satisfied kitten in his chest. Or rather, like a very well oiled machine!'

The doctor was right of course. As soon as he left I went back to Crow and stood watching him for a few moments. His respiration seemed fairly normal; he had a normal body temperature; but when I laid a hand upon his chest . . . his heart purred, 'like a very well oiled machine'!

All that had been twenty-four hours ago. Now night was upon the house again and I had dozed briefly in a chair beside my friend's bed. It was hardly surprising that I myself was tired: I had watched over Titus Crow's recumbent form continuously, taking a break only to grab a bite to eat.

I awoke feeling cramped and clammy. Crow's bed was empty, the blankets thrown back. I realized what had roused me – noises from my kitchen, recurring now, the clatter of plates, my kettle whistling, the dull thud of the refrigerator door closing.

'Titus?' I yawned, leaving the spare bedroom and making for the kitchen. 'Are you all . . . right?'

The last word fell flat from my mouth as I reached the kitchen door. He certainly looked all right! Two plates on top of the open refrigerator were piled with cold meat sandwiches, coffee steamed in a large jug and Titus Crow, with a leg of chicken in one hand, was methodically searching the cupboards for an elusive something. He was even mumbling to himself through a bite of chicken about civilization going all to hell!

'If you're looking for the brandy,' I said, 'I don't keep it in here.'

He turned and saw me, put down his chicken leg and bounded over to me, gripping my hand in a firm if greasy greeting. 'You old dog!' he rumbled, his voice showing a strength and vitality rare in the older man I had previously known. Then he grinned, his eyes brighter than I remembered them, and said, 'No, no, Henri, I've *found* the brandy.' He showed me the neck of a bottle protruding from a pocket of the robe I had left for him on his bed. 'I'm looking for the corkscrew!'

He began to laugh and I joined him, the two of us roaring with laughter until it hurt, literally laughing till we cried. Then we ate and drank and laughed some more, remembering old times. The night flew by as we reminisced, often in more somber moods but inevitably in delight at this reunion, the two of us, fit and well. Much later, slightly drunk and filled to capacity with food, I sat back and watched him carry on alone as if he would empty my pantry. Finally replete, one might almost say bulging, he stood up and stretched and asked me where his cloak was.

For a moment I misunderstood. 'Your cloak? You mean that rag you had thrown about your shoulders when you . . . arrived? That and your Arabian Nights trousers are stashed in a box under your bed.'

'The Arabian Nights!' he answered with a grin. 'Not

too far wrong, Henri. That cloak of mine is fitted with an antigravity device. Makes all your flying carpets look clumsy!'

'An anti – ?'

'And the old clock? Do I remember falling out of it into your study?'

I nodded. 'You do, after raising a storm I thought was going to do for me, yes.'

'Then let's go in there where I can have a look at Old Faithful. He's looking a bit battered, I imagine, the old clock, but there's more work for him yet. One more trip at least. That is, if I gauge my man right.'

'Your man?'

'You, de Marigny, you yourself!' he answered.

That started it off! Here he was, the living answer to every question I had asked myself since waking with a broken body in my hospital bed, and though we had talked and laughed and reminisced together all through the night, I had not once thought to put these all-important questions to him. Now, however, the dam was broken and I began to gabble uncontrollably. Words tumbled out of my mouth, questions piling themselves one on top of another until, comfortably seated in my study, with dawn already spreading pale fingers over the horizon beyond the bay window, Crow held up his hands to quiet me.

'I'll tell you all, Henri,' he said, 'all, but all in good time. I'm tired now and I can tell that you are, too. The journey was long and fatiguing. I've rested and the food and drink have done me good; this reunion of ours here on Earth, safe and sound and hardly the worse for our various adventures, is marvelous. But once I make a start I don't want my story to lag through weariness. It's a tale that will take a long time in the telling anyway. Right now, however' – he got up and moved over to the enigmatic clock in the corner, reaching to wipe a smudge of some sooty deposit from the great dial – 'now I just want to check over the Old Fellow here, then take a shower, and then it's me for bed for the rest of the day. I'll sleep like a baby, and this time for the sheer luxury of it, not just because I'm exhausted. If you get some rest, too, we'll be able to take all this up again this evening.'

Disappointed though I was I saw his logic. 'All right.' I nodded. 'Just answer me one thing. What did you mean when you said that the clock would be making at least one more trip, a trip involving myself?'

He seemed surprised, then cocked his head on one side to look at me in a curious attitude that I well remembered of old. 'Why, can this be that same lover of mysteries I once knew?'

Puzzled, I opened my mouth to ask his meaning but he cut me off before I could get started. 'De Marigny, I've been to the veriest corners of space and time, I've known a diversity of alien worlds and dimensions. I've lived in the pavilions of Ghengis Khan, journeyed to distant Yuggoth on the Rim, talked with incredible intelligences spawned in the hearts of suns. I've hunted on the mammoth plains of Northumberland, fourteen thousand years ago, with King Conan's own forebears, wandering the very forests and wilds where, twelve thousand years later, Hadrian would build his wall – and I was there, too, during that wall's construction!'

He paused to study the erratic sweep of the four hands about the dial of his clock. '. . . I've been trapped on the shores of a prehistoric ocean, living on my wits and by hunting great crabs and spearing strange fishes, dodging the flying dinosaurs which in turn hunted me. And a billion years before that I inhabited a great rugose cone of a body, a living organism that was in fact a member of the Great Race that settled on Earth in unthinkable abysses of the past. I've seen the cruel and world-spanning empire of Tsan-Chan three thousand years in the future, and beyond that the great dark vaults that loom at the end of time. I've talked telepathically with the super-intelligent mollusks of Venus' shallow soupy oceans, which will not support even the most primitive life for another half-billion years; and I've swum in those same seas ten million years later when they were sterile, after a great plague had destroyed all life on the entire planet. Why, I've come close to seeing the very birth of the universe, and almost its death! And all of these wonders and others exist still, just beyond the thin mists of time and space.

'This clock of mine sails those mists more bravely and surely than any Viking's dragonship ever crossed the gray North Sea. And you ask me what I mean when I talk of another trip, one involving yourself?

'When I return to Elysia, Henri, to the home of the Elder Gods themselves in a dimension bordering upon Orion, there will be a place for you in my sky-floating castle there. Indeed, you shall have a castle of your own, and dragons to bear you to the great festivals! And why not? The gods mated with the daughters of men in the old days, didn't they? And won't you only be reversing the process? I did, my friend, and now the universe is mine. It can be yours, too!'

Part Three

1

At the End of Time

(From de Marigny's recordings)

It would verge upon the impossible to attempt a description of the actual sensation of time travel, de Marigny. Frankly, while traveling through time – and I have done that aplenty since last I saw you – there is very little *time* to think about it! The mind, you see, has to tune in, to become one with the machinery of the space-time machine, to cleave psychically to the very being of the clock. As you know, I was once telepathic to a degree; well, this talent has recently returned to me tenfold. It has been strengthening in me ever since leaving Blowne House on that night of the winds so long ago.

I was and still remain highly psychic; I pick up vibrations which are beyond the sensory perceptions of most other men. Most people are psychically blind, and how may one explain colors to a child blind from birth? Similarly I am unable to explain this sixth psychic sense of mine, or how I managed to control the clock by meshing with its psyche. If I make it sound as if the thing is not a machine but a being in its own right, well, it very nearly is . . .

However, most of that is well away from the point, which is that I am unable to explain the sensation of time travel. Even the precise control of the clock still eludes me. Mind you, I am particularly clever at piloting the thing through space – on that I pride myself – but it is a far different matter to pilot a vehicle through time, which is completely against man's nature.

And of course it was for this reason that our first

attempt at traveling together in time was so nearly disastrous. I had very little idea really how to begin to use the
clock. I am astonished now that I dared even try it, and
you knew even less of the thing's mechanics. You knew
only what I had tried to tell you about it. To think that
we dared to brave such an adventure, and that we both
lived to talk about it!

But anyway, it took me all my time – again that word,
though frankly it conveys very little to me now – merely
to hang on mentally to the element of the omniverse
which the clock became; to try to grip the 'controls' of the
thing with my inadequately trained mind while it slipped
and slithered on a careening course to and fro across the
fabric of the entire space-time spectrum. And whereas the
clock itself was built for this kind of work – it is quite
simply a vehicle for transdimensional travel – man never
was intended to endure such stresses. I had to fight against
all the forces of order, forces which were bent upon
keeping me in my correct and designated place and time,
determined not to let me break away from my own sphere
of existence. And moreover, I had to try to keep you with
me, de Marigny.

Finally, when I was beginning to believe that I could
hang on no longer, when I had almost given up trying to
bring the clock under my control and was about to let go
and the devil take everything, then I sensed that my
vehicle had abruptly steadied itself, that it was hurtling
now on a straighter, truer course. I knew then that I had
been attempting to exert too great a measure of control,
like the novice driver whose lack of dexterity causes his
shiny new car to leap and bound. This craft had been
designed for a gentler touch than mine, but at last I
seemed to be gaining, albeit fractionally, in my understanding of its many and complex subtleties.

And that was when I realized that you, de Marigny,

were slipping away from me. In turning my attention to this mental symbiosis of man and machine I had relaxed my grip on you. I cried out to you to stay with me, to follow me, to mesh your mind with mine and become one with me and the machine, but it was too late, for you were already gone!

I had no idea how to check my machine. It was a demon steed bounding through the years, and having no reins I could but cling grimly to its streaming mane. You were gone, lost in the seas of time, and I could not even begin to know where or how to search for you. And almost as if you had been a human anchor chaining the time ship to your own age, now that the chain was broken it leaped along the timestream ever faster, its vibrations attuned to the rushing, dizzying currents at time's very rim!

Now I turned all my psychic perception to a greater penetration of the clock's being and, despite my horror at your loss in unknown voids, I found a mad euphoria in the sensation of sheer speed as the centuries sped by with the ticking of a clock or the beating of my straining heart. Now my more mundane senses came into play, though in a thoroughly extramundane fashion, for projected through the sensory equipment of my vessel, which I later came to think of as scanners, I saw the known constellations flying through space in a terrifying spiral, speeding up even as I watched until their tracks were blinding whirls and the passage of alien galaxies showed as stupefying tracks across the sky.

I knew then that at this rate of acceleration eternity itself must soon rush to a close, and no sooner had this terrific thought dawned on me than for the first time I heard Tiania's voice. You have heard her voice, Henri, when Ithaqua attacked us in the void. Just as she warned us against the Wind-Walker, which I thought a mere

101

mental projection of the CCD, so she warned me as I rushed ever faster into the future.

'*No, my love,*' she said. '*You are too rash! Stop! Stop now! Only the End lies that way!*'

A guardian angel? The mind of the clock in which I ate the æons speaking to me telepathically? A voice of madness, my own, ringing in my head as my mind crumpled under stresses and visions never before experienced, never meant for experiencing by a mind of man? All of these things I considered, all flashing instantly through my thoughts – all rejected. You have heard that voice, Henri . . .

I heard it. I knew it was Love and Beauty and Truth, and in that same instant I commenced a frantic mental search for my vessel's brakes.

Now, Henri, sit yourself in an automobile, get it in gear, top gear, then push the accelerator down to the floor and watch while the needle creeps up and up until it moves off the scale and the road becomes a blur beneath your wheels. Then take your hands from the steering wheel and throw all your weight against the brakes. This, in effect, is what I did!

Of course, given the circumstances I have just described, you would very likely die. Almost certainly you would be a hospital case and your car would be wrecked, but whatever the end results they would all be physical. My journey, however, was along no merely mundane road, neither was I subject to inertia or gravitational stresses as we know them, nor could I be said to actually feel the result of the abrupt temporal deceleration in any physical way, *but mentally . . .*!

There was no windshield for my body to hurtle through, no hard concrete surface to receive me. Welded to my machine, I simply decelerated along with it, but at the instant that deceleration began all my perceptions shot dizzily forward in time, to the limit of time itself, affording me glimpses of the dead black tombs which wait for all matter and energy at the very end!

I perceived it, I recognized it and in the next moment, like an elastic band stretched almost to breaking point and then released, my psyche snapped back into place within its fleshy house; and in that same instant I let go all control and surrendered myself to what I knew must be death.

But of course I was wrong. It was not death; I was merely stunned. The mind of the clock, with which my own mind had been in some sort of symbiotic rapport, had taken the brunt of the shock. No, I was simply unconscious, suffering from . . . from a badly bruised psyche, if you like.

When I came to I was very cold. I was dressed quite lightly, just as I left Blowne House, in slacks, a silk shirt and a smoking jacket, and the cold seemed to be penetrating through to my very bones. My face lay in dust. Turning, I saw that I lay half in, half out of the clock, in a dust bowl of a valley between low hills whose crests were gray against a dark blue sky.

At first I thought it was late evening and that a great, swollen moon hung in the sky at the zenith, but an orange moon?

And something was nuzzling at my neck!

I cried out and rolled away from whatever it was, leaping to my feet and immediately staggering and falling as my senses whirled in an attack of nausea. The clock remained open, enigmatic as ever, its aberrant ticking strangely faint. Something crawled slowly in the purple pulsing light from its open panel.

The thing was some eight or nine inches long, deeply furred like a great caterpillar, featureless as far as I could

103

see. The scene swam momentarily before my eyes. I carefully felt my reeling head and drank air deep into my lungs, or at least I tried to! Now what on Earth was wrong with my lungs? Nothing, it was simply that the air was very thin. Then I must be high in some mountainous region, which alone might explain the cold and the rarity of air. I was far in the future, that much I knew, but how far?

The crawling thing, moving very slowly, was now levering its furry body up and into the pulsing interior of the clock. Whatever it was, this creature, it seemed to have done me no harm. I certainly wished it none. Unless one is prepared, the clock can play hideous tricks. It is not only capable of traveling in space and time, it can also transmit matter into space and time while remaining stationary itself! I somehow knew, I was aware, that I had nothing to fear from the furry creature; it was harmless as a kitten without claws. So before it could cross the threshold into the clock's transdimensional interior, I stepped forward and caught it up. Instantly it snuggled into my jacket like a cold kitten would, and I knew that my body's heat had been the attraction which had first drawn the creature to me. Instinctively I called it Puss, stroking its deep fur as I peered about at the twilight hills.

'Puss,' I told the creature, 'I would get a better view of things from the top of those hills. What do you say we climb them and see what's become of the world, eh?'

The soil of the hillside was very crumbly, flaky with a sort of gray-brown rust, but here and there small horizontal burrows offered footholds as I climbed the fairly steep incline. I saw two more of the furry creatures as I rose up out of the valley, and then another emerging from its burrow. Toward the crest of the hill an even larger group of them gathered about a greeny-gray shrub whose brittle, withered twigs and drooping leaves they appeared to be eating. I did not break my climb to discover how this was accomplished but placed my odd little friend among its cousins at the shrub and carried on until, heaving and gasping for air, I stood wearily upon the crest of the hill.

And that was when I felt the first pangs of an incredible fear, a dread that set my teeth to chattering even more than the numbing cold, and the hair to bristling at the nape of my neck. No, it was much more than merely fear. I actually stood in awe of immensities whose like I had only ever guessed at, which now lay behind me in the wake of my fantastic journey. For this was indeed the twilight of Earth. I stood at the deathbed of a planet, and if proof were needed then that proof now hung like a ghastly, leprous sickle low in the sky over distant mountains. It was the moon, and the pregnant orange orb directly overhead could only be the sun, once golden and fiery but dulled now and dying in its turn!

A faint, eerie wind stirred the dust of ages at my feet as I gasped painfully at the thin air, turning slowly in order to take in everything of this time-ravaged scene. My vantage point stood up a little from its immediate surroundings, as if I stood upon the rim of a crater, and I guessed that this could well be the nature of that declivity in which my machine now stood. Meteoric impacts must surely be far more frequent now that time had so attenuated Earth's atmospheric envelope. I looked back at the clock, behind and some distance below my position, and felt reassured at the sight of the weird purple glow in whose pool it silently stood, like some alien spacecraft in the valleys of the moon.

Then I turned my face once more to the incredible scene that lay outside the crater wall, that picture of a planet at death's door. As I have said, distant mountains supported a thin-horned leper-moon, but even the mountains seemed flattened somehow and lower than they ought to be, as if weighed down by æons of gravity and worn away by the countless sands of time, until now they brooded like huge unmajestic humps on the far horizon.

Between myself and the mountains, beneath this hideous midday sun, a vast flat plain extended, gray-mottled and reddish in places as if rusted. Was not Mars once equally red in the eye of a childhood telescope? And had I not wondered if those great red sores had once been towns, and the straight and inexplicable lines between them highways?

Earth – this? The third planet from the sun, green and juicy and lush with life, howling in its season with nature's fury and lapped by giant oceans – this? This dry dust bowl of rust and weary lichens, of dumb, furry caterpillars, feeble winds and chill, lifeless air – Earth? Impossible! And yet I knew that it was so. And again I wondered how far, how many billions of years I had journeyed into tomorrow.

I shivered and blew into my cold, cupped hands. It was my intuition that I had not strayed far in space during my journey through time. I mean that while knowing my machine had advanced me fearfully far into the future, I believed that it had continued to occupy its original geographic location in space. If I was correct, then it seemed plain the machine must be fitted with some mechanism to make automatic compensation for planetary motion and alterations in surface levels, for surely in the absence of such compensation the clock might materialize anywhere at the end of a time-jump. High in the air, underground, even beneath mighty oceans as the continents rose and fell like the interminable waves of some leaden sea throughout the ages.

So I stood now not far from the spot where the walls of Blowne House had once sheltered me from the elements, even against those malign elementals of the air which tore our refuge down about us as we fled, you and I, de Marigny, into time. And here it was, noon, with the old sun directly overhead, and chilly as a London November! It was an awesome sensation, to stand there atop that crater's ridge, in a twilight land at the end of time . . .

As the cold worked itself deeper into my bones I started to beat my arms across my body, watching my warm breath crystallize as it plumed off into the thin air. I decided then to walk around the rim of the crater to its far side. Perhaps there would be a better view from there. At first I walked slowly, taking care not to fall and tumble down the steep crater wall, but shortly I began to hurry, as much as the thin air and my labored breathing would allow, as it dawned on me that hope sprang yet within me. What if . . . what if . . . supposing man lived yet within this withered husk of a world? Perhaps, deep down beneath the starveling crust, closer to the warm core, the spires and columns of great cities reared even now, their subterranean sidewalks teeming with life and, and . . .

My hopes for mankind sank abruptly low as I finally reached a point on the crater wall from which I could gaze south at what was once London, the greatest of capitals, now a great gray desolation! Then, to the west, twin fires blazed briefly in the dark blue sky, distracting me as they raced to earth. Meteorites at noon! My eyes followed their balefire to the horizon, then I turned my gaze southward again. What of the green downs of Surrey, Kent and Sussex? Away beyond the sprawling flat scab where once London had proudly stood, as far as my appalled eyes could see, stretched only that same endless gray wasteland.

I shuddered again as a feeble wisp of wind blew the dust of forgotten millennia over my shoes, and I felt an ache in my heart that I knew had little or nothing to do with the bitter chill of the air. It dawned on me then that

I could never leave this place, this future Earth, until I had satisfied myself against all hope that indeed she was barren of human life. With this in mind I began to slip and slide back down the inner wall of the crater to the clock. So far I had not tested the thing as a vehicle in the normal sense of the word, as a machine for traveling in three dimensions as opposed to four. Now would be as good a time as any.

My first trip was a very short one, more of a hop, really. I simply piloted my craft across the bottom of the crater. Of course there was no window I could look out of, and no controls as such. I merely plugged myself in mentally to the mind of the clock and moved it in the direction I wished to move. The clock's scanner system served me far better than any window would have done, for I could see far more clearly than through any Earthly sheet of glass. The whole process of the exercise was ridiculously simple, and the clock completed its first test trip by following a low mid-air trajectory and coming to rest without the slightest bump. Moreover, though I had witnessed the clock's movements in the mental scanner, I had experienced no physical sense of motion during the short journey. Patently my machine traversed space no less efficiently than time!

2

The Last Race

(From de Marigny's recordings)

My second trip was somewhat more adventurous. I flew
the craft up over the lip of the crater to the gray plain
beyond. By now I was starting to experience a great
pleasure in my increasing ability to control the clock, and
so I determined to move on at once in search of . . . of
what? Hope springs eternal, and I felt there had to be at
least a chance that I could find the vestiges of mankind.
Just what this need of mine really was, this suddenly
insistent urge within me to find in this unthinkably distant
future world some recognizable remnant of man, I cannot
really say, unless it was simply the loneliness! No man
before me, no Robinson Crusoe, not even the first lone
astronaut, had ever been more remote from his fellows
than I.

I *felt* remote. It shocked me to think that, by all normal
terms of reckoning and depending upon how long I had
lain unconscious at the foot of the clock in the crater, I
had been in my home on the outskirts of a teeming
metropolis only a few short hours ago. And yet it was
billions of years since I was last in the world of men and
in the company of a friend, you yourself, de Marigny,
removed from me now by countless gulfs of space and
time.

However, in addition to this insistent and poignant urge
of mine to search the Earth for some revenant of man's
lost glory, I now felt a desire to test the clock's vehicular
speed. Fortunately I was wise before the fact in this latter
trial. I took the clock up, way up out of harm's way, until
in my mental scanner the now thin atmospheric envelope

was plainly visible against the curve of the Earth. I must have risen to a height of some fifteen to twenty miles, and right across the indigo sky meteorites large and small were burning themselves out in fiery descents. Up there I set course to the left of the leper-moon and tentatively opened up my mental throttle. The Earth smoothly commenced rotating beneath me. As my speed picked up, in a sudden surge of exhilaration, I fed fuel to the motor of my machine – and much more than I intended!

Immediately the scanners blurred; the screen in my mind became indistinct and seemed to tremble with a rushing darkness shot with lines of fire. In that same instant, in something akin to panic and believing something to be terribly wrong, I canceled all of the clock's forward motion.

Again there came the mental shock of instant and complete deceleration, but in no way as devastating as that traumatic temporal shock I had known. Almost immediately my psychic scanner cleared to afford me an unobstructed view of the clock's surroundings.

We hung stationary, my vehicle and I, and my momentary terror was now completely forgotten in the breathless contemplation of what I had wrought with that one petty burst of overexuberance. I knew then that my scanners had been working all along, that things had only seemed to blur because of the fantastic speed I had achieved! All mathematical impossibilities to the contrary, the clock had defied Einstein himself! I had traveled, for something less than one second, at a speed which must have been in excess of that of light!

And this time my machine had followed no parabolic trajectory around the curve of the Earth. Why should it when I had not demanded as much of it? Indeed, my last mental instructions had directed the clock, albeit

110

obliquely, at a spot ahead of me and to the left of the sickle moon.

And I had reached just such a spot!

To my right, half in black shadow, half in dull yellow and pinkish gray light, the moon's great pitted orb loomed huge, and away behind me Earth's grim gray disk floated like a tarnished coin in midnight vaults.

I knew then that I had a machine in which I might very easily fly out beyond the farthest stars and, despite all the unknown and unimaginable terrors of such a voyage, or perhaps because of them, I admit that I was sorely tempted.

But there was something I had to know first, about which I must be absolutely sure before I could contemplate any other adventures in this amazing craft of mine, and that was the question of man and his continuation or extinction. To my knowledge, there was only one place where the answer might be found; and so, more carefully this time, I set my return course for the gray disk of Earth.

How long I spent orbiting the Earth at a height of some fifteen miles and on a course designed to allow an eventual observation of the complete surface I cannot say. I know that I was completing each revolution in something less than two hours, and that therefore my relative speed must be in the region of fifteen thousand miles per hour, but I kept no count of my revolutions for my concentration was equally divided between control of the clock and observation of the transient terrain below. I know that toward the end of my search, when I believed that at least I had found what I was looking for, I was very tired and hungry and I had lost all sense of direction and orientation.

Below me it was late evening, and the very last rays of the dim sun, sinking over the curve of the Earth, struck silvery sparks from some mile-high object towering way down by the shore of an æons-dead sea.

I slowed my craft and swooped lower, hovering at a safe distance until the sun had set proper, before determining to bring the clock down for the night at a spot some five or six miles to the west of that gigantic artifact whose merest outlines I had glimpsed from on high. As I settled my craft down to a landing lighter than the touch of the most weightless feather, I searched the land to the east for lights. Surely, if the edifice I had seen was a building of sorts, the place would be illuminated at night? But there again, what if it was simply a deserted, unused entranceway, a vast construction guarding a door to those inner worlds I had envisioned deep within the dead crust and that much closer to the still-warm core of the planet? In any event, other than the transient flaring of frequent meteorites, there were no lights, and so I settled down to sleep in the warm interior of the clock, determining that in the morning I would fly to the strange structure and perhaps satisfy that craving of mine for knowledge of man's ultimate station.

And here I find that I must attempt something of a description of the clock's interior.

The clock is, well, its interior is – how might one describe it? – greater than its external dimensions might suggest. By that I mean that it reverses all the demonstrable laws of geometry. Its internal 'angles', like those with which the ancient Cthulhu spawn were familiar and which were used in the construction of their nightmare sepulchers, were non-Euclidean. It was my first thought that to achieve this compact enclosure of a large area within a smaller space, hyperspace principles must be involved. Such concepts make difficult and highly conjectural theories as Möbius-strip mathematics seem as easy as the ABC by comparison. In this, though there was no way I could have known it at the time, I was actually understating the clock's fantastic properties. While I myself can now visualize and understand its basic principles, still it is literally impossible for me to describe them in anything other than the most commonplace terms or by use of the feeblest analogies.

What I said before, about the clock being a matter-transmitter as well as a space-time ship, has some bearing upon it. And yet perhaps such a statement gives an equally incorrect impression. Let me say instead that the clock is linked with all points in space-time. If the universe consisted of a two-inch cube composed of eight one-inch cubes – the three mundane dimensions, plus time and four others – then the clock would *always* lie at the exact center of the two-inch cube, where the innermost points or corners of the eight hypothetical dimensions of time and space meet. A mental push will send the clock itself traveling along a line parallel to any four of these dimensions at the same time. Of course my illustration ignores the fact that there are an infinite number of space-time dimensions, just as there are an infinite number of stars in space, but the same principles apply.

So within the clock, where all these interdimensional lines of force are gathered together and concentrated, there an untrained or inexpert adventurer may 'take a step' or 'fall' in any of an infinite number of 'directions', while the shell of the vessel itself remains static at its focal point of existence. Psychically then, the clock *is* everywhere and everywhen, but it can only *be* somewhere physically when directed by a second psyche, that of its user.

I fear I've lost you, de Marigny, but don't let it worry you. I've chewed the thing over countless times and I still occasionally lose myself!

And still I haven't described the clock's interior, have

I? Well, picture the thickest London fog you've ever seen, a solid wall of swirling gray through which you can't see a hand in front of your face. Now then, take away the dampness that invariably accompanies such a fog, and similarly remove all the physical phenomena you usually associate with it. Finally, let the pavement beneath your feet gradually lose substance until it too is gone, but without incurring any sensations of imbalance or falling, and there you have it.

The clock retains a temperature as nearly that of the human body as makes no difference, and provided one can plug in to its psychic receptors, then one can be perfectly comfortable. You could pack an army into that clock, de Marigny, and you could make *all* of them comfortable! When I'm tired I imagine a couch, and I lie on it. Picture that, me asleep on a couch, in a hyperspatial dimension, at a junction of unimaginable forces, and all within the confines of something that looks just like a grandfather clock, albeit one which has very little to do with any chronological system devised by man!

But to get on with my story.

I was up at dawn, if that gradual lightening of the sky, in which the stars never quite managed to extinguish themselves above the monstrous desert of Earth, could ever be called a dawn. The waning orange sun was rising in the dark blue of the eastern sky. And yet, despite the fact that the sun was dying, still its rising was my undoing, for of course the enigmatic structure I so desired to investigate lay in just that direction, to the east. Pitifully dim though the sun was by the standards of this twentieth century, still it was bright enough to throw the face of that towering edifice into shadow. Because of this I found myself approaching the thing blind, as it were, and I did so to within a distance of some three and a half miles. The base of the skyscraper (so I had come to think of it, though its actual purpose was as much a mystery as ever) lay in something of a declivity, but for all that the thing must still have stretched a good three-quarters of a mile into the thin air, while its column was easily a third of that distance in diameter.

At this point something about the shape of the thing caused me to halt the clock's slow forward motion. It almost seemed as if I stood at the feet of a giant, and I had not yet made up my mind that this giant was friendly! Nor was this idea too far fetched, for indeed the shape of the thing, seen in silhouette, was somehow statuesque.

I decided to circle about it and thus observe it from a position where the dim sun would not be shining directly into my eyes, but no sooner had I taken this decision than yet another factor arose to deny me a clear, unobstructed view of the thing. The sun, climbing steadily now into the sky, was warming however remotely the tenuous air of the valley in which my giant stood. A fine mist was rising, clinging to and climbing the steep and strangely suggestive outlines of the structure, so that by the time I reached that point to the north from which I had hoped to view it, the combination of ground haze and rising, writhing vaporization had obscured all but its pointed summit. That summit, however, I could now see quite clearly: a great curve of a silvery hull and sharp prow tilted at the sky, sleek fins gleaming in the weak sunlight. A spaceship, held aloft in a giant's hand, symbol of man's domination of the stars and of his exodus from this dying Earth!

My heart gave a wild leap. This was more than I had dared hope for, better by far than the thought of the last members of the human race burrowing in the dry earth like so many miserable worms. Impatiently I waited while the sun completed its work and the feeble haze began to drift lazily down from the gargantuan it so thinly veiled. And soon those disturbing proportions I had noted before began to emerge, but this time clearly and unmistakably to my shocked eyes!

My mouth went dry, my mind utterly blank in an instant. I could only stare . . . and stare . . . while my jaw dropped lower and lower and my hopes for mankind plummeted into unfathomable abysses. For perhaps a full half hour I stood there beside the clock, until, gripped by an emotion like none I had ever known before, I stumbled once more in through the panel of that purple-glowing gateway to forgotten times and places and carelessly hurled myself back, back into time, perhaps to a time when man lived and loved, fought and died and gloried on the green hills and in fertile valleys of Earth.

For the immense metal statue holding aloft that silvery symbol of galactic exodus was made neither by nor yet in the image of man. Vastly intelligent were its builders, yes, and plainly proud of their ancient heritage, a heritage which predated mere man and now patently antedated him . . . *It was a beetle!*

3

The Cretaceous

(From de Marigny's recordings)

Fortunately, de Marigny, prehistory and the flora and fauna of bygone ages were favorite subjects of mine in my younger days. I kept a tray of fossils at Blowne House for years, stony fragments I myself collected as a boy: ammonites and belemnites, a tiny bony fish from Eocene Leicestershire, a beautifully preserved 280,000,000-year-old trilobite from Permian Yorkshire, even *Archaeopterix* wing-fragments from the cycadeoid forests of the Jurassic. Traveling back through time in a blind panic-flight from the thought of those nameless beetle intelligences which at the last inherited the dying Earth and left a monument to indicate their galactic destiny, I had no idea that my more than average knowledge of the prehistoric world would be so soon put to practical use.

My plan – not really a plan as such, more an instinctive urge to get back to the eras of man – was simply to find a recognizable period of history. I would work my way back from there – perhaps I had better say work 'forward' – to my starting point, or even to a point a week or so after my departure in the time-machine. It all depended, of course, on if I was able to get the clock's mechanics down to such niceties! And while I talk about my panic-flight, still I was not in such a desperate hurry as to forget what happened toward the end of my first trip in time, when I almost overshot time itself. I was not about to make a second mistake of that nature, perhaps ending up in a mass of superheated plasma just recently hurled out from the sun!

Thus it was that after some time, rousing myself from a

state of morbid moodiness, I attempted to use the scanners. Now use of the scanners in normal circumstances – by that I mean during journeys in three-dimensional space – had proved to be comparatively easy, but traveling in time was a far different kettle of fish, and particularly traveling *backward* in time. Picture, if you can, a gigantic panoramic film run in reverse at many thousands of times its normal running speed and perhaps you'll understand what I mean.

I had taken my craft up out of Earth's atmosphere. The sun and moon were no longer distinguishable as such but had become continuous lines of light weaving in fantastic patterns through space, similarly the whirling constellations. I could discern nothing of the Earth beneath me but a constant flurry of fantastically transient cloud patterns and a tidal blurring of the coastal regions between oceans and land masses. I slowed down and brought the clock lower into the atmosphere.

The sky immediately turned black, only to be lighted up a second later by an impossibly hurtling full moon, mercifully bright and yellow as I had always known it, as opposed to that pitted, leprous horror at the end of time. And then came an incredible blaze of sunlight as the familiar flaming orb of Sol shot up from the *western* horizon to race east across the sky. In another second it grew dark again, and then once more the moon rocketed into view.

Here was an interesting point. Because I was not seeing all this with my eyes but psychically, there was no retinal image left to distort my view of Earth during the fleeting periods of darkness. It was because I saw something during this sequence of dark periods that I slowed down even further. I glimpsed a row of red and yellow lights blazing in a line that from my height seemed certain to be artificial, like some vast system of street lighting. I was wrong, and but for the clock's near invulnerability the end of my adventures in space and time would have come right there and then!

The Earth of course was stationary below. I mean that the clock was making its own compensations for planetary motion; it was rotating through space *with* the Earth, directly over that spot I had fled from in the now far distant future. So I plunged lower still through the dense stuff of what I took to be clouds. Too late I realized that this was not cloud but tephra, and that directly below me the throat of a monster volcano was belching lava-bombs, smoke and fire at me in a spectacular eruption. The row of lights was simply a great volcanic rift in the earth, from which at fairly regularly spaced points in its length the cones of active volcanoes thrust threateningly upward. Lightning flashed ceaselessly in the roiling tephra clouds, striking the time-clock again and again before I had recovered my wits sufficiently to move my machine laterally out of the way.

But about that volcano, de Marigny, and particularly about the lightning – just try to picture it! Of course I was still traveling backward in time, and so the lava-bombs were all hurtling up toward the clock from an area outside the actual radius of the volcano, to fall into its heaving, bubbling throat. And the lightning was not striking at me from the tephra clouds but seemed to be striking from the clock to the clouds! In any event I was unharmed, and the clock was barely scratched.

Once clear of the volcanic range I slowed my temporal speed more yet until the moon hung still and bright, if redly tinged, in a sky so dark that the stars seemed merely to flicker dimly above, and then only with difficulty. I brought the clock down to a landing there when I judged that dawn was not far away, but I stayed in the clock until the sun was fully up. My reason for doing this was very

119

simple: using the clock's scanners I could see my immediate surroundings even in the dark, but once I left that strange vessel I would have to rely solely on my own five senses. So I waited for the sun to come up before opening the panel and stepping out into a weird, fascinating and deadly world.

And it was then, striking through all my wonder and delight – the origin of which I will explain in a minute – that I first realized just how hungry I was. Oh, I was tired, too, terribly tired, but it was purely a fatigue of mind now. The clock had taken much out of me, sapping emotions as hard work saps physical strength. Even so, despite this emotional weariness, I was astounded, amazed, yes, and delighted. Do you see, Henri? Now I knew where I was. Perhaps I should really say I knew *when* I was, for I was back, way back, deep in the prehistoric world of the Cretaceous!

The Cretaceous was the last period of the Mesozoic, one hundred million years ago! It was also the Age of Reptiles, when the dinosaurs were lords. When giant *Archelon* turtles and mosasaurs swam in soupy oceans that were not nearly as salty as they are now, and scythe-winged *Pteranodon* called hideously to his mate as he winged on creaking leather through rich warm skies beneath billowing, soaring clouds.

It was an age of primal things – colors, odors, sights, sounds and sensations – so that even the wind felt different against my skin. It was Earth in the glory of youth, with all of creation insane in a frenzy of experimental trial and error, building new life-forms and changing them, destroying and then building anew. And the thought of man had not even crossed Nature's mind, would not for another ninety million years!

Men? Why, Nature did not build things as puny as men in those days! They were the days of python-necked

Brachiosaurus; of tank-like *Triceratops*, beside whom a rhinoceros would seem the merest toy; of *Tyrannosaurus*, who bellowed and strode the land on powerful piston legs, king of all the dinosaurs, ruling his cycadeoid domain with a tyrant's lusts and rages. Even the mollusks were monsters in those days, like titan-valved *Inoceramus*, which dwarfed even the greatest of today's *Tridacna*. Oysters, too, proliferated in those youthful seas, producing pearls as big as a man's fist, pearls that the ages have since reduced again to calcium dust. It was on the shore of just such a Cretaceous coral sea that I now found myself.

I knew it was the Cretaceous, I recognized it as surely as I would King's Cross or the tones of Big Ben, without stepping more than a dozen paces from the open panel of the clock. It had chiefly to do with that fossil collection of mine that I've mentioned. Favorites among those fossils were certain ammonites from this period, hard, lusterless things, drab as gray pebbles on a beach; but there in that coral pool upon whose edge I stood played myriads of these very creatures, alive and glowing in a morning sun that already drew mist up from the damp sands. Weirdly coiled, octopoid *Helioceras*, unicorn-horn *Baculites* and intelligent-eyed *Placenticeras*, all were there, groping with tiny tentacular arms, darting on squid jets, swimming in crystal waters that teemed with uncountable struggling life-forms. And lifting my eyes to the crashing ocean beyond I caught a glimpse of spray-wreathed *Tylosaurus* as the head and back of that primal sea serpent broke the frothing waters. In distant skies enormous, fantastic shapes flitted: *Pteranodons*, flying reptiles, darting to snatch bony fishes from white-tipped wave crests.

Oh, yes, without the least shadow of a doubt, I recognized this age, the Cretaceous. And I knew, too, that my physical hunger, the emptiness in my belly, should not go long unabated.

Close by, within a hundred yards landward of the beach, a low volcanic vent was steaming, its lava lip glowing red: there was my cooking fire. And here at my feet great crabs and lobsters, creatures halfway between trilobites and crayfish, moved on segmented legs in jeweled waters. Palm-like trees with large, strange nuts grew further along the shore, cycads and flowering trees, too, doubtless bearing fruit. Even as I gazed a small furry mammal sprang down from one of the nearer palms, scampered to the next and up into its green shade. Oh, there was food enough here, more than enough. Why, if a man had a rocket-launcher, doubtless back beyond that low range of volcanic mountains, in the cycad forests, he could bring down ten tons of meat with one shot – if he had the nerve! I would be satisfied with a lobster, and fruit for dessert and perhaps the milk of a coconut to wash it all down. I might even find myself a spring, with water that never had to recycle itself to remove detergents or DDT.

Now then, was the tide in or out? I scanned the beach for a tidemark and found it, many yards down from where I stood. To the rear of the clock the sand was yellow, unwashed. Nonetheless the pool at my feet with its many denizens showed quite clearly that the sea had recently reached this spot. Perhaps the tides were irregular, perhaps they had not quite settled yet to the pull of the moon. I had best move the clock back, higher up the beach to where the first palms and cycads fringed the feet of the volcanic hills. The volcanoes themselves did not worry me greatly; a few lava-bombs lay scattered about but the majority of them were old. That line of livid cones I had passed over last night – the night to come? – lay some miles west, behind this lower range.

I found a spiked branch of coral and speared myself a large wriggling lobster-thing, killing it immediately with a rock that severed its head from its body. Then I carried my breakfast back to the clock. I moved inshore to the fringe of palms, and sure enough the ground held a scattering of great nuts. As I hefted one, there came a liquid swishing from within its globe. Fruits there were, too, and I tentatively tasted one that looked like a small pear. Its juice was sweet, tangy and pleasing but like nothing I ever tasted before. This was a primal taste, from which lesser tastes might later distill themselves. Indeed it was heady, that taste, so that later I sang as I roasted my lobster in its shell on a coral spit over the fiery breath of a volcanic blowhole.

Feasted as royally as any lord, feeling a contentedness of soul experienced all too rarely in a lifetime, I ambled back in the warm sunshine toward the clock where it stood shaded beneath swaying, coarse-grained palms. In an instant, as I passed where I had not walked before, I was brought back down to earth with a jolt. There, in the dark yellowish soil at the edge of the palm clump, was a footprint – no, a clawprint! Huge, it was, that deeply imbedded impression of a hind foot whose owner, I knew, towered twenty feet high and weighed as many tons. Three claws fore and one less prominent behind, the greatest carnivore the world has ever known had made his mark: *Tyrannosaurus rex*, king tyrant of the giant reptiles!

I have never been a coward, but at sight of that monstrous indentation the hair on my neck prickled in almost preternatural dread. Since the end of the Mesozoic the world has never seen such rampant, unbridled, sheer animal ferocity in any living creature – no, not even in man himself – as in *Tyrannosaurus rex*. This print was a powerful reminder that I trod ground other than familiar, other than the safest, where man never trod before. I knew that the longer I stayed the more certain would be my eventual meeting with the creature who made this mark or others like him. I decided on the instant that as soon as I had rested I would be on my way. I would move forward, forward in time to the age of man, leaping the æons in my time-clock and only pausing to check my progress and eat.

First, though, I would rest, and then I would collect a store of the great nuts and roast myself another lobster, perhaps two, to take with me. The last was imperative. Though I could foresee little difficulty in what I intended to do, who could say for certain that a future opportunity to replenish would present itself? Of course, the need might never arise, but . . . And before I went, why of course I must scour this shore for seashells, for half a dozen of each variety that I could find; and I had to pass over the mountains in my clock to see the primeval forests and their denizens, to fly above the lizard-lands in safety and watch the great beasts at play – and at war!

And yet when I awakened, though I had intended my sleep to last only until midafternoon, it was already late evening and far too dusky to think about gathering seashells, not on that shore, at any rate. There were too many things to worry about in the Cretaceous night. I had earlier set a pair of nuts down beside the clock; now, sitting in the late evening beneath the palms and gazing out over the moonlit sea, I pierced one of the nuts with a coral spike and drank its refreshing milk. In the morning I would drink from the other, then crack them both for their flesh.

The night was warm. The moon, while it was as bright as I had ever known it, seemed smoother somehow, faceless. The stars, though many of their constellations appeared amply familiar, were dim, due to volcanic ash high in the atmosphere. Of course, for explaining the unscarred surface of the moon, that lunar orb was too young yet to have gathered many craters. Indeed its haze might even suggest that it had a faint atmosphere of sorts, not yet drifted off into space . . . A fascinating place, this Cretaceous.

As it grew darker still I opened the panel in the front of the clock, allowing its eerie dappling to illuminate my seat on a large stone. Great moths, attracted by the light just as they are today, came to visit me, soon becoming a nuisance as they fluttered in the purple pulsing light. Then they became more than a nuisance.

I have never been a moth fancier, indeed most insects are offensive to me one way or the other, but in the Cretaceous some of these nocturnal lepidoptera had wing-spreads of eight inches and more. When I put my hand up to keep one of these from fluttering in my face its fur-edged wings stung me! Likely the creature lived on the poisonous pollens of strange night-blooming flowers. Enough of that! I retreated into the clock and continued to observe the weird night from the safety of its interior.

To my back, several peaks jutting up from the line of hills glowed with volcanic fires. Far along the shore down at the edge of the sea, some shadowy beast splashed and snorted. The sea itself was quiet, the wind of day having dropped to a gentle breeze. Though I rarely smoke, I would have vastly appreciated a good cigar right then, and of course I should dearly have loved a glass of good brandy. I had neither, but I did have one of those intoxicating fruits. Nibbling on this I eventually drifted off into a shallow, troubled sleep.

No, that may give the wrong impression. My sleep was not troubled by nightmares or those nameless fears that waken you in the night drenched with sweat and frightened but unable to recall the threat. In fact my dream was quite vivid and ineffably beautiful, I could say haunting. Indeed, it haunted me for a long time after. No, it was only disturbing in that I sensed, even dreaming, that this was much more than a dream . . . a vision! There were elements in it hinting of an almost telepathic communication, albeit an unwitting one.

I dreamed I was in a tremendous hall or room of fantastic angles and proportions. A curving, high-arched ceiling towered over me like the dome of some hollow mountain. Everything, the gargantuan-paved floor, the distant walls and clouded ceiling, the pillars whose ornate columns supported high balconies lost in rose petal clouds of mist, everything was of crystal. Milky crystal, mother-of-pearl crystal, pink and blood hues of crystal glowed everywhere, like the interior of a splendid conch of the seas of space, letting the light of alien suns shine through its translucent nacre.

Some vague titanic Eminence of similar hues stirred upon a vast seat or throne in a distant curtained alcove. I held my breath, knowing that this was what disturbed me so; this being whose misty form behind luminous pearl-dust drapes flashed fire from jewel-adorned members. I did not wish to see the being more clearly; I was glad that it sat far off, that its form was hidden by the crystal sheen emitted by the walls, roof and pillars of this, its palace. I knew, you understand, that this place I was in belonged to the Eminence upon the throne, that being whose presence filled me with a subconscious, psychic unease.

Then my attention focused on a figure in the center of the gigantic room. There a scarlet divan, low but of great surface area, like an enormous pillow, supported a figure at once human and inhuman. It was a woman, with her back to me, and I was glad that this was so for no face could ever hope to match the perfection of that body. I have known women in my youth. I remember beautiful women, but never has any woman I ever knew looked like this.

She was clothed in a cape of faintly golden bubbles, with a high collar laid back by the weight of hair cascading over it. That hair, it was . . . can green describe it? Highlighted by emerald mists and aquamarine coils, it massed in ringlets down her milk-of-pearl back to a waist delicate as the stem of a crystal wineglass. The cape concealed little. Of bubbles itself, it merely softened the outlines as bubbles do. She knelt, her legs drawn up beneath her and clothed in wide-bottomed trousers of the same spun-gold bubbles. Thigh and hip, waist and back, arms and slender neck and rich, glossy, emerald-flashing hair, all were encased but not enclosed, not concealed, by precious foam-of-gold. No man could look upon this vision and not gasp. Fires I had believed forgotten since my youth raced in molten streams through my body, driven by a furnace heat. And yet, even in my longing, I was sad. No woman's face however lovely could match the beauty of this woman's body. No, Nature herself could never conceive of such a face. But I had to know.

I moved forward, approaching until a perfume distilled of no rare orchids but the flowers of her own milk-of-pearl skin drifted to me. She was so close now that I could touch her. My fingers burned, tingled, ached to stroke that hair, turn that head to me; my eyes desired so to gaze upon that face, even though I knew I must be disappointed. I moved around her, passing over the huge cushion without feeling it, as one moves in a dream. Now I could see . . . her face!

I dared not cry out for fear she would hear me and flee, the thought of which I could not bear. I could no more bear that thought than I could bear the sight of her face, a sight mortal man was surely never intended to see. And yet I was seeing it: the pale pearl brow from which an emerald ocean sent lustrous waves and wavelets cascading down the spun-gold strand of her cape; the huge eyes of deepest beryl, in which a man might drown, open wide and staring; the mouth, quite beyond my meager powers of description, with its perfect cupid's-bow of pearl-dusted rose, turned down now over teeth whiter than purest snow that bit the flesh of the bottom lip in distress. The whole lucent face was a slender oval, with arching emerald eyebrows almost long enough to melt into the verdure of temples, elfin ears like the petals of rare blooms, a nose so delicate as to go almost unnoticed. She radiated a distillation of Essence of Woman, human but quite alien. A woman – but a goddess, too!

Her eyebrows were drawn now in a frown, and still she bit her lip. The infinite depths of her eyes were worried. Her expression hurt me with concern for her, that she should ever feel the need to worry. She studied a great crystal set in the center of her huge cushion, a sphere of shining brilliance to which I eventually managed to drag my eyes from her face. I stared for a moment, and the crystal cleared to show a scene at first unrecognized. There were star-spaces streaked with a comet's blaze, but then that shooting star loomed close and I saw that it was no comet but . . . my clock!

Faster and faster the vessel fled down the void, speeding on an immaculately straight course down to a blackness that loomed in the crystal, a blackness in which no tiniest gleam of light showed. The stars were gone now, leaving nothing but an empty void ahead and an irresistible force that pulled the great clock faster yet toward some unknown doom.

'Kthanid!' the woman on the vast cushion cried, half glancing over her shoulder to where the hidden Eminence sat upon its alcove throne. 'Kthanid, I must go to him at once or he is lost, my beloved, who you promised me so long ago!'

. She had spoken to the Eminence in a voice as wondrous as her face and form, and drawing breath to do so her perfect breasts had lifted, heaving in anguished agitation. Again I glanced at the crystal sphere. Faster still rocketed the clock, its shape beginning to distort, twist and flow. It was my clock, my vessel, and therefore the obvious concern of this goddess must be for me, but how? Why . . .?

In my dream – I will call it that, though I know now it was no such thing – the Eminence stirred behind its pearl-dust curtains, jeweled members writhing and tiny crystal bells chiming as drapes briefly billowed. It answered her, but with no voice of sound. In my head I heard the Eminence speak, and by her actions knew that she also heard.

'*Child – Tiania – you must know this: if this man dies now – and if you are with him when he dies – then you may yourself be hurt even unto death.*'

'Wise one, if he dies I will die also, of a broken heart! That I know, for I love him. It is why I must be with him, why I must try to help him.'

'*He is most human, this man; the blood of his own kind is stronger than ours in him. His mind may not be able to guide his vessel away from the Black Hole. You may only join him in spirit – true – but such is the pull of the Black Hole that even your spirit may find itself fast. If you cannot help him – if you fail – then you go down to the Black Hole with him!*'

'I know it, yet I must go to him, now, before it is too late!'

'*And you desire my help?*'

'Oh, yes, Kthanid, yes!'

'*I cannot deny you, therefore I will help you. It has long*

129

been my thought that he may be – great – this man. I sense his presence even now. I suspect that you are his magnet even as he is yours. If indeed he has the germ of greatness within him, then it would be a matter of great neglect not to help you. So ride the thought-winds, child – and hold fast to this Great Thought I send you, to help you on your way!'

Instantly the lights in her eyes went out, her lashes furled down like the silken sails of færie ships. She sighed once, deeply, then gently curled herself about the crystal sphere, its orb cloudy now and empty of visions.

And abruptly the scene contracted, shrank, as if a giant's hand had snatched me up from it. The beautiful creature curled upon the great cushion melted to a tiny halo of life about a glowing seed-pearl; the alcove of the Eminence dwindled and its misty drapes became as the tiny, dew-spangled webs of dwarf spiders; I passed into the vaulted ceiling of rose crystal and my dream collapsed in the wake of returning consciousness.

I awakened in the clock with a cry of pain, pain that I was separated from the woman of the dream.

Dream? Had it been a dream?

4

Marooned in Prehistory

(From de Marigny's recordings)

Hours later, after I had breakfasted and flown the clock down to the wet sand where the sea now sullenly retreated, while I absentmindedly gathered gem-tinted shells unknown to man except as drab and colorless rocks, I still pondered the dream or vision, whichever it had been. So engrossed was I with it that I passed off the first trembling of the earth beneath my feet as normal volcanic activity; such seismic shocks must be frequent in an area literally riddled with volcanic vents.

With a thousand damp and glistening shells in the bowl of a broken nut, lifting my eyes from the contours of the conches to the line of smoking hills, I felt that pulse of Earth and strangely it set off chords of memory. The voice of the girl, the woman, the goddess in my dream had been . . . had been the same voice that came to me as I crashed headlong into the future in the clock, as I hurtled toward the End! It had been that voice of warning I heard even as I applied mental brakes against the closing of time! But who, where, what was she? And she had said she loved me . . .

Now why should I connect a warning of disaster from a beautiful creature of dreams with a volcanic rumbling deep in the ground? Was it simply a hangover from my past experience of the burrowers beneath, the automatic suggestion of danger in connection with any movements of the earth? Or was it something deeper, of the subconscious? Perhaps I had better get back to my clock.

Wasting no more time in pondering the enigma, I tucked my shell collection up under one arm and set off briskly back toward the time-clock. Even as I started out there came again that subterranean trembling, accompanied this time by a low and ominous rumbling. Black smoke coiled up now from several pinnacles and crests along the line of low hills, and as I lengthened my pace to a clumsy run across the damp sand there came a loud explosion from out at sea, and then an even louder one, followed by a tremendous blast that threw me down on the sand while the earth commenced a violent shaking.

There followed such a hissing and crackling that I immediately turned my face toward the sea, to the source of these threatening sounds. A fantastic manifestation drew my awed attention. Something was beginning to happen out there, something preceded by a flash of lightning from a sky already darkly turbulent and accompanied by a mad swirl and rush of ocean, a sudden howling of wind and a column of smoke and tephra that reached up into the sky with astonishing speed. Then, through the smoke and abruptly hissing rain, I saw the outline of a tremendous bulk steaming up from the sea. A newborn island, crying out as it struggled from its watery womb!

Shuddering, jerking, a massive pinnacle of gray-black rock and slag was climbing from the boiling waters. And flame, too, gouting up redly in a sudden barrage of liquid rock from the emerging volcano, blasting down in the form of white lightning from a now blue-black sky. And water – a shock wave of panicked ocean!

The clock, my one means of returning from this place, from the Cretaceous back to the ages of man, lay directly in the path of a fearful wall of water that even now heaped itself up far out at sea to begin the awesome plunge landward. Despite the lurching of the earth beneath me as I struggled to my feet, despite the sucking of the wet, quaking sand, I tried to run. Perhaps I might have made it back to my vessel in time if yet another tremendous seismic shock had not chosen that exact moment to throw me down once more in the sand and pebbles.

And I was still there, some fifteen to twenty yards away from my coffin-shaped refuge, when the great wave crashed down on me, crushing me to the beach until I thought I must drown, then sucking me up and hurling me headlong on its rushing crest until finally I was thrown down again in a clump of great palms. There, as the first rush of water subsided, I managed to cling to the bole of one of the primal trees and so save myself.

There was no chance yet to spot my vessel amid the crazed howling of the elements. Stumbling out from under the lashing palm branches toward higher ground, it was all I could do to support myself against the tearing wind. Oh, of course my concern for the clock was of the greatest – I was filled with a terror of my vessel being lost forever – but even so the instinct for immediate personal survival was uppermost. Glancing back as I stumblingly climbed the gradual slopes, I could see that a series of secondary shock waves was already forming concentric circles about the island out at sea; it would not be long before they, too, rushed in to further flood the lowland areas.

Well, time passed. Though those lesser shock waves did not reach as high as the first, still they continued to form until well into the afternoon. Watching from my vantage point in the foothills, I saw them breaking all through the day in gradually lessening fury along the great curve of the beach in both directions. The ground rumblings had eventually ceased, too, as had the sporadic eruptions in the hills behind me. The newborn island stood steady now in the gray sea, sullenly smoldering.

A sort of lava dam had been created out in the ocean, forming a great basin in which those waters thrown landward by the initial emergence of the volcano were trapped. Also, it seemed that the shoreline must have settled somewhat, for while the arms of this newly formed bay did not completely shut off the stretch of water between the new island and the mainland, still that water did not seem to be receding to its previous level. And if the ocean did not recede . . .

My God, Henri, but that was a monstrous thought! To be trapped here in the Cretaceous, with my time-clock lost beneath the shallow but viciously denizened waters of this volcanic bay, in a prehistoric world of great beasts and primal plants. What chance would a mere man have in a world ruled by dinosaurs, an age of constant struggle for survival? And there I was, stranded in those Cretaceous foothills, with afternoon all too quickly growing into murky evening.

As night drew near and the elements less wild, the hum of insects and raucous cries of bat-lizards began to come in to me from the surrounding wilderness of foggy heights and crags, particularly from the now heavily misted beach. Of course! Down there must be a wonderful feast of stranded fishes, mollusks and crustaceans for the *pteranodons;* indeed I could see large numbers of the flying lizards flapping in from over the ocean as the warm, heavy haze of the beach developed into a full blown fog.

Now, complementing the clinging clouds of moisture-laden air that rolled up from the sullenly washing ocean, there came the odor of things too long out of water, a far stronger smell than I had ever known in London's fish markets. Little wonder that the flying lizards had been attracted so soon to the scene of the recent upheaval. I would not be able to go back down to the beach tonight, perhaps not even tomorrow. But what was this? Here I was sitting in these foothills, surrounded by a rapidly thickening wall of fog while night quickly set in, dreaming like a madman of tomorrow! My God! Would there be another tomorrow for me?

Quickly I found myself a tiny cave in a steep escarpment of rock, large enough to cram myself into but leaving no room for anything so superfluous as comfort. Then, marking the location of my shelter, I left it again to search out a great palm leaf from which to strip a long, sharp, pliant splinter: a weapon against any unwelcome attentions I might attract from night-wandering beasts of prey. Still feeling far from safe, and while there was yet enough light, I sought out from the volcanic shale of those foothills a flat slab of slate about the size and thickness of a paving stone. A further twenty minutes of pushing and struggling saw me inhabiting my uncomfortable hole in the rocks, weapon in hand and pointing out through a narrow crack between the edge of my new slab door and the side of my tiny cave. As darkness fell, miserable though I was and – I freely admit it – desperately afraid, I finally fell into fitful slumbers.

Twice during that dreadful night I awakened, once to the eerie creaking of leathery wings overhead – a sound that had my nerves silently screaming for at least ten minutes before it finally faded into the background hum of night insects – and the second time when something tugged at my sharp fang of palm splinter where it projected slightly from its aperture. A nervous, involuntary thrust of this weapon as I awoke sent whatever creature it had been – possibly one of those tree-dwelling mammals I have previously mentioned, certainly nothing very large – scampering off unseen with a shrill cry of fear and pain into the night mists.

By midmorning the fog had dispersed and the sun was blazing down from a sky of purest blue. The last of the

135

gorged *pteranodons*, their sac-like bellies grotesquely distended, had flapped away along the beach or out to sea. Behind me, higher up in the hills, solitary smudges of smoke drifted lazily above volcanic sources. It seemed completely impossible that only a few short hours ago Nature had displayed such a disastrous fury of elemental creation, and yet now a great new stretch of ocean lay flat and calm, lapping at the edge of those fringing palm groves that so recently had stood well back from the beach. I calculated that the waters had crept at least one hundred and fifty yards further inland from the level at which I had last seen my clock.

I made my way slowly down to the beach, picking a path through an appalling assortment of rotting, ravaged marine corpses of various sizes, from tiny translucent bony fishes to shark-like things up to eight or nine feet in length, to the water's edge. The sea, as I have said, was flat and blue, mirroring the sky. An occasional fish could be observed to leap clear of the warm waters in a burst of desperate acceleration as it fled from greater dwellers in those sparkling shallows. Even as I watched a particularly ugly, square, serpent-like head viciously broke the surface only a few score yards out from where I stood.

I shuddered despite the fact that the weather was so nearly tropical as to drench the deteriorating rags of my clothes in perspiration. I had been thinking of swimming out there, of making a series of dives until I found my clock. It was out of the question – I might make twenty-five yards if I was lucky! On the other hand, why couldn't I build a raft and simply paddle out until I could actually see the clock in those crystal waters? That way I would only have to risk one solitary dive. I refused even to consider the possibility that my vessel might not work under water! But if I did build a raft, would I find the time-clock in the place where I believed it to be? What if yesterday's upheaval and tremendous shock waves had moved it, perhaps even burying it beneath the silt of this shallow seabed?

Well, that last was a distinct possibility certainly, but it was no kind of thought to dwell on for any length of time. A raft would at least enable me to find out one way or the other.

I looked around with more purpose now. Following yesterday's violence the sea, despite whatever life-and-death turbulence there might be beneath the surface, had grown singularly calm. All along its quiet edge giant palm branches were strewn; it should not be too difficult to lash two or three of these together.

A sudden rage came over me and I cursed the newborn volcano, shaking my fist at it where –

The creak of leathery, membranous wings drew my instantly terrified eyes from their angry contemplation of the smoldering infant cone standing out in the sea's blue expanse to the skies directly above me. Winging down in a narrowing spiral came one of those hideous, hammer-headed scavenger-lizards, a *pteranodon*, blotting out the sun with its shadow as it descended directly toward me. Without a doubt, I was the thing's target; it uttered a hungry, raucous cry and its eyes, red as the pits of hell, burned unblinkingly on me as it fell from the sky. I felt the cooling fan of its great wings, with a span all of twenty-five feet, and then I ran wildly, desperately along the edge of the water.

Closer yet the wings of that pursuing horror beat at the air, until one of them struck me like a leather club as I zigzagged amid the rotting refuse of the recent upheaval, sending me sprawling with my head and shoulders pene-trating the spear-like fronds of a fallen giant palm branch. Quickly I scrambled into the shade of the branch, pressing my body to the wider stem and peering up through the lesser leaves at the sky-lizard as it settled in a violent stirring of rancid seaweed and damp sand to lean its evil head inquiringly forward in avid contemplation of my refuge.

As I pressed closer to the great palm stem the *pteranodon* saw the movement of my body through the umbrella of fronds directly above me. Quick as thought, its murderous beak came down to slam into the thick branch, ripping away a strip of coarse bark and missing my head by inches. I smelled the horror's vile exhalation of breath – perhaps I even tasted it, so thick was the overpowering fetor of decay – but then, before that dreadful beak could descend again, a shrill screech and fanning of air announced the arrival of yet another sky-lizard. Now there were two of them, with but a single thought in their tiny minds.

Then, crouching beneath that fallen palm branch while two of the prehistoric past's most terrible children battled for the right to devour me, I saw what might just be a means for survival. Sooner or later one of these great flying reptiles must win the fight outright or at least frighten the other off, and then it would not be long before I fell to a vile, darting beak. But right now I saw a refuge that might just be a little more difficult to penetrate than the comparatively flimsy green foliage now protecting me.

There, where tiny wavelets washed coarse grasses only fifty feet or so away from my temporary shelter, a great coiled shell like some vast ammonite lay, but empty now of whatever species of octopus had built it. The bell-like mouth of this monster was like a small calcium cave, well over two feet in diameter. Now, keeping one eye on the battling *pteranodons* while their horny lizard feet hopped and stamped and their beaks darted in angry conflict, I scrambled out from under the fallen branch. I took my chance to make a run for the coiled shell, and . . . it moved!

I skidded to a trembling halt as the great shell swiveled on the grasses at the edge of the sea. A huge plated claw extended from the shadow of the bell mouth to snap shut with a pistol-shot report only inches in front of my chest. One stalked eye, then a second, edged out warily from behind the massive claw, the two swaying and observing me intently where I stood transfixed with terror. A hermit crab, by God, the biggest of its species I could ever have imagined!

Now the pink, hairy, paddle-like arachnid legs curled out from under the stalked eyes and over the lower rim of the shell's mouth. They touched and felt the ground beneath, spread themselves and braced against it, then with hideous speed the thing scuttled forward, bearing the vast shell with it!

In that moment I knew that I was done for. To this day I don't know exactly what happened to prove me wrong. The claw, I could have sworn it, was actually closing on my head and upper body when once again I was sent sprawling by a blow from a flapping leathery wing. One of the sky-lizards must have noticed my flight from beneath the palm branch and had hopped after me. Doubtless it regarded the attack of the crab as a threat to its own proprietary rights. There again, perhaps I flatter myself. It could be of course simply that the *pteranodon* preferred crab meat to my own untried, completely conjectural texture and taste. Whichever, the great crab saw the danger it was in, snatched itself back and its walking appendages commenced a rapid, jerky retraction – but not rapid enough.

The fetid beak darted over my stretched-out form to pluck the soft-bodied crab from its shell in one lightning-like snatch. The writhing victim screamed hideously, harshly as, in the next instant, its juices squirted where the flashing beak split its black-veined body-sac. I was drenched in nameless muck as I gathered my wits sufficiently to scramble unceremoniously, and completely uncaring of the fate of its most recent resident, feet-first into the safety of the great shell's bell mouth.

I slithered backward, and as I went I snatched up from the sand a long, dagger-like *Baculites* shell, holding its sharp point outward. Further back yet I forced my body, until the curve of the thick shell shut off my view of the outside world, until my hips would go no further down that smooth, vacant throat. Then, trembling in a fever of reaction and terror, I waited for whatever was to come next.

The crab was still screaming, but weaker now. Its harsh, rasping emissions soon turned to a quiet rattle and a lessening, sporadic clicking of claws. Then there was only the splintering of shell and rending of flesh, and the occasional indignant squawk or threatening, hissing cry. Obviously the two sky-lizards were sharing the crab, however unwillingly. I hoped that their tiny minds would forget all about me in the general festivities.

It must have been all of an hour later when I heard the heavy flopping of wings and fading, raucous cries that announced the departure of at least one of the *pteranodons*, perhaps both of them. I waited for half an hour longer, hardly daring to breathe, before squirming my body forward until the curve of the shell's mouth formed a crescent of light with the curving main body of the shell itself. A crescent of daylight, with a distant palm bending in a freshening breeze off the sea. I used my elbow to edge myself forward a few inches more, and froze!

Sitting there waiting for me, wings folded back, its head cocked expectantly on one side and its evil red eyes gazing unblinkingly, almost hypnotically into mine, was the

140

second *pteranodon*! Oh, no, it had not forgotten me, this creature. Perhaps its now departed colleague had filled itself with the doubtless succulent flesh of the crab, but this one had obviously not been satisfied, would not be until I, too, had been made a meal of . . .

But not if I had anything to say about it.

I slid backward again until I could only just see the sky-lizard, then hurriedly further back as it experimentally tried its head in the mouth of the shell. No, I was safe for the moment, it was unable to reach me. The great wedge-shaped head and beak simply could not maneuver within the shell's mouth. In fact as the *pteranodon* pushed harder, twisting its head as it sought to close with me, that huge wedge of head and beak jammed. In something of a panic the sky-lizard attempted to withdraw, actually rocking the vast ammonite before its head came free. For a moment or two then there was silence, but in the next instant my head was ringing to the reverberations of a series of savage blows on the exterior of the shell. Within those hollow acoustical confines the sound was deafening, a burst of machine-gun fire!

God almighty! Could the shell hold out against such a battering? The whole coil seemed to be vibrating about me. Surely it would shatter into a thousand pieces at any moment, exposing me like a bark-bug in a cracked cocoon to the beak of a hungry woodpecker! But mercifully the sharp blows soon ceased.

Following a long period of silence, thinking that perhaps the creature had given up at last and moved away, I eased myself forward again. He was still there, peering at me just as intently, his head cocked on one side as before. As I stared back at that monster I couldn't help but think of a line from *Aepyornis Island* by H. G. Wells: 'A great gawky, out-of-date bird! And me a human being, heir to the ages and all that.'

Oh, I know, the creature in Wells's story was a true bird and mine was a reptile; but my plight was much the same as that of Wells's hero, infinitely worse, in fact. He at least had been located in his own time: *Aepyornis Vastus* had been the odd-bird-out.

So the afternoon crept by. At intervals I would ease myself forward to peer out from the mouth of the great shell, invariably to find my *pteranodon* antagonist still laying siege on that exit with what seemed to me the patience of a prehistoric Job. Occasionally, too, there would come a burst of staccato pecking at the outer wall of the shell, to which I soon grew accustomed. And strangely enough, apart from my slight hunger and thirst, and not to mention the horror awaiting me outside, I found the coiled shell very much preferable to that pebbly crevice of the previous night. It dawned on me that I was perfectly safe where I was. Following fast on the heels of this realization my state of extreme nervous tension, the rigors of which, by then, had been sapping me for over twenty-four hours, subsided into a relaxed weariness that soon gave way to sleep.

Suddenly there came an assault upon the shell that almost tipped me from its bell mouth before I was properly awake and bracing myself against the sides of the cavity. What had it been, this rude awakening? My sleep-dulled mind could not quite grasp it. There had been a rumble as of distant thunder, then a vast stirring of the ground that tilted the shell on its side, almost tipping me out. This had shaken me roughly awake, and –

Again the ground rocked, jolting the shell wildly up and down, shaking me violently and threatening to cast me loose from my position against the curving walls. There came a frightened squawking from outside in the night and a lurid orange glow shone dimly even through the coils of my ammonite refuge. This could only mean volcanic activity, a second eruption!

Above the low rumblings of the earth there came then a frantic flapping of leathery wings and the sudden *hisss* of swirling waters. I could hear the *pteranodon* squawking and blustering as it rose high in the disturbed air, and as I crawled from the mouth of the mammoth ammonite I saw the sky-lizard's wildly fluttering shadow cast by the glare from the distant mountains.

Out at sea the volcano was on the move again, sinking this time as secondary cones broke the surface much further out. A rush of cool water swirled about my feet, lifting the huge shell and floating it away along the beach. Hastily, with the water rising quickly to my knees, fearing a shock wave of water such as had left me in my present predicament, I backed up the beach to slightly higher ground. The expected shock wave did not come, however; instead, the disturbed water quickly subsided.

Out near the cone the whole surface of the sea sprayed up suddenly in foaming white crests, and I could see that the new volcano was quite definitely sinking. Way out beyond the reef it had formed, at a distance of what must have been five or six miles, many fires shot the darkness with lurid light, hissing and roaring as they spouted flames from the sea. Plainly I had slept all through the night, for already dawn was showing on the horizon. Even as I watched, the edge of the sun crept up to illuminate a fantastic scene.

The sea was on fire! For mile upon mile the surface of the water was lit by submarine explosions; geysers of superheated water shot into the air; turbulent waters tossed and rushed in an utter confusion of currents. Behind me the hills seemed to burn as rivers of lava began

143

to course down them. Away to my right these lava streams had already reached the water, sending sheets of steam hissing and searing skyward. And then a wonderful thing happened.

The last of the waters washing about my feet began a hurried retreat and, as the sun rose higher and the volcanic activity out at sea grew more furious, that retreat became an absolute rout of receding waters. Down went the reef in a sundering of ocean, back to its watery origins, and the blazing cone with it. A tremendous cloud of steam rose up then that turned the sun into a pink glow, washing the entire horizon in rose and blood tints.

The whole beach jerked and tossed now, no longer in violent spasms but rather in short, spastic rhythms that kept me adjusting my balance as I watched the spectacle of the red, retreating waters. They were in full flood now, leaving the beach bubbling and slimy and scattered with gasping fish and flopping shapes behind them. Why, at this rate –

At this rate the time-clock would soon be exposed! Somewhere out there in the mud and pebbles my time-machine lay, just waiting for the retreating waters to leave it high and dry.

I started down the beach in the wake of the fleeing ocean, beginning to run across the coarse wet sands as the sun rose up above the volcanic mists to turn the entire Cretaceous scene pink and gold. The sand sucked at my feet and various stranded creatures snapped at me in their death agonies as I sloshed past them. To my left a huge shadow grew up from the misty beach to flop awkwardly in a shallow pool. I barely gave it a second glance, however, barely recognized it as a vast *tylosaurus*, as a second shape, one with which I was far more familiar, suddenly appeared in a swirl of black, receding water.

The time-clock! There it was, half buried in wet sands, its narrow end pointing at thirty degrees to the sky, its face buried deep in muck. My vessel, my gateway to the future, to the world of men!

Through a pool of warm water I splashed and struggled, dimly aware that something huge splashed after me, but I was interested in one thing only: to regain my clock and find a way to dig it from the clinging muck. Now I was almost upon it, falling beside it as finally I tripped and sprawled in the trembling, quaking sands. My hand touched the clock's peculiar wood-like texture. I trembled then in a cold sweat of frustration and fear. It would take me hours to dig the thing out, assuming that I was to have the chance!

Far down the beach seaward a massive wall of water was gathering, piling itself up for a titanic onslaught on the land. But I must at least try. Even as I began scrabbling at the wet sand and pulling uselessly at the heavy bulk of the clock a shadow fell upon me and a primal scream tore the salty, misted air.

I hurled myself flat and headlong as a monster flipper slapped down at the spot where I had crouched, spraying me with slimy pebbles and mud and half lifting the clock from the grip of the sand. The great jaws of the stranded *tylosaurus* struck at me, missed, fastened in terrible anger on my half buried vessel. Balanced on its massive foreflippers, the creature slammed its rear quarters time and again down onto the sand to assist its jaws in their action of tearing the time-clock up from its boggy bed. At last the time-machine came loose, was tossed a dozen yards as easily as a man might fling a light chair, landing on its back, face up.

As the ground began to rock more violently and the *tylosaurus* again turned to snap at me, I scrambled after the clock, diving on it and groping for the hidden mechanisms that would open its panel. The great sea beast flopped after me, its body thudding down on the wet sand with each convulsive heave of gigantic flippers.

For some time a roaring had been growing in my ears, and even as the frontal panel of the clock swung silently open I looked up to see an awesome wall of water bearing down on me like some monstrous express train! That wave was all of fifty feet high, white-crested, curling and roaring and hissing like all the demons of hell and quite as fearsome! I hurled myself in a headlong dive into the clock's eerily illuminated interior, and as the panel clicked shut behind me felt my vessel picked up like a toy and carried away on the crest of the wave.

The *tylosaurus* was gone at once in the mad torrent of water. An instant more and my mind had meshed with the clock's and I was climbing up, up to the clouds while below me, viewed in the scanners, the great wave crashed inland, carrying all before it . . .

Three days later I left the Cretaceous and set course for the future. During the intervening time I managed to collect a marvelously representative selection of shells to replace the collection lost at the onset of that first disastrous volcanic outbreak. I undertook the task this second time far more carefully, choosing a beach far from volcanic regions. I also gathered an ample supply of the great nuts, to sustain myself should my journey prove to be a long one.

Ah, if only I could have guessed just how long it would take to return to my own era. But there, I could never have guessed, could not possibly have had any idea.

On the third evening following the recovery of my vessel, as the hot disk of the sun sank down behind wild and primal mountains, then I said my silent farewells and took leave of the Cretaceous forever. I had seen as much as I wanted to see of the vast and teeming swamps and forests, jungles, lakes and oceans; and certainly I had had my fill of that prehistoric world's denizens. All scientific interests aside, my own time called to me from across future ages.

So it was that lifting the time-clock up again to the skies, I meshed my mind and psyche with those of my vessel and turned the prow of that fantastic vehicle in the direction of tomorrow.

Part Four

Introductory Note

Since it has been part of my task in the preparation of this work to divide it into its various parts, chapters and sections, and to provide titles, and since the following part (despite its length) is composed mainly of fragments, I have chosen for it simply that title, 'Fragments'. I have however subtitled separate sections within the whole.

This has been necessary due to the fact that while my safe at Miskatonic University was more or less fireproof, it was not completely waterproof. The flames that devoured the old university during the Fury did little harm to the tapes, but the flood waters of the freak storm which later deluged the ruins most certainly did! Whole sections of the tapes, I fear, complete and complex statements of not inconsiderable length, have been lost.

I have used the usual system of ellipses, three or four periods to mark breaks in what I judge to be sentences and paragraphs; I have similarly prefaced new paragraphs apparently springing from the broken narrative. Excessively large or long breaks I have marked with a line of asterisks and/or comments.

With the opening section of the following part my task was not so difficult, as the tapes were more or less complete. In general, however, this part of my work toward preparing the manuscript for publication was by far the most trying, particularly for one whose interests prior to this task were anything but literary.

Arthur D. Meyer

Fragments

(From de Marigny's recordings)

1 The Thing in the Vat

. . . And that, de Marigny, was when I first met up with the Hounds of Tindalos. Yes, those same Tind'losi Hounds of the Cthulhu Cycle: vampires of time that haunt the darkest angles of the fourth dimension, foraging abroad from the temporal towers of wraithlike Tindalos to hunt down unwary travelers.

I knew them of course through my familiarity with the pantheon of the Cthulhu Cycle and its legends, remembering them from the references they are afforded in the old occult works. Nevertheless, and though I ought to have been at least partially prepared by such knowledge, when I sensed them about my time-ship, and particularly when I actually first saw them in my scanners, they were so patently evil that my very soul shuddered!

And yet they are so difficult to describe. They are what one might expect to find if all goodness were taken away: an uncleanliness without living form, and yet embodied in vaguely batlike shapes, flapping rags of evil, vampirish drinkers of life itself. Of course, if we are to take the olden records as gospel, then in certain circumstances the Hounds are capable of materializations in three-dimensional space. I can only say that I have known innumerable clashes with them since that first time, but not once have they followed me out of time into normal space.

They exist, you see, in time itself, 'amid time's darkest

angles', as it were. Which means of course that they exist at a different temporal speed from life as we know it. Ah, but when one travels in time, then one moves in their element.

. But that first meeting.

As I have said, I had set my course forward from the Cretaceous, toward the present era, intending to slow down and stop at intervals of time until I reached a period subsequent to that of our departure when we fled from Ithaqua's elementals of the air. In this way I hoped to avoid the obvious pitfalls of temporal paradox.

It was as I was about to make my first halt in time that I became aware of the Hounds.

They were like shadows in the scanners, distant tatters that flapped almost aimlessly in the voids of time; but as they in turn sensed me their movements became imbued with more purpose! As they drew closer, I saw that in fact they had shape and size and even something approaching solidarity, but that despite all of these attributes there was still nothing about them that even remotely resembled what we know of life. They were Death, the worms in a dead man's skull, the maggots fattening in a rotting corpse. They were the Hounds of Tindalos, and once recognized they can never be forgotten!

Now they swarmed toward the clock, ethereal wasps attracted by a juicy apple of time in which I was the succulent core, and as they fluttered darkly about my hurtling vessel I heard their hellish chittering. They were batlike, and they communicated with batlike voices. Or were their chitterings simply expressions of delight that here they had found some unsuspecting traveler in time? Knowing instinctively that they were evil – I knew it as surely as I knew that they were the Hounds of Tindalos – I nevertheless thought myself safe in the body of the clock. Very soon, however, I discovered that this was not the case.

If my time machine were a sphere, Henri, then I might have been safe, for the Hounds fear perfect curves. But of course the clock is of hard angles, and the Vampires of the Void are one with all the angles of time. There are ancient Greek documents which, along with certain esoteric translations, might explain all of this far better than I ever could. What I am saying essentially is this: the Hounds could reach me, even through the incredibly hard material of the clock's walls. The first I knew of it was when smoke seemed to pour from all the interior angles of my vessel, angles I sensed rather than saw, you understand. And then awesome feelers entered into my refuge to fondle me with their chill, a chill that threatened instantly to draw off all of my body's heat – all of my life-force – and leave me stiff, frozen and dead!

I instantly accelerated, only to discover that the Hounds were endowed with that same power. They, too, were capable of controlling their rate of passage through time. Similarly, when I hastily slowed down and turned to race into the past again, they were amply capable of pacing me, closing with the time-clock once more to recommence their foul gropings and draining of my life-force.

Desperately, while yet hurtling backward through time, I further maneuvered my vessel in space. That is, I consciously sought to avoid the Hounds of Tindalos, whose element is time, by throwing my vessel through space. In this my blunder was twofold. One, I lost myself hopelessly. Two, my ploy did not succeed. Certainly I had fled through space, but I had still been traveling in time as I did it!

One cannot avoid the Tind'losi Hounds in time. There is only one way to escape them: the time-traveler must revert back to the three mundane dimensions. I should

154

have known it at once, but it's useless to cry over spilled milk. When, at the very last moment, I did revert back into normal space, it was to find myself utterly and hopelessly lost! Gone the Hounds, and with them any chance of an early return to my own time, my own place.

I had no way of judging, you see, how far I had accelerated into the future, no way of knowing how many æons I had traversed in my flight back into the past. And when you consider the fantastic leagues, the light-years of space that the clock can consume in mere instants, why, I could be out beyond the Milky Way, while back on Earth the ice sheets might even now be reaching out from polar regions to freeze the woolly mammoth on the plains of Siberia.

I repeat, I was utterly, hopelessly lost.

From then on, for what I judge now must have been a period of at least a year of normal time – I find difficulty now, you know, in thinking of time as in my old pre-transition period – I wandered the space-lanes, and occasionally the corridors of time, seeking some clue, some signpost to the planet of my origins. It was toward the end of this period that I again braved time in a direction I hoped would take me toward my own era. I was actually searching for a period in which I might recognize the constellations, which in turn might lead me home. Instead, I again chanced upon a foraging party of the Hounds.

I say chanced upon them, and yet it is more than probable that in fact they were lying in ambush. Yes, it seemed they were waiting for me, and I became aware of them only in the last instant, as they were actually fastening on the clock! To be surprised like that is disconcerting to say the least, de Marigny. Picture yourself in a car, driving down an empty street, when suddenly a child steps off the curb only a few feet in front. Your brakes are out of the question; you are too close to the child. You hold the steering wheel in your hands, however, and while your foot is reaching for the brake you are able to turn the wheels.

I was in a vaguely similar position, except of course that it was my own life I had to save. My immediate reaction, I suppose, should have been to switch out of time into the mundane three dimensions. To this day I do not know why I did not do so, unless the Hounds have that same ability of the greater powers of the CCD to get into men's minds and dull them or turn them to their own purposes. Anyway, I turned my 'steering wheel' instead, and sought a path through the massed ranks of the Tind'losi Hounds. And indeed there seemed to be a path, a clear route through time that they had not blocked.

Fleeing down this sole avenue of egress, I saw my mistake too late: there were more of them waiting for me behind dark angles. Yet again I was obliged to fly both in space and time simultaneously, and yet again I found that in the end all escape routes were blocked. Only then, it seemed, did I remember the three mundane dimensions and revert back to them, and only then did I discover how cruelly the Hounds of Tindalos had fooled me!

They had maneuvered me into a perfect trap, forcing me to revert to normal space – or at least reminding me that I could do so – at that exact second of time most propitious to their cause, which I knew then was to destroy me completely! Hurtling out of time but yet speeding through space, I emerged in three dimensions to discover myself already rushing down upon the surface of a gray world. The vast bulk of the planet was there directly before me. There was no time even to think – an automatic application of mental brakes had but minimal effect. The lower atmosphere rushing by in a stream of sparks that formed a flaming tail, I plunged, a meteorite, tightening my mental controls of the time-clock, but it was already too late. The bulk of the world below rushed up to embrace the clock, to flatten it to its bosom of mountains and plains.

I threw my hands up before my face, at least, I think I tried to . . .

I became aware of a vast room filled with a variety of machines and obscure electrical mechanisms for all the world reminiscent – no, the very duplicate – of some mad scientist's laboratory out of those old horror films of the thirties and forties. Over the tiled floor of this tremendous laboratory, in and about and all around the towering consoles of incredibly complicated instruments, trundled a squat, rubber-wheeled robot of multiple appendages and faceted electrical eyes. It paused every now and then at one bank of dials and levers or another to make speedy but delicate adjustments. The whole scene was soundless and I seemed to view it through some distorting element, like faintly frosted glass. Either that or my eyes were not functioning properly.

My mind, too, was very foggy. Snatches of memory were there, I recall, from all my years of youth and middle age, but much was missing. For example, while I knew dimly who I was, I did not know where or how I came to be where I was. My awareness, which had seemed to be instantaneous, was incomplete, as if I were a machine, suddenly switched on but not yet warmed to the task of existing.

Then it dawned on me that I was hardly aware at all. I could not feel my body, could not close my eyes or even blink. I felt no sensations whatever. Where, for instance, was the tightening and slackening of the chest that goes hand in hand with breathing? Where was the sense of flowing blood, the pulse, which I personally have always been able to feel or hear in my head? But I was given very little time to ponder these things. In any case, such questions would all soon be answered.

All at once, as far as I could make out, having paused to observe the readings on a metal mushroom of gleaming dials and flashing lights, the robot spun quickly about while its faceted eyes all swiveled in my direction. The thing looked at me. Then it rushed toward me, its rubber wheels blurring over the tiles while the upper appendages of its metal body became suddenly galvanized into fantastic tremblings. Three of its five eyes flashed through an astonishing range of color combinations.

The thing came right up to me until, achieving some sort of perspective and clarity of vision at last, I could see that it stood almost man-sized. It reached out an appendage toward my eyes, a rubber-tipped claw of sorts. As this tool began to close over my right eye I tried to scream, to turn and run, to throw up a protective arm before my face, and nothing happened! My brain was pouring commands to every part of my body but –

My body? Had I been capable of laughter then indeed, at that exact moment of time, I might have laughed hysterically, though I think it more likely that I would have screamed. For as the mechanical claw steadied itself to close gently on my right eye and shut out sight in that orb, so my left eye witnessed this action reflected in the many facets of the robot's own five crystal lenses. It also saw the vat of electrolytic fluids bubbling and the thing the vat contained: a thing like a flattened, wrinkled, elongated bladder. It saw the glowing plastic tubes that protruded from the grayly pulsing mass in the vat, and also the naked organs with which those tubes were tipped. In short I saw myself, the mortal remains of Titus Crow: *a brain in a bowl, with stalked, lidless, bloodshot eyes*!

The human mind, despite its circumstances, or perhaps because of them, is mercifully equipped with a means to shut out sensations and sights which are completely unbearable. Happily what remained of my brain in that robot laboratory upon an alien world still retained this facility. A blackness engulfed me in which I was to know no dreams but only a long drawn out longing for death rather than the ultimate horror and madness of the thing in the vat.

2 Robot World

So began my transition, de Marigny.

My next awakening was one of longer duration but no less horrible, though this time the climax did not cause my mind to shut down, seeking safety in unconscious oblivion. As it happened, the shutting down was done for me, automatically. But in many other ways that second awakening was very different from the first. For one thing, the scene in the great laboratory was now accompanied by sounds, the sounds one might expect to hear at the heart of a giant computer: a mechanical clicking, as of a thousand typewriter keys; a whirring and fluttering, similar to the shuffle of programming cards; the hiss and sputter of controlled electrical energies and the distant, subterranean thrummings and vibrations of great engines.

When the robot – custodian? – of the place saw that I was once again conscious, it approached in far less agitation than before and, astonishingly, spoke to me, in a neutral but not unpleasant English! 'I see that you are aware.' Two of its eyes swiveled down to peer steadily at something below my sphere of vision, then joined the other three in staring at me in a manner more than merely mechanical. I detected an air – I could swear it – of something approaching pride in the metal scientist, for such the robot later proved to be.

'Yes, you are aware, and you hear me, but do not try to answer. You will not have a voice until much later. At that time we will be able to talk, but until then I must rely upon the intelligence imparted to me by your friend here. He is guiding me in your reconstruction and we are making slow but steady progress.'

My friend? I found that with a little effort I could move my eyes, making them follow the direction clearly indicated by a movement of one of the robot's upper appendages. There in a cleared space, its back to the wall of the laboratory, stood my time-clock. It was undamaged, as far as I could tell, and as I saw it many memories rushed in to fill the blank spaces in my mind, particularly the memory of falling in the clock like a meteorite to the surface of a gray world!

But what had the robot meant by calling the clock my friend? I was not to find that out for some time.

'I am told,' the robot continued, its voice remarkably human if hollow, 'that life-forms such as yourself suffer certain disturbances of mind originating in diseased or damaged members or organs of your bodies, and that such disturbances are known collectively as pain. This condition, I am led to believe, is as distressing to you as rust or lack of lubrication would be to me; indeed more distressing, for you are incapable of disconnecting the offending member or organ or of switching it off from your brain while the necessary corrections are performed. Moreover, I am assured that this pain is quite capable of bringing about a general debility in your entire system. Since it is important that you are not further damaged during this period of your reconstruction, I would like to know if you are now experiencing pain. If so I will switch you off immediately until I can find and remove the source of such distress. So that I may do these things, you may reply in the affirmative by moving your eyes to the right, or in the negative by moving them to the left. Are you in pain?'

Immediately, and with less effort this time, I moved my eyes to the left, then back again to stare at the robot. I could feel no pain whatever. Indeed I could barely feel my eyes, while the rest of my body remained a mere vacancy. (All this time I had kept my eyes averted from any shiny surface in which I might see unmentionable things reflected.) But now the robot's upper appendages were trembling and quivering; its faceted eyes were swiveling here and there like those of some freak, hybrid chameleon; its voice, when at last it spoke again, was full of what might only be called, well, if not emotion, certainly an unprecedented machine excitement!

'You . . . you see, you hear and you reason! You . . . you really *are*!' For a moment longer this weird metal creature exulted, then said, 'But there remains much to be done, and once more I must consult your friend before continuing my work. It were better, I think, if I switched you off.' He – already I thought of the robot as a male entity – reached out an appendage toward an area to one side of me and to the rear of my sphere of vision, pulling into view a large mirror on wheels. 'But before I do I would like you to see how we have progressed, your friend and I!'

I tried to close my eyes then but found that I could not do so. The attempt was an automatic reflex which, if I had been able to bear the sight revealed by the mirror, if I had looked closer, I would have seen to be impossible anyway. One cannot close eyes that have no lids! Instead I remembered the robot's words of a minute or so earlier and simply moved my eyes, all too slowly, to the right.

'Pain!' The robot actually seemed to gasp, recognizing my signal on the instant. Then he turned and sped rapidly away to operate a red switch in the center of a nearby console. Once again darkness descended, but not before I had fearfully, in dreadful but irresistible curiosity, turned my eyes back to the mirror.

Oh, yes, much had been done. Work upon my reconstruction was truly progressing:

My eyes were attached to my brain as before (the latter was now much more brain-shaped), but now they had been embedded in nubs of living flesh, in rudimentary sockets. There were twin, raw, wrinkled orifices, one at each side of the brain, with metallic cones attached to them by slim copper wires: my ears, I supposed them to be. There was an esophagus of flexible plastic, supported at the back by the first bones – or were they, too, plastic? – of a spine, which in turn had hanging before it a black, baglike thing that I took to be my stomach. Lungs, liver and kidneys were there, all artificial and none seeming to be working, all loosely attached to one another in a network of gristly filaments of synthetic protoplasm or plastic. And where my heart should have been, there hung a cluster of connected plastic balls, five of them spaced evenly about a shining metal nucleus. The whole visceral obscenity, with the exception of the stalked eyes and the metallic cones, swam or floated in a large transparent tube of yellow fluids.

And so my transition progressed. Periodically I would be made to awaken, to be shown my latest physical acquisitions, the most recent steps in my path toward completion. It seemed to me that my robot super-surgeon worked lovingly, and with tremendous pride in his craft. I watched myself grow in his mirror, saw my body gradually taking shape. Step by step I was brought back to full existence in that laboratory, and I marveled as each bone

– many of them plastic duplicates, for most of the originals were ruined beyond redemption – was made to fit into place within my semi-synthetic body. I saw my limbs take shape, and felt memories waking as my damaged brain healed itself or was repaired. And always and ever the robot talked to me, explaining how all this had come about, how it was that my jigsaw puzzle being was in process of reconstruction in his laboratory.

It seemed that my disastrous arrival upon the surface of the gray world had been witnessed by the robot, who at the time had been on a lone interplanetary expedition in search of life! His own planet, a world of subterranean hives and corridors, utterly devoid of organic life, was fifth from the sun in a system of six worlds and eleven moons. That was where I was now, on the fifth planet, but the gray world whose surface had so rudely received me had been the second from the sun, 680 millions of miles away toward the system's center. The robot had transported all of my parts and the clock, too, to his home world. There he had commenced . . .

. . . but in any case it had been my good fortune – no, let me not understate the matter. It had been a fantastically fortunate coincidence – not only that the robot had seen me crash to the surface of that gray planet, but also that he had been perhaps the one and only mechanism of his race who could ever have . . .

. . . T3RE, however, possibly by virtue of his years of random thought and his inbuilt capacity for endless physical and theoretical experimentation, had developed his own ideas with regard to organic life. His theory of the origin of species was that robots were not there in the beginning, but that they had been created originally by and in the service of superior organic life-forms. In short, I suppose you could call my friend a mechanical Darwin!

Eventually there came a time when I could no longer

be completely switched off, when only my conscious mind would respond to T3RE's control. This simply meant that my brain was whole again. Moreover, my id must be intact – I could hope, I could dream! And during those periods when the robot scientist labored his labor of love – and in the case of T3RE I am sure that so utterly unmechanical a phrase is not at all out of order – when of necessity my surface consciousness must be closed down to spare me the embarrassment of pain, then indeed I did dream.

As often as not the dream was recurrent, but though the main setting was known to me of old, this time it came to me that I *only* dreamed, that these subconscious sensations were merely pictures out of my own mind. They were not, as had been their prototype, of telepathic intensity. There was of course a vast crystal hall and a gossamer-clad goddess who cried crystal tears, while the rumbling thoughts of some being great beyond words fumbled to comfort her grief-stricken mind, and misty drapes trembled before a huge, alcoved throne upon which the Eminence himself stirred in emotional agitation. Such dreams were not good.

Then came that long-awaited awakening when I found myself with a working voice (I had already had several that did not work) and at last I was able to put to T3RE all of those questions I had saved up during my period of enforced muteness. Of course, it was a great moment for the robot, too, for at last he had a genuine, self-attestable specimen, albeit a reconstructed one of sentient organic life. Soon he would be able to . . .

'. . . as I myself am – was – organic,' I told him. 'We called them presidents and prime ministers and dictators and kings. They were all human beings. At least here you are all equal.'

'An equality leading to the utmost boredom, at least

until I found you!' he answered. 'And make no mistake, you are still organic, the greater part of you. But tell me more about this world of human beings. Were there no robots, no computers?' He was vastly interested.

'Oh, yes, there were computers. There were robots, too, though none so advanced as you,' I told him.

'And the machines existed in companionship with you human beings?'

'They were' – I was forced to admit it – 'man's slaves. Men made them.'

'Slaves? They were not companions? Men made them?'

'They were machines, as you are a machine, but they were simply not individual enough to be companions. They were heading that way, though. Certainly I knew men who loved their automobiles!'

'Ah! I see. They were of a low order, these robots, as are the T6's and T7's.' He turned from me where I hung in my complicated life-support tube. For a moment his crystal eyes stared across the laboratory at my time-clock, then he turned back to me. 'And yet your robot, the time-clock that brought you across time and space, is of an exceptionally high order, higher, I would say, even than a T2. It surprises me that he deigns to talk to me at all.'

'Oh, yes, the clock is a high-order machine, all right,' I answered. 'But it was made by organic beings of *such* a high order that by comparison I am not much better than those lowly, single-celled organisms and primitive animals which you tell me you have found on distant moons.'

At this revelation T3RE grew very excited. 'Then my theory may very well be correct! I have long suspected that it is a basically illogical presumption that we robots were here in the beginning. We have no sexual reproductory apparatus; we are incapable of generation by fission, though that is certainly the nearest we get to organic reproduction; we devise new models for specialized tasks, of course, but these have to be assembled from components which are, as separate units, insensate. Who, then, built the first robot?'

'We have a similar theological problem on my world,' I answered, as T3RE turned from me, switching off my conscious mind as he trundled almost absently away to ponder, no doubt, his last question. 'But there on Earth,' my subconscious mind continued to itself, 'there we ask ourselves who made God!'

It was not until very much later, during a period of wakefulness when T3RE had once more called me up from the netherworlds of subconscious mind to his robot laboratory, that I thought to ask him how long he had worked on me. The answer was not immediately forthcoming as we had to work out a satisfactory chronological system. It was based on the speed of light, in units of the length of time it took light to race from the primary of T3RE's system to his home planet. Finally I discovered I had been in the robot's care for no less than forty-seven years. Of all that time I had spent perhaps one hour awake, and of that hour all of fifteen minutes had been taken up in mutual conversation!

It had taken T3RE ten years merely to duplicate his first living red corpuscle. My nervous system had taken much longer, was still in process of reconstruction. My brain, too, had been a major problem: not its repair and assembly but the replacement of lost memories and complex nerve and motor areas. In this T3RE had relied solely upon my friend the time-clock.

What I had never known – what I could never have guessed – was that during my journeys in the clock through time and space, not only had I been one with the clock's psyche but the clock had recorded in its own memory banks all of my memories and thoughts! I have never discovered just why this was done; I fancy that it is normal procedure, that time-clocks such as mine always retain copies of the psychic identities and memories of their users.

At any rate, T3RE had fed these recordings back into my reconstructed brain using an infinitely delicate electronic system devised by the clock and himself. Now my body was almost complete, a composite but nearly perfect Frankenstein built mainly of synthetic parts, but yet retaining all of its original passions and humors, hopes and aspirations, pleasures and fears.

And in another twenty-three years, perhaps three or four hours of consciousness, I was ready. Ready for T3RE's final tests, when he would link up in a series of operations all of my millions of synthetic circuits and give me back my body. Then I would be lifted free of my life-support tube complete again as a man, a man like no other.

'When you have undergone all your tests,' he told me toward the end, 'when you are ready to recommence your journey, for your friend the time-clock tells me you are destined to complete a great journey, then I will . . .'

. . .'And what of yourself?' I asked him. 'Your future?'

'I do not matter. I have no God. My emotions are based mainly upon your own, which I tried to duplicate electronically within myself before you first regained consciousness. The clock explained these emotions to me. It was not a very successful experiment: I cannot even dream! You are superior, you and your clock, both of you. He can dream; he has many memories, even those of many beings before your time, he tells me. He has, yes, a psyche, an id. I do not matter, no – but you? – both of you must go on, to your journey's end.'

3 The Transition of Titus Crow

When I awakened next it was to a sort of chaos in the laboratory of T3RE. Other T3's were everywhere. Many of them moved about the laboratory, three or four clustered around my tube. At least half of them were almost indistinguishable from T3RE himself, while others had different arrangements of appendages and were obviously constructed to perform different tasks. Finally the robot directly in front of me spoke and I recognized him.

'That was your first test!' T3RE told me. 'You woke up yourself, without stimulation. Is there pain?'

'No, but there is – I have feelings! I can feel my arms and legs, my fingers. Is it finished?'

'It is finished,' cried T3RE in a sort of mechanical delight. He was a robot for sure, but in that instant he seemed more human than any real person I had ever known. He was whirring nervously on his wheels back and forth in front of me, his upper appendages waving, his five faceted eyes all aswivel; he acted for all the world like some excited schoolboy with his first model airplane, about to propel it on its maiden flight. And, more amazingly, his enthusiasm seemed to have infected his visitors!

'I am communicating with them on radio wavelengths,' he explained. 'They cannot speak in your tongue, indeed they have no tongues as such. Nor had I before I built into myself the necessary components. Even so, they are not as efficient as your organic vocal chords. Now we must see if the rest of you is equally efficient!'

I felt myself being lifted, tried to turn my head to see

what was going on, and my head turned! A sort of dazed disbelief enveloped me then; I felt quite drunk. At last I was back in control of my body! But what degree of control did I have? In an instant I was trembling in the grip of many emotions, and fear was not the least of them. Often before I had compared myself with the Frankenstein monster of fiction, but what if I should prove to be no less a monster? A stiff-limbed, mechanically jointed, uncoordinated mass of synthetic muscle and plastic parts?

A harness of some soft material lifted me from the tube and set me slowly down on the tiled floor of the laboratory. Though my feet touched the floor, and I actually felt them touch it, the harness lowered me no further. 'Is something wrong?' I inquired of T3RE.

'I will lower you slowly,' he answered, 'to give your body a chance to orientate. If anything goes wrong, tell me.' He moved a lever on a nearby console and the harness lowered me a few more inches.

Now I braced my feet against the floor and stood upright. I shrugged my shoulders free of the harness. I lifted my hands and looked at them, then tried a spontaneous whoop of joy and relief – and nothing came!

'My . . . my voice!' I gasped. 'What . . . what is wrong with my – ?'

'You must first learn to breathe if you wish to expel air violently,' T3RE told me. 'You have lungs, but from now on they will only be of use to you in speaking. I decided long ago that yours was a most inefficient circulatory system, and that – '

'Are you trying to tell me that I don't need air?' I cut him off.

'Only for the activation of your vocal cords,' he answered. 'But come, this is nothing to worry about. In fact your new system is far more efficient. You will be able to exist unprotected in all but the most corrosive atmospheres. I thought this would be better for you, in view of the journey you have ahead. Come, now, there are other, more important things to be tested. Walk, run, jump – try out your body! I need to see you function. Breathe if you wish, if it seems normal to you. The atmosphere in here has been adapted to suit your old constitution; see what your taste buds think of it. And then I have food for you, and drink: synthetic proteins and carbohydrates extracted from the oils of the earth!'

I sucked air into my lungs, tasted it, expelled it – and suddenly I exulted! Strength filled my body, I could feel it: an abundance of vitality, the sure knowledge that I was a new man, quite literally! I turned to the great mirror that stood beside my now empty tube and stared at myself.

Oh, the man who stood there, reflected in that mirror, was Titus Crow, little doubt of that, but he was a younger Titus Crow, revitalized. And he was complete! I knew that, just staring at myself. And yet I was more than complete. Not perfect, not by any means, for despite the wonderful blend of synthetics and flesh and metals and bone and plastics and hair that I now was, despite all this I was still human. And human beings are far from perfect. But I was a damn sight nearer perfect than had been the old man who fled the Tind'losi Hounds and smashed himself to pulp on the surface of a dead gray world!

'T3RE,' I finally said, 'you have worked a miracle. Many miracles. There is no need at all to test this body of mine; I know that it is an excellent body. And there is no way for me to thank you for what you have done.'

'You have thanked me enough,' he answered, 'in that I now know that my theory . . . all these colleagues of mine: they, too, are now aware that . . .'

* * *

. . . had known any practical way to get T3RE into the time-clock at that time then possibly he would have come along with me. As it was we said what we could of farewells, and so I took my . . .

. . . for where I was headed: well . . . list of possible three-dimensional directions which just might take me back to Earth. The route was designed, in any case, to send me close to galaxies and star clusters and nebulæ where, with a bit of luck, I might suddenly recognize some constellation or other and thus find my way home.

Such a route-card of interstellar space seems quite ridiculous, I know, but nevertheless that's the way I tried to do it. Not quite 'turn right at the blue dwarf with the tri-planet system and head for the binary with the spiral nebula at its left', but pretty much that sort of thing. Yes, I suppose it must seem ridiculous, until one considers the sort of speeds my craft could accomplish. If you are working with speeds in the region of tens of thousands of miles per hour, then of course you require a very accurate scientific course to get you and your target arriving at the same spot at the same time. Not so with the time-clock! I could simply pick a star in the sky and go there, and at almost that speed!

But of course there is only one Earth, and I soon discovered that the planet of my birth might just as well be the proverbial needle in the haystack as far as instant success was concerned. One thing I did have, however, and that was patience.

4 Roman Britain

. . . in the end, can wear extremely thin, and I proved to be no exception to this rule. Not that my journey could be said in any way to be boring. On the contrary, for I had my pick of alien worlds to explore, and many of them were beautiful beyond words. Others, I must add, were frightening beyond words.

. . . as close to Venus, and not only in time, for . . .

. . . wonderful as any that the science-fiction writers ever dreamed of; more, because they were real! But the telling would take so long that it must wait until another time. Perhaps, de Marigny, if ever you decide to join me in Elysia, and I'm sure you will, then we'll be able to swap adventures with each other. And if . . .

. . . back on Earth. And I *knew* it was Earth. Third from the sun, with a moon I knew and loved as every human lover since the beginning of time has loved it; green and beautiful as no other planet except perhaps Elysia, which isn't really a planet anyway, is beautiful. Oh, it was Earth, and not too far removed from my own time at that, for England's shores were sharply etched against the blue of the sea as I fell toward . . . could see that there was a . . . fields of the North . . .

. . . boy herding sheep. In my excitement as I brought the clock in to a landing I had not bothered to pay attention to my exact geographic location; I only knew that I was somewhere in Yorkshire. No doubt the lad with the sheep would be able to put me right . . .

. . . to run away! Perhaps he had seen me land and thought me some sort of flying monster. A minute later I had managed to catch up with him and bring him to a halt. I held his shoulders and looked him straight in the eyes, letting him see that I was only a man, if a somewhat weirdly dressed man, for I was clad only in a soft leathery loincloth, a leaf torn from an alien palm on a tropical planet.

And yet by then I had discovered that the shepherd boy's own garment was no less surprising. It was formed of little more than a body sheet of rough cloth, with a few stitches to hold the thing in place, like a crude poncho. He kept rolling his eyes longingly toward a far-off huddle of stone towers and outlying huts with smoke rising into the blue summer sky, and trying to pull away from me while crying out in a tongue which at first I did not recognize. Then I caught the fact that he wanted to go home. Home to – to *Eboracum*!

Eboracum! The name given by the Romans to York! I was home on Earth, in the very land of my birth, but hundreds of years too early, in Roman Britain! You can have no idea . . .

. . . boy further. Once he was used to the idea that I meant him no harm, and hearing my stilted, rather poor Latin, he soon regained his composure. The governor of Britain, I discovered, was Platorius Nepos, and three years earlier work had commenced 'far to the north' on Hadrian's Wall. Roman Britain in the year 125 A.D.! . . . that I was so close to home, the merest hop through time in the clock, and –

Ah, but it was not to be. Close to where I had landed stood a villa, and now that I knew *when* I was I realized why, when I had flown the clock down close to the place, the building had struck me as being rather Old Mediterranean in style. Later I was to discover that the villa was the retreat of a retired Roman senator, one Felicius Tetricus, and that because of a local uprising some miles to the northwest he had stationed sentries and watchmen in and around his villa's grounds. These men were of his own household and very loyal to him, which was my downfall. Perhaps if they had . . . course they were on the lookout for just such persons . . .

. . . talking to him. At any rate I saw this fellow in a jerkin and leather skirt, with sandals on his feet and a shortsword at his belt. He seemed friendly enough, despite an evil scar across one cheek, but as he came up to me and started to speak I saw his eyes flicker strangely and, simultaneously, heard the shepherd boy's cry of warning. Someone behind me! I whirled, saw a second man leaping – and then the heavy pommel of his sword crashed down upon my temple and I fell, unconscious, to the heather.

When I came to I was in a bed of silks and linens, in a room whose balcony overlooked a paved veranda surrounded by a garden of flowers. From my bed I could look out and actually see the garden. I could smell the flowers' heady perfume. There is no other smell in the entire universe as sweet as the flowers of Earth, unless it is that fragrance of my own Tiania's slender neck.

Well, I was eventually attended by a physician in a purple toga, an elderly man who would not talk but simply clucked and bathed my head, applied some cooling liniment and changed my bandage. Finally, before he left me, he told me that I must rest. I had been in Tetricus' villa for three days, and at first the master of the house had despaired of my life.

'You can consider yourself lucky,' he told me obscurely, 'that you resemble Titus Tetricus so well!'

My mind was all foggy, in fact I was in a fever, and so perhaps I didn't entirely know what I said when I answered: 'But I *am* Titus!'

When he heard this the old physician turned quite gray, then backed away, mumbling to his gods and making a series of esoteric symbols in the air with a forefinger. Not long after this, before I could drop back off to sleep, Felicius Tetricus himself . . .

. . . was a period when I kept swimming up out of my fever for a few minutes and then sinking slowly back. During one of my semiconscious bouts I heard old Tetricus and someone else – I think it was the gnarled physician – talking about me in lowered tones. Tetricus remarked on my likeness to his own dead son, Titus, killed in a chariot race across the moors and buried these three years. The bereaved father had offered up prayers to all the gods of earth, air, fire and water – particularly the latter, Sul, who seemed to be Tetricus' patron deity – that his son be returned to him. And now? Could it be that his prayers had at last been answered?

Might this stranger not indeed be Titus, returned from the land of the shades to his doting father in the form of this stranger? And was this man really a stranger? Had he not admitted that his name was Titus? True, he was older than Titus Tetricus had been at his death, but that had been three years ago. Did the shades, too, age then? The man had an athlete's body, of that there could be little doubt, and he was no simple Briton. Patently his was a noble . . .

. . . more Felicius had looked upon my troubled, feverish face and form, the more sure the old Roman was becoming that I was his son reincarnate, that . . .

. . . came to proper. I found Felicius at my bedside. My fever seemed much abated and my head much clearer, and I remembered what I had overheard of the old man's superstitious half-belief in his son's resurrection in my body. I determined that if it seemed in my favor to do so, I would put Felicius' fancies to my own use. By that I mean that it . . .

. . . thing I asked about, therefore, was the clock, which I called a 'shrine' to all the gods of the air. I did this just in case those assailants of mine who had knocked me down and brought me here, nearly caving my skull in with their enthusiasm, had actually seen me land. It seemed to me . . .

. . . had it brought into the villa, though he had seen little use for so inordinately heavy a thing. Now, however, he was glad. If it was indeed a shrine, then he would offer up prayers to it that I had been delivered unto him. But what was I really, and where did I hail from?

Well, I obviously could not tell the truth. For one thing I doubted if Tetricus, a very down-to-Earth man for his sort, could even grasp so completely outré a concept as time-travel. Instead I feigned loss of memory: all I could remember was my name, which was Titus.

. . . hear nothing of my moving out of bed. I was to spend a further week in enforced recuperation, until my head was fully healed. In fact my head was already fully healed, and long before the end of the week Felicius caught me pacing to and fro in my room and asked me what was wrong. I told him I needed to worship, that he must take me to my clock. He skated around the subject, walked me around the villa and its grounds, literally gave me free run of the place, except for certain locked rooms in the . . . servants. There, too, I was introduced to Thorpos, a huge Nubian whose . . .

. . . absolutely no way! More and more it seemed that Felicius was becoming enamored of the idea that I really was his son, and I had to play along with him. That seemed to me the only way I might ever. . .

. . . while they hadn't seen the clock actually arrive, they had seen me step from it! Felicius was no fool; he certainly did not intend that his son, recently returned to him from beyond the pale, should ever be recalled! He wasn't going to let me anywhere near that clock, not as long as he could help it. So what was I . . .

. . . unwilling to use force against the members of the noble's household, and so I tried at first to bluff my way past the ever watchful Thorpos. I might as well . . . failed, I then attempted to bribe the Nubian. He was very polite – I was his master as much as any man could be – but his orders came direct from Felicius Tetricus and they were . . .

The big black must have informed Felicius that I was still trying to get to the clock, for the next day I was called to the old man's chambers and chided over the matter. If I wanted to offer up prayers, I was told, there were temples in Eboracum I could visit, not to mention Felicius' own private shrine in the grounds of the villa itself.

For a fortnight then I was completely obedient to the old man's whims, simply biding my time and trying to allay his fears that perhaps I desired to leave the hospitality of the villa. This was in no way easy, for . . . and in the end I made the fatal mistake of letting Thorpos find me wandering in the servants' quarters, trying the doors in the middle of the night. I simply wasn't made to be stealthy. And how could I possibly make out after that that I was not trying to get away from the villa, away from Felicius Tetricus?

Some few days later I heard it whispered among the servants that my clock had been taken out and buried on the moors. I made what worried, discreet inquiries I could, all useless, and it didn't take long for me to understand that Felicius had put a terrible price on the head of any man who dared even mention the clock to me! That was that, then. Since it seemed I . . .

. . . simply continue to bide my time and hope that eventually I could talk the Roman noble into revealing the clock's whereabouts, I settled to my far from uncomfortable existence in Felicius' household.

And it was that way for the better part of a year. I waited and tried my best to ignore the ever-present anxiety that nagged at my insides, that the clock might be lost beyond redemption, and only . . . good at subterfuge, the type of trick I've never much cared for, but I . . .

. . . many months. For a period I was even driven to consider violence upon the person of Felicius Tetricus himself, but when the opportunity came I could not bring myself to do it. And by then the old man was absolutely convinced that I was his son, Titus Tetricus, returned to him by the gods.

And yet the year had not been wasted, for I had struck up a firm friendship with the Roman philosopher, Lollius Urbicus (not to be confused with Q. Lollius Urbicus, who was to become Antonius Pius' governor of Britain in 139 A.D.) whose truly remarkable erudition and magnetic personality suited my own mental attitudes very well. At the same time, yet on an entirely different level, I had managed to find many outlets for that physical abundance built into me by T3RE. I was a man in my prime, with the strength and stamina of three men.

Much to Felicius' alarm I had taken up chariot racing and wrestling, all the sports of the games, and I had quickly grown to excel in them all. I had been tutored in the use of the shortsword and in the heavier British blade, even in the Scottish and Pictish long-handled ax. There came a time when it seemed that there was no weapon I could not master, but all of . . .

. . . instincts and love of knowledge always took me back to the sparse household of Lollius Urbicus, and there I would bury my frustrations in long hours of discussion and simple contemplation of the nature of . . .

Oh, certainly Felicius Tetricus tried to win me over. There was, for instance, always a party at the villa; the women he made arrangements with for my amusement ran from the wives of officers engaged on supervisory duties at the Wall to expensive local whores whose wares would have tempted any man, except perhaps one whose dreams were haunted by the face and form of a goddess. No, try as he might to make me his son, the weeks found me spending more and more of my time with Lollius Urbicus, with whom I had developed scholarly links completely transcending two thousand years of time and vast differences of creed, society and similar mundane concepts.

And it was in this affinity of mine with the Roman philosopher whose book, *Frontier Garrison*, back in the . . . seeds of a dilemma within a dilemma were sown, and they were seeds that grew and blossomed strangely in the end.

5 The Great Race

. . . that this Earth of ours was inhabited by many intelligent races before Man, some of them malign, as the Cthulhu Spawn, others benign and . . .

. . . in the writings of the elder Peaslee, Wingate's father, particularly in what he wrote of his peculiar amnesia during the years 1908-13 . . . that one of Wingate's principal interests had always lain in the Great Sandy Desert. Of course I can see that you are wondering just what all this has to do with my life in the villa of Felicius Tetricus in 125 A.D.. I will tell you.

I have mentioned this almost psychic affinity of mine

with the Roman philosopher Lollius Urbicus, the similarity in our thinking and the primal puzzles to which our minds were drawn as one. Now I want you to picture, way back in the dim mists of time, a great race of scientists dwelling upon the primordial landmass of Australia, which was yet to sink beneath the waves and rise again several times before the first man walked the Earth. This race is lost to man except in the most ancient of desert ruins, whose hints of an antediluvian super-civilization are mind-staggering.

These beings, creatures of multiple appendages that walked in much the same manner as garden snails and talked by clicking great claws, stood ten feet tall and were ten feet wide at the bases of their rugose, conical bodies. They had developed instruments through which they could send their minds out into space, or into the past or future, to displace the minds of other sentient beings and replace them. When this happened the displaced minds took up habitation in the conical bodies of the usurping Great Race. In this way scientists of the Great Race collected knowledge of all future and past civilizations, of every planet within range of their mind-swapping machines. And always they were on the lookout for fresh bodies to inhabit, young races into which, should the need arise, they might project their own minds en masse. As to . . .

. . . but Lollius! How it happened I will never know, but where it had undoubtedly been their intention to reach out from the dim past of 500,000,000 years ago to exchange a mind with my philosopher friend, well, the Great Race got me instead! To be a man, deep in silent contemplation the one minute – and in the next to find oneself inhabiting the body of some monstrous slug! The shock was tremendous, and were it not for the sheer stability of the shape of my new body I am sure I would have fallen over in a faint. There was no suggestion that this might be a dream or an hallucination; I knew immediately that it . . .

. . . to record the history of my own civilization, the Roman race, and in that instant I knew that I was the victim of a terrible mistake: I knew that Lollius Urbicus should be there in my place. But what to do? And what would become of me if these beings should suddenly discover that I was not the Roman philosopher they thought I was? I decided that for the moment I would attempt to bluff my way through, at least until I could see which way the . . .

. . . minds of divers races from every conceivable epoch of Earth time, and from hundreds of inhabited planets scattered throughout . . .

. . . conversed with the group-mind of members of a hybrid polyp race whose home world had been a moon of Mercury ages before it was drawn into the sun's destroying furnace; with the minds of two intelligent reptile creatures from dimly fabulous Valusia; with the utterly alien consciousness of a semi-vegetable entity whose hibernating body slumbered at the core of a vast comet which would not end its journey for ten million years, when at last its passenger would awaken. I talked with the mind of a Cimmerian chieftain, Crom-Ya, of prehistoric Northumberland; with that of Khephnes, an erudite Egyptian of the Fourteenth Dynasty; and with the mind of Wolfred Herman Freimann, who fought the Romans in the passes of the Teutoberger Wald. There were intelligences from . . .

. . . but that eventually . . .

. . . through me as easily as a windowpane. In a state of terrific apprehension I was taken before a council of scientists whose prime purpose and task was the correlation of the ages, the Masters of the Archives. And when they began to question me, then I knew that my problems were only just beginning. They wanted to know who I was and from which era of Earth's future. Then, when I answered, they desired to know how the mind of a man from the twentieth century could possibly have been drawn back from Roman Britain in the year 125 A.D.? . . . nothing else for it but to tell them of my travels through time and space in search of my own era, which I had fled in the face of insuperable adversity. And so . . .

. . . the time, during my examination, I was conscious of a kind of derision in the council members, frankly of their disbelief. Obviously they had made a great mistake, and plainly my story was one huge fabrication. Perhaps I was the philosopher they had sought, but the business of mind-transference had driven me insane. This was surely the only reasonable explanation, for even with all the technological advances the Great Race had made in the course of a million years of migration across the universe, not even they had discovered how to project their *bodies* through time, only their minds. How then could so rudely fashioned a being as myself have . . . and then built a machine with which to . . .

And that was when I broke in on them. I think I would rather be struck in the face than ridiculed, de Marigny, for . . . be made sport of by these vast intelligences, even knowing them to be incredibly superior intellectually to any man, was just too much to bear. I told them that I was not the builder of a machine for traveling through time, but that I had simply discovered the machine and learned its intricacies over many years. This interested them. What form did this machine take, they desired to know, and how had I discovered its use? And so I . . .

. . . such confusion! At first I couldn't understand it, but then it dawned on me that these mighty beings actually stood in awe of me! It had been when I mentioned the hieroglyphs about the time-clock's face, and the weird sweep of its four hands. That was when they had started to sit up and listen. And no wonder, for . . .

'. . . of the Elder Gods themselves!' said their spokesman. 'If you have learned to use one of their devices, then you yourself are of their kin. Only the finest of minds are capable even of knowing of their existence. We know of them, and we are to them what microbes are to us.' Then this great cone-creature began to cast patently fearful glances all about the great auditorium in which I stood. 'They are all-seeing, all-knowing,' he told me. 'They may be watching all that happens here even now!'

And the idea of these tremendous beings trembling at the thought of being observed about their business by the Elder Gods, and thrown into a panic that perhaps in the transference of my mind they had erred against the will of those Elder Gods, made me quickly reply: 'Yes, they probably are, and I don't think they'll be at all happy about this!'

'But you should have mentioned this earlier!' the spokesman protested. 'You have been here for three days now, and – '

'Three days of my time wasted, of their time!' I shot back.

'Will you allow us to make amends?' the agitated being asked me. 'We will send you back to your rightful body immediately.'

And that was when a wonderful idea occurred to me, a frightening idea, too, for I wasn't at all sure that it could work. But it was at least worth a try. 'I do not wish to be transferred directly back to my body,' I told them. 'I want you to transfer my mind back to the time-clock!'

'But surely this time-clock you have mentioned is a machine, without the necessary – '

'It has a mind!' I cut in.

'And do you know its location, relative to your own at the time we interfered?'

'No, only that it was close, buried somewhere under the earth.'

There followed a hurried discussion among the council members. Finally the spokesman turned back to me. 'We can try, but you must help. Your mind can only – live – for so long unbodied. If between us we cannot find this machine of yours, then you will perish. I will explain.'

And he did explain. I was told that after the transference, if I wished to wander mentally and unrestricted by flesh in 125 A.D., then I could do so simply by willing it. I would be almost, well, a ghost. In the meantime my body's present inhabitant would be snatched back into his own body far in the past. This would leave my human shell empty, a husk of flesh without a will, without a mind or spirit. Gradually, then, my free-wandering mind would lose its ability to move of its own accord, and soon my body would die. If I could not find the clock, and if I did not get back to my body in time . . .

The body is the battery, you see, Henri? And the mind is the power. Without the power the battery is flat, dead. Without the battery the power must escape, dissipate. The dangers were . . .

. . . they would attempt in the interval of transference to find the mechanical mind that powered the time-clock, and then to enter my mind into it. That, too, was something they had never done before: inserting a mind alongside another in the same body. Looking back now I can see that the risks were enormous, but at . . .

. . . arrangements had been made and I was to . . . energy . . . projection . . .

6 Back to the Clock

. . . that obviously they had not been able to locate the clock. I was back in my own body, back where I started in the villa of Felicius Tetricus. I was in the old man's chambers and he was seated at a table writing. He looked up thoughtfully, and he looked right through me!

No sign of recognition, no glimmer to even hint of my presence showed on his face. Was he ill? 'Felicius,' I began, stepping forward, but I heard nothing, and instead of moving on my own two feet I seemed merely to drift! And in that instant I became aware that indeed I had no body! My mind was free, not clothed in flesh, and somewhere within this household my empty husk must even now be dying for want of a governing spirit!

. . . such mental panic . . .

. . . old physician entered with a powder for Felicius. The ex-senator looked up at him and said, 'Septimeus, have you seen Titus?'

'He went out to walk on the moors, I believe, Felicius. He has been strangely unsettled these past few days, as you know, but today he seemed much more his old self. He seemed, when I saw him, full of life and curiosity. He'll come to no harm.'

'Huh!' the master of the house grunted. 'Doubtless he's off to visit with that simpleton Urbicus. Can't understand what he sees in that fellow!'

Lollius Urbicus! Could it be that my body lay at his house? But that was some miles away. I must hurry! Unaccustomed to this unbodied condition of mine I moved toward the open door, and as I did so Septimeus stepped in my way. I passed through him before I could

185

bring myself to stop! But I should have known it: a bodiless mind can know no barriers. Behind me as I passed out through the wall in the direction of Urbicus' place I heard Felicius say:

'You went quite white then, Septimeus. Is something wrong?'

And I heard the old physician's answer: 'I . . . it was as if someone stepped on my soul!'

Then I was on my way to the house of Lollius Urbicus, drifting in what seemed to me to be agonizing slowness over the moors toward the valley where his modest dwelling nestled. Worse than this frustrating inability to force myself to move faster, the thought came to me that indeed I was slowing down fractionally! What had that spokesman for the council of the Archives said to me? That if I did not return to my own body at once I would gradually lose my ability to move about? In a passion of frustration and dread, I finally came to the house of Lollius Urbicus, only to discover that he was not in, that I – or rather my body – was not there either!

Rapidly weakening now, or perhaps it was only my morbid imagination, I started back for . . .

. . . villa, I headed straight for Tetricus' chambers. There I found the old noble again in earnest conversation with Septimeus. 'Do you think it possible?' the ex-senator had asked at the moment I entered.

'It may well be,' replied Septimeus. 'And it would certainly explain his never-ending visits to Urbicus' place. The two of them would have to be in it together. The shrine was buried deep – I saw to that myself – but two of them working at it secretly could soon exhume it, I think. That is always assuming, of course, that they have discovered the shrine's burial place.'

Felicius' face darkened as he climbed to his feet. 'It would be most ungrateful of Titus,' he said. 'Come, gather a few of the servants together: Thorpos and Valerius and a handful of others. We'll go, you and I, to where the shrine is buried. If they are there I shall be most angry!'

Was it possible? The clock and my body both . . . I followed the two Romans as close to heel as a dog as they quickly prepared for a visit to the buried shrine. But by then I knew indeed that my strength was failing. The power of my mind was dimming, waning, I had difficulty in concentrating. But I must . . .

. . . over the moors. We were only a handful – rather, they were only a handful, for of course I was less physically than a puff of wind – Felicius, Septimeus, Thorpos and four others. Mercifully I found that simply following them was comparatively easy. It required very little conscious effort on my part to allow their embodied spirits to draw mine after them; but I had to fight off a constant weariness now, the urge to simply fall asleep. I knew that this was a sleep from which I could never awaken!

. . . perhaps two miles. I knew the little valley, for it was a place I had often visited during walks . . . wonder that I had never guessed that here my clock lay hidden, for its tomb was deep in the heart of a hazel grove beside a small stream . . .

. . . dimly now, only very dimly aware that here I must . . .

. . . . Septimeus' voice, all shuddery, saying that if ever a place was haunted, this must surely be that place. And Felicius must have agreed, for even as my dying essence began to permeate the ground, sinking down into . . .

. . . sensed that the group was moving away, returning by an alternate route to the villa. But by then I did not care; nothing had meaning any longer. A great peace seemed to be falling over me like a cloak of darkness.

My spreading, disintegrating spirit sank ever slower

into soft earth, all sentience radiating outward and disappearing in abysses of disembodiment, drawn toward Earth-heart whose warmth is that of the cradle of all souls, and –

And however weak, however insignificant, something of the spirit of myself, some infinitely tiny particle of the intelligence of Titus Crow penetrated or was absorbed into the time-clock.

And simultaneously there came a pinprick of light in Stygian darkness, and an infinitely distant voice cried out to me: 'Titus, oh my Titus – let the clock help you! Only ask of it, seek out its being with your mind, even with a tiny spark of your mind. The clock is yours to command!' And as quickly as it came the voice was gone, leaving only . . .

. . . Tiania! And her voice crying out to me had awakened and aroused all that was left of life, even disembodied life, in me. 'Seek out its being,' she cried: 'the being of the clock, its mind, its psyche. Seek it out and command.' And I did!

The pinprick of light became a floodlight, a magnificent expanding beam of light and knowledge and reason that dispelled darkness and left my spirit whole, intact, with the clock once more mine to command more properly – but buried still! And somewhere my poor body lay, even now growing colder, colder, its capacity to support life dwindling, blood congealing, brain gelling . . .

. . . urgency gripped me, I . . . must be very loosely packed. The question remained: would my time-clock be able to surface, push the tons of earth above out of its way and . . .

. . . with the merest pressure of my mind! It must have seemed like an eruption. Tons of earth geysering to the sky, and the time-clock a lava-bomb that . . .

. . . had doubtless seen the aerial display, indeed were

even now staring up at me, or rather at the clock, as I flew my machine in a great circle, desperately scanning the whole area of moors for sight of my empty shell of a body. All of them gazed skyward, fear staring straight out of their faces, terror in the trembling arms they threw up before their eyes. All except Felicius himself who knelt, oblivious of all else, on a path that wound in gorse and heather. And beneath his hands and bowed head, hidden almost in the white folds of his flowing toga under which his shoulders moved in unmistakable emotion as he sobbed shamelessly – a motionless form!

. . . my body down there, and if Felicius and his party had not come across it first then I might . . . to set the clock down close by. All others fled, even Thorpos, save the Roman noble whose faith . . .

'. . . gave you back to me,' he said, 'that you are theirs to take away!' He turned to the clock and cried: 'Merciful and almighty shades, whose wisdom . . . eternal and dwell . . . but only give him life again . . . this shrine!'

What better time then to attempt what must now be attempted? If I succeeded, Felicius would be at peace in the belief that the shrine had taken me off again to the land of shades, and that he had been instrumental in his prayers for my deliverance from Earthly death and decay. And if I failed? But in any case, I had no time left to . . .

And so I once more left my body behind, although on this occasion it was a body fashioned of no woman's womb but the hands of alien gods of Eld. I projected my mind or psyche or what you will out through the portal of my vessel, which opened at my command, even though that was unnecessary, and into the still cold form of that flesh which had been Titus Crow.

Instantly I felt my body about me, like the shelter of a room entered out of a storm. Felicius immediately jerked his hands from me and I heard him gasp. I opened my eyes and looked at him, at which his jaw fell while his white crown of hair seemed to stand straight on his head. He staggered back from me as I climbed easily, smilingly to my feet. I marveled at this body T3RE had given me that life should spring so readily in organs which, by human standards, should surely already be falling into corruption!

'. . . no fear, Father mine, who has brought me back again from death's dark door that I may now return to the land of shades, there to live in peace and glory. But promise me this: that never more will you try to call me back from them whose shrine this is.' I turned toward the clock. 'And I . . . that you, too, will live out your span of years in peace and tranquility of mind and spirit, until you are called in your turn to the great beyond.'

Now I could not honestly say where the inspiration sprang from to use those exact words, but wherever . . .

For Felicius threw himself down before the clock to bathe a moment in its eerie rays, and as the door swung silently shut on me I heard him say, 'This I promise!'

It was only later, as I sailed the time-stream for home, that I thought to ponder . . . and of course I had known all along that Urbicus had been one and the same man as that author of *Frontier Garrison*, in which he had told his story from the viewpoint of . . . Only the fact that I had not wished to tamper with the past, and that . . .

. . . is it not written, among many other strange things, that there occurred in that year a mysterious volcanic eruption of soil and stones in the vicinity of a villa some five miles from Eboracum, which sent a cloud of dust and pebbles and soil almost half a mile into the air and shook the moors over an area of many miles?

It *is* written, de Marigny, and thus it was.

190

7 The Black Hole

So I had set course for the future, and this time I had dared hope that my journey might not be long. Indeed, it should not have been long, less than nineteen hundred years! Never since leaving Blowne House to fall in ruins, as Ithaqua's elementals of the air beat at the place with their hurricane wings, had I been so close to my own age. Nineteen hundred years? It was nothing! Had I not journeyed through hundreds of millions of years of time, traversing whole epochs as if they were mere minutes? And had I not crossed limitless light-years in my venturings in the voids of space?

Ah, but Cthulhu and his hosts were also aware that I was moving quickly toward journey's end, and it was not part of their plan that I should succeed in returning to my own time. Since they were in constant telepathic contact with those vampires of time, the Tind'losi Hounds, and since time was the element I must cross in order to regain my own period, it would not be too difficult for them once more to thwart my efforts. It was *not* difficult.

Of the Hounds themselves, one might almost be willing to return to a belief in the so-called supernatural when confronted with them; but since we know that there is a supernatural, and that it is merely the phenomenon of an alien science wherein mundane concepts hold little water . . .

. . . were herding me, those nightmares, a great flock of them and I was the only sheep. No unlikely analogy, that, for it really was as though a multitude of wolves chased one lone sheep; myself, and that soon they must bring me down.

Forgotten now was any dream of returning to my own time; it would be sufficient to come out of this alive, my soul intact! It dawned on me that to escape them I might simply halt my clock's motion in time, but that might mean a crash such as I had known when pursued by the Hounds to the world of robots. They might be simply maneuvering me into just such a position again. Then I had not known that I might also fly my craft through solids, even through the hearts of suns, with impunity. Instead, knowing that I must crash I *had* crashed, for my mind was linked with the clock and I had instinctively ordered it to halt, literally to crash against the surface of the robot world. Now I knew differently, that I could have driven right through that planet if I had wanted to, but such belated knowledge had not helped me then.

And supposing that the Tind'losi Hounds had now arranged a similar surprise for me in the universe of three dimensions? No, not until it was absolutely necessary dared I . . .

. . . me utterly! Why, this was Tindalos – Tind'losi – itself! There, sailing the time-winds, doomed to the temporal mists of the fourth dimension just as the Flying Dutchman was doomed to sail the foggy seas of Earth, there was the ghost city; the black-spiraled citadel and seat of these disembodied vampires! They had driven me to their place, shepherding this frightened sheep to the slaughter; and out the butchers came to meet me, pouring from the dark turrets and black corkscrew towers of a city wandering in time. I have described them before, de Marigny, and you assure me that you yourself have seen them in monstrous dreams. Still, the memory is awful, even now!

What to do? How to avoid them, escape from them, when even now their flapping, pulsing, poisoned feelers sought me out through the fabric of the clock? Immaterial themselves, the substance of the clock's shell was no barrier to them. They came through it like, like ghosts through a solid wall. For of course they were ghosts, disembodied entities doomed to sail a city over the temporal tides!

They were the same black rags of yore: rags with glinting eyes, flapping threads of wings and groping, soul-sucking feelers. And now those feelers were upon me, in my mind, fastening on my soul, sapping my life as Arctic ice draws all feeling from flesh and leaving me quite as numb. And then Tiania's voice came to me as so often before. This time, however, she had no advice, could offer no succor but only add her own mental cries of horror to my own.

Weakening, feeling my life-strength sapped and dimming like the flame of a candle in a bell jar, suddenly I saw my chance. They had closed in on me, the Hounds, clustering to my coffin-ship like bats to the walls of a cave, but beyond them the void of time lay clear before me in one direction. In that direction rode dark Tind'losi itself, empty now of its hideous inhabitants, and so I used up what was left of my rapidly waning mental strength to ram my faltering craft in that direction, scattering the Hounds in a flurry of fluttering, chittering rags behind me. Straight for their damned city I drove, straight to its heart and out the other side like an arrow through misted cobwebs – and knew too late that yet again they had tricked me!

Driven to this point in time, trapped and on the point of being mentally devoured, I had seen one egress and had taken it, but the Hounds of Tindalos had left no egress! I knew it as soon as I felt that nameless power, that force that pulled the clock now faster and faster, against all my efforts to rein it back. But wait! This was a force that must exist over vast distances of time; surely it was so, for even now I was hurtling over the aeons. Did it also exist in three-dimensioned space? Dare I now stop the time-clock's temporal rushing, reverting back to those three dimensions of my natural heritage?

Shrieking their mental fear, helpless as moths caught in the candle's flame, a dozen rag-things which had thought to follow too close behind me whirled past, tumbling head over heels, as it were, in the grip of the same tremendous force that held me. If these beings that dwelt in time could not fight this awful attraction, then what chance did I stand?

I slowed the aeon-devouring flight of my vessel until it emerged into the mundane three dimensions, but not in any mundane place! For still the clock hurtled, not through time now but space, and yet drawn on by that same dread attraction. Faster and faster yet it plummeted, falling through space.

Falling? Gravity!

I was caught in a gravitational field of incredible force, which of course had extended in time as well as space. But in all my traveling in space I had never experienced this before; no sun, no giant star I had ever passed by in the clock had affected the course of that vessel of mine in the slightest degree. What, then, was the source of this enormous power?

The Hounds of Tindalos were gone now, left behind in time, their enforced habitat, their prison forever, and yet I saw that I was in no less a . . .

. . . Behind me the stars, shrinking in the awful voids of space; ahead of me an empty blackness, a midnight that grew as I plunged headlong down its throat of pitch. All my power over the time-clock seemed dead, departed, as if it had never been. I could move my vessel neither up nor down, left nor right, and all efforts to slow the clock in its rapidly accelerating rush were useless.

One by one the stars behind blinked out, until blackness stretched in all directions. I had passed into a region where it seemed as if light was bent back upon itself, a region of such ferocious gravitational attraction that nothing might escape its lunatic pull! As this thought passed in a twinkling through my mind I knew suddenly where I was, and I remembered that dream I had known so long ago. I remembered those words uttered by the Eminence as it sat upon its alcove throne behind curtains of crystal and pearl-mist:

'If you cannot help him – if you fail – then you go down to the Black Hole with him!'

The Black Hole! And now other memories flooded my mind: of scientific concepts and theories I had known in my own time, particularly the popular one of a black hole. The theory describes how a giant star, collapsing in upon itself to a tiny diameter, develops a density of billions of tons per cubic inch of matter; this incredible mass would exert a gravitational field from which not even light itself might escape!

That was a black hole, and here I plummeted headlong into one!

Already my velocity must be enormous! And now I began to feel the tremendous strain on the clock and my own mind and body. If I could only swing my vessel to one side of the center of this unthinkable attraction, use its speed, like the swing of a giant pendulum, to fling myself away into free space on the other side. The idea caught, was immediately rejected. I was grasping at straws and . . .

. . . ridiculous thought; why, plainly . . .

. . . twisting, distorting, the time-clock's very atomic pattern commenced an elongation, a liquid flowing apart, and I knew my being, my human body, must also be subject to this horrid atomic viscosity. Was this the end, then? The clock's mental scanners were dimming – not that it mattered greatly for there was absolutely nothing to see outside the vessel's shell – but the symbiotic sensitivity of their feel was dying in my mind's eye. I was rapidly losing all control, all contact with my time-ship.

What use to fight any longer? Toward the end of this last trip together, the clock and I would simply spread out, become an almost two-dimensional rain of component chemicals falling still toward the gravitational center. We were doomed, the clock and I!

'*No, my love, my Titus, there is a way!*'

The voice of the goddess, and more than a mere voice this time: a presence, a spirit! 'A way?' I asked, hope springing eternal within me, even as time itself slowed down with my velocity. 'What way?'

'*You have not explored all the possibilities, my love. Kthanid has explained it to me: your vessel is not restricted to time and space alone.*' I could almost feel her marvelous green tresses against my cheek, her urgent lips against my ear.

'But how can I – I don't understand!'

'*You have taken control of the vessel with your mind. Its controls are in your mental grasp, but you have not yet mastered all of them!*'

'Other controls?' I answered. 'Yes, I believe there are other controls. But they are meaningless to me.' I could feel the time-clock spreading out about me, and the very atoms of my body with it. 'I don't understand the other controls, can't use them!'

'*The controls you do understand are useless to you here. Release them! Do it now, love, before it is too late. Then take possession of those unknown controls. It is the only way!*'

The only way! I released what remaining mental grip I had on the . . . she had said, could it be so? Had I been merely taxiing a plane around the airfield, never once attempting to fly? . . . meaningless they might be, and their purposes . . .

And if I failed? Then the spirit of my goddess would go down to the Black Hole with me!

Freed now from those previous mental restrictions I had been imposing, the vessel sped faster still; wider its sundering atoms spaced themselves, and mine too. Desperately I sought to manipulate, activate those sections of the clock's complex psyche hitherto avoided. No good! My mind was human; this damned device, this impossible vehicle had been built by gods! And goddesses?

And then, knowing that I turned to her for help, she spoke to me again. And now she, too, was desperate: *'Not that way, Titus! There are dimensions other than the four you know. Do not try to draw back from the Black Hole, nor yet to circumvent it. Simply move . . . away from it!'*

At last I had the answer, and now I meshed myself deeper still into the clock's inhuman being. We were one again, the clock and I, and finally I recognized an escape route – no, a hundred escape routes *away* from the fiendish pull of the Black Hole. I chose one of them barely in time, melted into it!

Instantly the scanners opened like windows in my mind, affording me one fantastic, horrific glimpse outside the clock before I sent my vessel darting into yet another previously unsuspected alleyway between dimensions. For in that first there had been a blue ocean of light filled with drifting figures of rainbow hues and starkly geometric design; and in and about these aimless, helpless patterns ambitiously dark and slender cylinders had roved, snapping up the slower shapes as large fish devour small ones. My flight from that place is most easily explained: those black cylinders had been immediately aware of the clock, and even as it appeared among them they had darted in my direction!

Ah, but whatever they were, they could not follow me between dimensions!

Only then, emerging into that second parallel dimension, did I realize that my goddess had left me once more. I heard her beautiful voice, retreating in my mind, its telepathic echo bidding me farewell:

'*I go now. Kthanid sends me a Great Thought to guide my spirit home. Take care, my love, that we may be one in Elysia!*' And then she was gone. I sent my thanks silently after her, to follow her through what I guessed must be many eternities to her home in Elysia.

Now I could look about me at this new place, ready on the instant to slip away again between dimensions should danger threaten. But no, no danger here. Here I moved through vast orange spaces in which, afar, scarlet jewel stars twinkled against a background of red-tinged infinities. Flat disk-shapes with the diameters of worlds but no apparent thickness whatever, spun by; between them tiny, flat diamond shapes moved in obviously intelligent journeyings. A cluster of these diamonds were . . .

. . . this strange dimension, to a place which I hoped would be many light-years away from the monstrous Black Hole of my own universe. Only then would I dare make the trip back through the dimensional barriers, which my vessel penetrated like sunlight through shallow water.

When at last I fancied that . . .

. . . hopeless! . . .

. . . to starvation. Such was my hunger by then that I cared not a damn whether I set the clock down on an alien world in an alien time, or on some prehistoric . . .

. . . own longed-for universe of three dimensions, no,

198

four, for now I accepted time, too, as my element. And thus, no worse for my many ordeals, I . . .

. . . not Earth, however, nor had I the remotest idea in which direction my home planet lay. Still, there . . .

8 Of Alien Life-Forms

. . .hinted at . . . those many worlds of wonder I visited after leaving the Cretaceous . . . different again, with . . . tell you?

De Marigny, you know how there are creatures that dwell in the most inaccessible, inhospitable places above, on and under the Earth and in her oceans? I am talking about life-forms you can find in any handbook of zoology, as opposed to those fearsome beings of the Cthulhu Cycle with which we are now so familiar. Well, there are also creatures which exist in the most obscure and random corridors and corners of time, in lost and unthinkable abysses of space, and in certain other twilight places which are most easily explained by referring to them as junctions of forces neither temporal nor spatial, places which by all rights should only exist in the wildest imaginings of theoreticians and mathematicians.

. . . wonder how this can possibly be; one might as well ponder Hans Geisler's photographs of great burrowing bivalves which suck up sustenance from the aeon-deposited muck of the Taumotu Trench, six miles deep in the sea; or the microbes that thrive in the mud of boiling geysers. And if one considers . . . multiverse . . . impossible?

Suffice to say, then, that there are extreme forms of life within and without this universe of ours. And I know it to be so for I have seen or learned of many such forms.

For instance:

. . . intelligent energies in the heart of a giant alien sun who measure time in ratios of nuclear fission and space in unimaginable degrees of pressure! There are wraithlike biological gases which issue at the dark of their moon from the fissures of a fungoid world in Hydra, to dance away their brief lives until, exhausted, they die at dawn, scattering the sentient seeds of mushroom minds which will sprout and take root, and whose crevice-deep roots will in turn emit at the dark of the moon euphoric, spore-bearing mists of genesis.

There is a dying purple sun on Andromeda's rim whose rays support life on all seven of its planets. On the fourth planet there are exactly seventeen forms of life, or so it would appear. On closer inspection, however, a zoologist could tell you that these forms are all different phases of only one life-form! Consider the batrachian and lepidopterous cycles of Earth life and this might not seem too astonishing, until I tell you that of these seventeen phases two are as apparently inanimate mineral deposits, six are aquatic, two others amphibious, three land-dwelling cannibals, three more are aerial and the last is to all intents and purposes a plant while all of its preliminary stages (excluding the mineral phases) were animal! And to . . .

. . . the time-stream of a distant and utterly alien universe, a one-dimensional entity argues continually with its past and future selves on the improbability of space! And beyond . . . life as a terminal disease?. . .

. . . I mention all of these things, Henri, to help you in the first instance to understand the diversity and tenacity of life, but mainly as an introduction to what I . . .

NOTE: Here the contents of almost a complete tape have been lost.

ADM

9 The Lake of Doomed Souls

. . . Hyades, though I did not know that then. Indeed I knew nothing of the whereabouts of my present refuge, neither in time nor in space. When a man flees for his life in the dark he takes whatever route is open to him; he only looks before leaping if he has time. One thing I knew for certain, though: this was not Earth. Never in any period of our planet's prehistory that I know of has it looked like that! And God forbid it ever look that way in the future.

There were moons, Henri, strange moons whose orbits were about other moons as well as the parent planet, so that they seemed to circle or spiral across the sky. And the stars – they were black! I suppose, looking back on it now, that those things alone should have told me where I was, but my mind was so badly battered and bruised that I was hardly capable of knowing anything, merely of accepting. And one thing I accepted gratefully: for the nonce I was again free of Them, the vampires of time, the Tind'losi Hounds.

Well, I was exhausted and I slept. In that dreamless sleep, still ephemerally attached as my dormant mind was to the psyche of the clock, I knew that day had come and that a sun, or suns, had walked the sky, and that now night was once more upon this weird world. Surely enough, when I awakened I saw in the scanners that black stars hung again in the sky; the ashen moons were spiraling in sulfurous, ocher heavens.

I knew instinctively that I dared not leave my vessel, no, not for an instant, for the atmosphere of this world would kill me as surely as immersion in sulfuric acid. Not a comforting thought, that . . .

. . . of oppression. How may I describe it? It was a feeling as vague really as the dim and nighted landscape, and yet ominous.

Suddenly it came to me that I must not simply sit there waiting for something to happen. I knew, you see, that sooner or later something *would* happen. It was the type of feeling you get standing too close to the lip of a vast cliff gazing out over far horizons. No, not vertigo but rather a presentiment, the sudden realization of infinity and one's own insignificance, an awareness of the presence of vast powers. And even with the shadows lengthening grayly, then shortening, constantly and weirdly dividing and uniting under the spell of oddly orbiting moons, still I did not know where I was. Not even as I lifted my clock up and forward, to drift lazily over that pallid, alien, fog-masked landscape . . .

. . . that the milky fog now rolled like the waves of an ocean, a sea of undulating fumes white as the snowy domes of *Amanita phalloides*, and just as deadly, rising from some mordant sea. No, not a sea, a lake.

I saw it as my vessel passed into a region where the cloud-waves rolled less densely: a lake of murky depths the very sight of which, so still, without a ripple to stir its surface, tugged at the roots of memories that slumbered uneasily but would not waken.

A numbness was on my mind, Henri, engendered of unplumbed mysteries, mysteries not alone of the lake. That was only a part of it. I felt perhaps as a dying man feels in that moment before death; or as a baby before it is born; or a soul before it is reborn. Yes, this world, or more accurately this lake, might easily be the rebirthing place of souls – *or their graveyard*!

Ah, now I knew this place – as Alhazred knew it in the

desert, and Castaigne in New York; as Schrach, Tierney and others have known it – as every dreamer knows it at least once in life. And once is as much as most can bear, too much for many. Rearing in horror then above those depths, mentally lifting my coffin-clock up through an agonizingly leaden atmosphere, a succession of names and associations of half-remembered elder myths and monstrous legends flooded my mind.

I thought of Demhe and Hali, and knew it was the latter lying beneath me even as I rose slowly to the sky. I seemed to hear the songs Cassilda's dead voice sings, but knew them to be only the eerie ululations of someone, something else! I sensed the dread approach of the King in Yellow, knowing that his scalloped tatters still shrouded Yhtill; and, seeing a sudden swirl of mottled yellow far down near the milky shore of the lake, I knew also that my torpor had dissipated only just in time. Then, lifting higher and more freely, I saw behind that flapping yellow mote down on the shore the shadows of a moon, and behind those bloating fungi shades the jagged towers of lost Carcosa!

Then came the real horror, that which I had most feared. For rising up now behind me in that mordant lake from which, in the words of the poet, '. . . dreamers flee in nameless dread,' a great tentacle stretched, dripping bubbling acids as it lashed viciously in the wake of my fleeing vessel. It was a Cthulhoid tentacle, I knew, belonging to that prime evil's half-brother, the whistler of Cassilda's songs. Hastur had reached up from the depths of the prison Lake of Hali, sending a pseudopod to trap me but mercifully sending it too late!

Faster I climbed, completely free now of the morbid mental sloth that shortly before had held me in its languid arms, until red rays reached out to me from over the rim of the prison planet and massive Aldebaran bathed my time-clock in the warmth of her ruddy light.

And now with the horror of Hali behind me, as I sped out into the Hyades, it dawned on me that indeed I was not far from the planet of my birth. Not far? No, a mere sixty-four light-years, but a moment of concentration. Ah, but in which direction? I was sure that my very rudimentary . . .

NOTE: At this point another lengthy part of the narrative, consisting of a third of a spool of tape, is lost.

ADM

10 Atlantis

. . . Sidney-Fryer's translations from the Atlantean of Atlantarion? Man, I was there when they were written in the original! In that same period, something like fifteen thousand years ago, I saw the foundering of Atlantis. Saw it? I was very nearly part of it . . .

. . . awesome cataclysm, de Marigny! It saw the end of a land, of a people, of an era – the end of a period of poets who knew the true meaning of beauty, whose like can never be known again. I may say that of all . . .

NOTE: Here the break in the narrative is not so extensive, and my opinion is that the lost matter is not of great importance. In any case the narrative from this point on is more or less complete.

11 Outside!

. . . that at last they had succeeded in hounding me into a place of utmost evil. I sensed it in the same instant that I passed between incomprehensibly layered zones of hyper-space-time into that other place. There had been a sudden, short-lived blast of mental exultation, of fiendish delight, from the pursuing Hounds; their echoes seemed to follow me as I slipped sideways away from those fluttering, chittering rag-things into that parallel dimen-sion. And their unholy . . . anticipation, warned me that here . . . something which, while it must be allied to the Tind'losi Hounds in hideous purpose, in the overall alliance of evil forces, even they stood in awe . . . A power so monstrous that . . .

. . . dread; I had heard again as so often before Tiania's voice crying in my mind. And oh, the hopelessness that rang in that beautiful telepathic voice before it, too, was cut off:

'*Not there, my love. I cannot follow you or help you there. I cannot even penetrate the veil in Kthanid's crystal! Not even a Great Thought can follow you there, and there is no returning from –*

'*No, Titus! NO!*'. . .

. . . could not stay here, and yet I could not leave!

It had been contrived that I might place myself in a region from which I could not escape; and once again, in fear and loathing of the Hounds of Tindalos, I had obligingly done just that. But what else could I have done?

Desperately now I sought to plumb those depths of my vessel's psyche wherein I knew lay the controls to open the gates between dimensions, those same controls I had manipulated to break through into this place, as I had used them to escape the Black Hole and other horrors. But now they were . . . gone! There was only an emptiness where they had been.

And outside, exterior to the clock, there stretched an infinite darkness. No stars hung in that all-embracing wall of seemingly solid jet. It was comprised of a blackness without the tiniest glimmer of illumination, as if suddenly I had been plunged into the heart of some titanic block of black marble, and yet not like that. For black may be defined as a color and this was an absence of color, an absolute absence of light. No, it was more even than that: it was the absence of everything. It came to me that there was quite literally nothing beyond the walls of my vessel, neither time nor space. This time I had gone – *away* – from everything; the time-clock – and I had quite literally moved *outside*!

Why, I asked myself, should these restrictions suddenly have been placed on the clock's previously unlimited capabilities? My vessel was now like an ocean-going liner confined to port, and an alien port at that. Desperately I attempted to burrow even deeper into the time-clock's . . .

. . . perceived that there was something out there after all, a movement, a disturbance in the darkness far away. This impression came to me through the clock's fantastically sensitive scanners. There being nothing else in that whole immense blackness to detect, the scanners had finally sought out this most distant disturbance to bring to my attention. But in this I was made aware of several other things, namely: if the source of the disturbance was distant, then this place did not have an absence of space. Therefore, since it is an irrefutable law that space and time go hand in hand, time also existed here. And yet I knew somehow that this was a very different space, a very different time, a space-time continuum like no other.

The realization was instantaneous and went no further than that, for now the disturbance was closer, growing, seething in the scanners, its outlines beginning to make themselves clearer. For another instant I gaped, then drove my vessel away from the thing as it grew with fantastic speed from a distant amoeba outlined in eerie blue radiance to a spreading blot that put out groping, bubbling pseudopods. And along these pseudopods the thing seemed to shoot itself toward me, reminding me of some hideous octopus with its quick, jerky movements. But by then I knew that it was no octopus. I knew exactly what it was and where I was.

A different space, a different time – different because of an alien juxtaposition to nature – a place utterly outside nature, synthetic, manufactured! A dimension parallel with all four mundane dimensions but impinging on none of them, 'coexistent with all time and conterminous in all space' but locked outside nevertheless, behind barriers only the Elder Gods might construct. But barriers constructed to enclose what?

What else but that soul-symbol of most abysmal evil, that father of darkness, that frothing, liquescent, blasphemous shapelessness that masks its true horror behind a congeries of iridescent globes and bubbles; that primal slime seething forever 'beyond the nethermost angles', the Lurker at the Threshold – the noxious Yog-Sothoth!

I knew then that I was dead, de Marigny, finished, that already my life was used up and that all I had aspired to must come to nothing. My soul was lead within me, plumbing the very depths of despair, for there I was face to face with a being whose only peer in monstrousness is dread Cthulhu himself.

Face to face? Yes, despite the fact that I had in the

previous instant driven my vessel away from the thing! Certainly, for how might one escape a being who is conterminous in all space? I had no sooner hurled my craft in a direction away from that frothing obscenity than I found myself rushing toward him as he placed himself in my path! Time was no refuge either, for flinging my clock madly into the future I found the horror already waiting for me – no, rushing with me along the time-stream – and always, inexorably, drawing closer to me!

To and fro in space, forward and back in time. And through all of that silent, nightmare rush my hurtling vessel's scanners sought to obtain for me a clearer picture of the thing lurking behind those protoplasmic bubbles and globes. I caught insane glimpses of a purplish blue mass: a titanic primal jelly of wriggling ropes, bulging eyes and tossing, convulsing pseudopods and mouths . . . a super-sentient but nevertheless ultra-evil anemone from the deepest seas of screaming nightmare!

Closer still the horror came, while my attempts to avoid it grew ever more frenzied, ever more useless. Forward and back in time I plunged, then further back yet; to and fro and around and about in space. Faster and ever faster the pace grew, and closer the looming horror of Yog-Sothoth. All of those lightning mental reflexes built into me by T3RE were being taxed to their very limits, strained to the breaking point as I flung the clock through space and time in ever more intricate four-dimensional patterns. And through all of this those myriad bulging eyes of the monster stared and lusted. Its convulsing mouths drooled and chomped vacuously, and the mass of its throbbing body loomed over the clock as if to enclose it within some unmentionable amoeba.

It was hideous, indescribably hideous! Then suddenly, driven almost to insanity, gibbering and clawing at my hair in an attempt to force my mind to react faster and faster yet to the perils of that impossible chase, finally it happened. I drove my time-clock in two directions at one and the same time!

Impossible? Fantastic? Even I did not immediately understand. I, too, believed it impossible, believed that I had finally gone mad. Even now I do not completely understand the how of it, but I think I know the why:

I was hemmed in by Yog-Sothoth in space, enclosed in time. Driven finally to a frenzy of mental agitation surpassing any state of mind I had ever known before, torn between a number of choices of directions in which to flee, I had chosen two simultaneously. And I had hurled both the clock and myself in *both* of them! And wonder of wonders, the Lurker at the Threshold could only follow me in one! Bemused as I flashed both forward and back in time, Yog-Sothoth paused, and I took that chance to allow the split psyches of the clock and myself to flow back together again.

But in that last statement perhaps I mislead you. I brought the two materializations of man and vessel back into one phase, yes, and in so doing I repaired that rent I had made in the fabric of infinity; but the reparation was almost involuntary. It was simply a correction of something I knew could not be, made the instant after realizing that it could be and was. In any event, I then found myself free of the lord of that black demesne, but not for long.

The breathing space I had given myself, however short, was at least time in which to consider the implications of the foregoing phenomenon. Now, you must understand, Henri: it was not as if I had been two men in that brief instant of split personality. No, I had been one man, thinking as one man, reacting as one man, but existing in two places! A difficult concept even for me, but in that concept lay the seeds of my salvation.

If I could move in two temporal directions at once, into

209

both past and future simultaneously – is that a contradiction of terms? – could I also remain in the present simultaneously? Could I, in the present, move here and there simultaneously? And similarly in the future, and in the past? If this vessel of mine existed, however hypothetically, everywhere and everywhen, couldn't I with the application of my human psyche and superhuman mind – for indeed T3RE had given me a superhuman mind – be able to make the time-clock physically omnipresent?

I know what you are thinking, Henri, that only the gods are capable of such things. But didn't gods, the Elder Gods, build this craft of mine? Think of it: here was Yog-Sothoth, a prime member of the Ancient Ones, a being with the ability to reach any given location in the space-time of his own dimension almost instantaneously, but not several locations simultaneously! Only I had that ability, and in that I had the monster's measure.

Now, doubtless recovered from his initial surprise, he was coming for me again, walking the black voids on his pseudopod arms like some thinking slug of space. Well, if he wanted Titus Crow so badly he would have him! *He would have one million Titus Crows, and each and every one of them capable of a further million branchings, enough to fill this entire dimension end to end and top to bottom – a superabundance of Titus Crows!*

Throwing all caution to the wind then, uncaring of what cosmic calamities might accompany my next action, I achieved an instant and complete psychic meshing with my vessel. I became a sort of superhuman polyp as I commenced to divide in that instant, subdivide and divide again in all my manifestations to a point not far short of infinite. I became one mind governing a billion materializations, one psyche with the omnipresent awareness of a billion psyches. And in the next instant of time – the next few millions of years of time; for of course I had spread my materializations through all of Yog-Sothoth's time-dimension – a number of things happened.

First, the Lurker at the Threshold curled up on himself, writhing horribly and visibly shrinking. His telepathic anguish filled me with a mental agony that was almost physical. Yog-Sothoth was mortally afraid! Confronted with an enigma as unthinkable as this, I yet found myself capable of compassion. More than that even, I felt a tearing, sickening, intensely burning empathy for the horror, exactly like that which I had known as a small boy when a friend of mine poured salt on a snail!

Second, even as I realized that the devastating explosion of my myriad manifestations had torn a gaping hole in the fabric of Yog-Sothoth's prison dimension, so a voice called to me from the other side of that awesome gap. The mental voice I had heard before in what I had taken to be dreams. I recognized the voice of the being in the great alcove behind the enigmatic drapes in the hall of crystal: Kthanid, guardian of my own guardian angel! *'This way, born of woman, you, Titus Crow. You have opened the gate, now come through it!'*

And finally, drawing back my own and the clock's countless identities into the one original id, into one body, one vessel, I flew as bidden out through that fantastic rent from which issued now a beam of purest light – that same beam you saw me use against the Wind-Walker, Henri, or at least a beam issuing from a similar source. This ray, so pure and dazzling white as to strike physically, like a solid shaft, flashed over and beyond my darting vessel at something behind me. In my scanner I saw Yog-Sothoth, bloated again to his former titanic loathesomeness, rushing to escape his interminable punishment. He fell back, stricken as the beam hit him. And as he fell the portal I had torn in his prison wall slammed shut again, closing on him and locking him in as securely as ever.

211

All of these things happened, Henri, and one more thing. It was simply that flooding my entire being there came the realization that at last I was one with the Elder Gods, a lost sheep returned to the fold, a wanderer come home.

Home to Elysia!

Part Five

1

Elysia

(From de Marigny's recordings)

The voice of Kthanid, a supreme being, had called me
from vile vortices of nether-existence to Elysia, a true
garden of heaven! Elysia was home of the Elder Gods –
of which Kthanid doubtless was one – and home, too, of
the goddess whose telepathic guidance had succored me
through a score of danger-fraught situations.

Elysia is not a planet, or if so it is the most tremendous
colossus among worlds. There was, for example, no
horizon that I ever saw. Even from on high I could testify
to no visible curvature of the surface below me in the
great misted distances. There were beautiful mountains,
between and behind whose peaks the spires and columns
of delicate cities clustered. Beyond those golden balconies
and fretted crystal balustrades silver rivers and lakes
tinkled; and far and away behind all this, misted by
distance, yet more mountains thrust upward – and yet
more fairy cities sparkled afar – but no horizon! Instead
distance vanished in a pearly haze beneath skies that were
high and blue. Flying machines soared or hovered in those
skies or simply hung motionless. And through tufted
drifting clouds golden creatures like benign, majestic
dragons pulsed on wings of ivory and leather.

Some of these dragons were harnessed and bore proud
riders through dizzy heights of air, riders whose scales or
feathers or crests or iridescent skins set them aside from
mere humanity, or rather, set them in a higher mold.
These were the Elder Gods themselves, or their minions,
and not one of them displayed the slightest interest in my

time-clock as I passed between them now on an arrow-straight course beyond an emerald ocean toward the steep spires of blue mountains.

Completely numb from head to foot – awash with awe and wonder and pinching myself to make sure this whole experience was not simply some fantastic dream – I made no motion, no mental effort to check the flight of the clock as it rushed out of the utter blackness of Yog-Sothoth's realm into this place. And yet now I perceived that I passed at a very leisurely pace over fields of green and gold, and dizzy aerial roadways that spread unsupported spans city to city like the gossamer threads of a spider's web.

How could this be? How was it that while I had made no conscious effort to slow the clock we yet paced the skies so steadily? I reached mental fingers into my vessel's motor areas, its psyche or mind, and recoiled as a sort of slow, frozen electrical charge burned me! The time-clock rejecting me? I tried again, but to no avail. My machine, my time-clock, did not want to know me now, not at this exact moment of time. I knew instinctively then that I must not interfere, must make no attempt to pilot the clock or guide its course. Nevertheless, out of sheer human stubbornness, I tried yet a third time – only to meet a blank mental wall. I was no longer master but passenger, shut out of the engine room, not even allowed on the bridge.

T3RE's words came back to me in that moment: 'You have a great journey before you, you and your time-clock . . . he has told me it is so . . .' My clock had been like some lean hound, lost and wandering alone. I had found him, befriended him. We had roved and adventured together and now, by accident, we had come into his homeland. He knew and recognized the place. No use my hand on the leash, for he scented the hearth of home. If I tried too hard to curb him then he might turn on me, for even now his mistress called him.

His mistress . . . and perhaps mine?

Slowly the scanners dimmed. All my connections with the time-clock were breaking now, each joining thread parting. Now I was simply a man in a box, alone in the deepening darkness.

My last glimpse of Elysia before the scanners went completely blank was of the blue mountain spires, much closer now, lifting up to pierce cotton clouds. Then the darkness was complete and I was journeying blindly toward an unknown destiny in an alien, beautiful world.

After some little time I felt the slightest jolt as the clock came to a halt, and almost immediately the door before me swung open on a corridor that stretched away into softly silver distances. A corridor lined with . . . with time-clocks, just like my own!

No, not quite like mine. Certainly they were machines governed by a similar principle – the clocklike faces with their strangely erratic, twin-paired hands and curious hieroglyphs were ample proof of that. But these machines, the majority of them at least, were designed for forms other than those of men. There were some identical in every respect to that clock of mine, which I had mistakenly believed to be unique, but of the rest . . .

There were machines of silver and gold, others of glass or crystal, some of stone or at least of a material indistinguishable from stone, and at least one of a delicate bronze wire mesh. Some were quite tiny, no more than seven or eight inches in height; others were wide and tall, towering a fantastic thirty feet or more toward the glowing ceiling of the vast corridor. I could not help but wonder what sort of creatures might have need of these latter machines.

Then, as I gazed along the corridor of clocks, I saw that

I was not alone. Moving toward me strode a plumed, bird-headed being whose saucer eyes regarded me with an ancient intelligence. Costumed in a cloak of gold and wearing padlike sandals of golden mesh on his clawed bird feet, he drew close and paused to address me in softly clucking, inquiring tones in answer to which I could only shake my head. Rapidly then and with many a gesture the bird-man tried several different tongues on me, all without avail. His demeanor, despite his utterly alien aspect, was the very soul of polite friendliness. Eventually, after listening to a long sequence of hissing cachinnations, I said, 'It's no use. I'm afraid I don't understand a word you're saying.'

'Ah!' he replied at once. 'Then you'll be the Earthman Tiania is expecting. Stupid of me, I should have known at once, but it's been a long, long time since a man of Earth was here in Elysia. Let me introduce myself. I am Esch, Master Linguist of the Dchichis and adept in all known tongues, including the electric hum of the D'horna-ahn Energies. Whenever I meet up with a stranger I take the opportunity to practice my art. Right now, though, I am off to Atha-Atha VII to learn the language of the sea-sloth. Perhaps we'll meet again. Do excuse me.'

He turned to a globular clock whose base resembled, not surprisingly, the woven bowl of a metal nest and was about to enter when, as if on an afterthought, he turned and added, 'Oh, but I almost forgot. A lithard is waiting for you outside, sent by Tiania.'

'A lithard? Outside?' I answered uncertainly, staring about me. 'Thank you.' I began to take a tentative step in the direction from which the bird-man had approached.

'No, no, no!' he called out. 'I walk only for the exercise. You have no need of exercise.' He quite openly admired my muscular torso, then cocked his head on one side and gave a piercing whistle from his ridged beak. 'There we are. Now just you wait a moment and your lithard will come for you.'

'But –'

'*Auf Wiedersehen! Au revoir! Saph-ess isaph!*' he chirruped, waving a vestigial wing and entering into the nest-shaped clock. The machine immediately faded and disappeared from view.

Again I was alone in the corridor of clocks, but not for long. At first the sound was a mere – susurration, a murmur as of small winds or the sound of a distant ocean in a conch's sounding coil, but in a twinkling it grew to a regular throbbing, a beating of great wings. My lithard was coming for me!

To my left the corridor stretched into softly silvery distances as before; to my right a mote danced afar in the air between the glowing ceiling and the floor of the corridor, passing above the receding rows of space-time machines. Rapidly the mote grew to a shape, a winged outline preceded by outstretched head and neck. Just as quickly I began to feel the air stir on my cheek as the dragon – for the moment I could only think of the creature as such – flew toward me with a majestic beating of its great wings. A moment more and it alighted before me on the floor of the corridor, a living fragment from one of Earth's oldest mythologies. Here was the green and golden dragon of the Tung-gat tapestries, a beast such as might play in the Gardens of Rak! There it stood, *Tyrannosaurus rex* with leather wings and serpentine neck, a *draco* out of the Asian hinterlands but magnified many times over, and all of a natural green and gilt iridescence. It was harnessed in black leather where neck joined body with a saddle of hammered silver and reins of spun gold!

The massive lizard head towered high above me while huge eyes observed me, then a great rear leg bent to lower the creature's bulk, forming two scaly steps each half the height of a man. Amazingly, with a dull rumble, the creature spoke: 'Tituth, Tituth Crow! Tiania ith waiting.'

A lisping lizard! A . . . lithard! Could this possibly be the source of the naming of such creatures? I doubted it, but laughed nevertheless at the thought. There was no malice in my laugh, however, and as if it knew my thoughts the huge beast before me laughed too, throwing its head back on its scaled neck and booming until I thought the high ceiling must surely come down on us both.

When the creature was quiet I reached up and patted its great head, gazing in wonder into the huge black eyes. For a moment longer we studied one another, man and dragon, and then the lithard began again: 'Tiania ith –'

'I know, I know!' I cried. 'She's waiting for me.' Then, with all my senses dizzy and rushing, almost as if I was half drunk on the wine of pure joy, I put all other thoughts aside but those of the goddess. Leaping on my mount's knee, and from there to the ridged back where I swung easily into the saddle, I cried: 'Lead on, my scaly friend!'

The great head turned to regard me more soberly. 'Thcaly friend named Oth-Neth!'

'Bravo, Oth-Neth!' I slapped the great neck. 'Now take me to your mistress.' And mountain of flesh that he was, he stretched his great wings and we lifted up, impossibly light as a feather, and I gripped the reins hard as the corridor of clocks began to speed by beneath me . . .

The corridor of clocks stretched away and away, but before long Oth-Neth turned and flew into a side shaft that rose at about thirty degrees and at right angles away from the silvery main corridor until it emerged from the subterranean place into daylight. I had not been dreaming when I flew the time-clock – or rather when it flew me – over the fields and aerial roads and cities of færie Elysia. The same fantastic view now spread below me as before. Behind us were the blue mountains, in the heart of which lay the corridor of clocks, and before us the vast and splendid landscape of a world of opium dreams! A fragrant wind whipped my hair and lifted my soul to heights rarely if ever experienced before.

A sudden thought came to me and I stood up in my saddle to stretch myself out along the ridged neck of my mount. I shouted into one of Oth-Neth's tiny ears: 'Oth-Neth, I fear I'm hardly in any fit state for audience with Tiania!'

My hair was long and unkempt; my beard was wild and uneven; my naked body, while brown from the rays of several suns, was not nearly as clean as I would have liked it. Oth-Neth turned his head slightly and rolled back a great eye. 'Do you with to bathe?' He wrinkled a nostril. 'You thmelly?'

'Yes, I think I am rather . . . smelly, and I would love to bathe,' I answered him, somewhat abashed at his more or less accurate perceptions. 'And perhaps clothes . . .?'

But now the dragon seemed uncertain. The beat of his wings became fractionally less steady, then stilled completely as he drew them back and fell forward into a breathtaking, gliding swoop.

'You would bathe . . . thoon?' he asked. 'Before we get to houthhold of Tiania?'

'Yes, before we get to the household of Tiania,' I answered.

'Then there ith only . . . lithard pool. If that will do, I altho bathe. Later . . . bring you robeth.'

'That will do very nicely,' I told him, wondering what, exactly, the lithard pool could be but not wanting to appear ignorant.

'Good!' he seemed greatly relieved. He turned one wing into the wind, pulled his head up and transformed his dive into a circling, soaring climb that took us up, up to the cotton clouds and through them. Then he turned his head slightly to ask inquiringly: 'Do you fear . . . the high platheth?'

'No, I'm firm enough in the saddle.'

'And do you like . . . thpeed?'

I thrilled to the idea of riding a speeding dragon through the skies of an unknown world. 'I love speed!'

He blinked his great eyes. 'Tiania, too, like fly . . . fatht!' And with that his wings stretched out and back, doubling the speed of their beating in a moment. In but another moment we were caught up in a thermal current that whipped us faster and faster along dizzy paths of upper air in a thrilling, nerve-tingling ride that I wished might go on forever!

All too soon, however, it was over. Then we plunged down, down through the clouds and between the higher spires of a scarlet city, then down again toward a distant glittering blue patch in fields of green. The patch soon became a lake – the lithard pool.

Young dragons splashed in the shallows of glittering waters under the watchful eyes of warty matrons, while farther out more mature creatures raced above and below the surface, to and fro, with wings folded back almost in the manner of Earth's penguins. Occasionally they would leap up from depths near the center of the lake to burst fully into view in rainbow cascades of water that caught the warm sunlight and scattered it. Then they would spread their wings to climb high before plummeting again to the cool pool below. This then was the lithard pool, a lake of sporting dragons!

We settled in the shallows where Oth-Neth put down his great hind legs and spread his wings across the surface of the pool. All the younger lithards backed away to stand watching us. Their eyes were saucer-wide and, among the very young ones, a little frightened. In a matter of seconds all the excited activity of the pool had died down and all lithard eyes were upon us. Only the matrons politely turned their backs on my nakedness.

'What's wrong?' I questioned Oth-Neth. 'Is something . . .'

'Very rarely,' he answered, 'do mathterth bathe . . . in lithard pool.'

'Is it taboo, then?' I asked. As a stranger in Elysia I hardly wished to go against the grain.

'Not taboo, but . . .'

'You mean the masters frown upon it?'

'Not mathterth . . . lithardth!'

'But you didn't mention this be – '

'For you,' he cut me off, 'ith different.' Then he lifted up his voice and boomed deafeningly across the pool what must have been some sort of explanation of my presence. I caught only the name 'Tiania' in all he said. By the time the echoes of that dragon-cry had died away, however, the play was on again in full swing, and some of the younger lithards splashed over to us as I slid from Oth-Neth's saddle into the blue crystal waters.

One of these young ones, big as myself, covered with a soft velvet leather the color of marble, kept pace with me as I slipped easily into the motions of a powerful crawl. Closer he came, eyeing me intently, then he dived down beneath me to lift me up bodily sprawled across his neck. High out of the water he tossed me, letting me fall back with a splash. Indignant, I rose to the surface, only to find the bawling infant undergoing a thorough booming tirade from a vast and blotchy matron.

'No, no!' I cried at once. 'He was only having fun.' Oth-Neth, paddling over like some gorgeously painted

Loch Ness monster, translated loudly. From out near the center of the pool there came a noisy and concerted booming from an audience of more mature lithards.

'They approve of you . . . Tituth Crow!' Oth-Neth informed me. 'Now you bathe. I go . . . fetch robes.' Without another word he sank down into deeper waters, to emerge a moment or two later in a breathtaking fountain of spray. His great wings unfolded in the air and he was off, lifting ponderously at first, then more certainly, finally climbing to the sky and disappearing in tufted clouds and rosy sunlight.

So there I was, left alone for the duration to the tender mercies of the strange lithards, and never could I have imagined that to bathe in a pool of dragons might be such wonderful sport! No sooner had Oth-Neth taken his departure than a pair of young beasts came to me from the middle of the lake, hoisting me up out of the water and bearing me bodily to where a host of adult males and females splashed and cavorted. I became the ball in a game of catch, but such was the gentleness of the friendly lithards that I received not even the smallest bruise.

Then, tiring of hurling me through the air one to another, they formed a floating bridge of arched necks along which I ran, while one of them splashed and boomed after me in the water, trying to dislodge me from each successive scaly perch. Finally slipping from a great neck, I swam to the bottom of the pool, staying there for many minutes to study the decorative beds of freshwater oysters with their huge black pearls. As I rose in a slow spiral to the surface, two young adults grabbed me. They were males, booming in turn what were obviously questions, in answer to which I could only shake my head. A pity that all the lithards were not versed, like Oth-Neth, in English.

Then one of the lithards thrust his head beneath the

surface of the lake, whipping it out an instant later to display bulging eyes and panting, lolling tongue. He repeated this performance, but on the second occasion when he withdrew his head he plainly suffered no discomfort whatever. The whole thing had been a mime and now I knew the creature's meaning: he had asked me whether or not I found any difficulty in staying under water for long periods. In answer I allowed myself to sink slowly down into crystal depths, tickling scaly legs and staying down until my two new friends came after me. For this was one of the benefits of having a custom-built body, as it were. I needed lungs only for talking, and who wants to talk under water?

Plainly the two young lithards wanted me to follow them when they set off down toward the deepest part of the lake, their great rear legs sending them speeding into silent fathoms. Then, when they noticed how far behind they were leaving me – their speed was quite phenomenal – they circled back to grab me with their small forelegs and carry me effortlessly along between them. Down we went, down to depths I had not suspected, and in through a sunken portal whose interior was lit with a mother-of-pearl radiance. This glowing light apparently sprang from shoals of tiny organisms that swam in that entryway, luminous clouds that parted like opening curtains to allow us access to the mysteries beyond.

Deeper still we swam, through waters strangely warm and growing warmer, until suddenly the narrow neck of the channel opened into a great cave. There we surfaced, emerging into air in a cavern whose domed ceiling, adorned with sparkling stalactites, covered an area of what must have been at least an acre. Globes of artificial light hung near the ceiling, invisibly suspended in the air, sending down a dappling of green and mauve rays to give the place an appearance of soft contours and quiet, submarine shades.

We emerged from the pool onto a wide shelf where rested several matrons whose task, I soon saw, was the tending of hundreds of huge eggs – dragonspawn! The eggs rested in rows in hollows all along the sandy shelf, each perfect oval perhaps nine inches long and each one beautifully speckled in blue and gold. Under the watchful eyes of the matrons my lithard friends guided me down a path between the rows of eggs. Soon we stopped where the two dragons crouched to admire a pair of gold-flecked ovals, their subdued and reverent booming hinting to me that they must be the respective fathers of these hatchlings-to-be. After a minute or two of what seemed to me rather proud and boastful booming together, nevertheless undertaken in lowered tones, my friends indicated that it was time to go. I kneeled to touch the speckled surfaces of the eggs just once, to feel their smoothness, then the lithards led the way back past the matrons and again we entered the water, returning through the narrow neck of the cave to the surface of the lake.

Spying Oth-Neth on the far bank, I first said farewell to my new friends and then swam over to him. While drying myself in the sun I told the lithard what I had seen below the lake.

'You thingularly honored,' he answered. 'The Cave of Hope . . . it ith for lithardth alone!'

'The Cave of Hope?'

'Yeth. Not many eggth hatch. Elythia ith not Thak'r-Yon. Thak'r-Yon . . . home world.'

'Then why are you here?'

'Thak'r-Yon gone . . . ecthplode when thun nova. Elder Godth have pity on lithardth. Bring here. But Elythia ith not Thak'r-Yon.'

When I was dry at last, Oth-Neth handed me a pair of

soft boots, dark silk trousers straight out of the Arabian Nights, and a light cloak of some golden material whose wide fastenings crossed my body to buckle into the belt of my trousers. The collar of the cloak was decorated with large brass studs inset with black buttons. Oth-Neth explained the purpose of these studs: they were antigravity devices by means of which the wearer of the cloak might control himself in marvelous flight. Then the dragon pointed out similar studs and buttons set in his own harness, within reach of his short forelegs.

'All lithardth fly with . . . antigrav. The Elder Godth gave . . . when they brought uth from doomed Thak'r-Yon. Thak'r-Yon had low grav. But you try cloak . . . later. Now, Tiania ith waiting.'

'But my beard.' I tugged at the untidy growth. 'And my hair. I was never very vain, but to appear before a goddess . . .'

'Ah, yeth. Forgot,' he replied, drawing from his harness pouch a small jar of cream and a silver comb. The cream was a most efficient depilatory; my face was soon clean and smooth and I was able to set about combing the knots and tangles out of my hair. Finally, and before I could stop him, Oth-Neth produced a tiny spray and liberally doused me with a faint, not unpleasant perfume.

As I jumped into the saddle I said, 'Well, if I wasn't "thmelly" before I most certainly am now!' At which Oth-Neth threw back his head and boomed jovially. He sobered quickly.

'One more thing,' he said. 'Tiania not goddeth but . . . one of Chothen.'

'The Chosen?'

'Chothen of the Godth!' Then, and without a single further word, the great lithard stroked the row of studs set in his harness and bounded into the sky in a fanning of leather wings.

2

Tiania

(From de Marigny's recordings)

There are times in a man's life, no matter what previous wonders he has known, when the feeling comes that everything is a dream and he must pinch himself to wake up. I had known this feeling before, when faced with horrors too grotesque to be real – though they were! – and again on a number of occasions when realization of marvels beyond words had suddenly burst upon me.

Now it was this dragon-ride of mine toward a destiny I knew had called me all the days of my life – the feel of my healthy, strong body, alive and burning bright, seated in the saddle of a fabulous beast snatched straight out of Chinese mythology; a journey more fantastic than dreams themselves. I was actually riding a dragon through the skies of an alien world, enroute to the household of Tiania, Chosen of the Gods in her sky-floating, garden-girt castle high in the cotton clouds of Elysia!

Down below, the fields formed a giant patchwork quilt on which some child of the djinni had thrown his toy cities of crystal, with yellow and silver ribbons for roads and bright pieces of broken mirrors for lakes and pools. I laughed with the heady exhilaration of it all, and Oth-Neth laughed too, baring his teeth and booming into the tiny clouds that flew apart at the unspoken command of his thrumming wings.

Then ahead I spied an island in the sky. It was literally that, an island, a massive slab of rough rock floating in a sea of air. It looked for all the world as if it had just crashed down from some titanic cliff in space, except that its topside was planted with lush grass, trees and flowers, and its precipitous edges were walled and grown with orchid-sprouting creepers. And set back in a garden of fountains and pools, where strange lilies exhaled exotic perfumes, there rose a granite-walled, wide-windowed ornamental castle. Sweet-smelling stables stood at the rear, close by a clover field in which a group of sated dragons slumbered in the shade of mighty trees. The household of Tiania. A world of its own that looked down upon Elysia even as the great soaring birds of the upper air look down upon the fields and cities of Earth.

We alighted first on a cobbled path before the outer walls; with a single bound Oth-Neth carried me in beneath a high archway, coming to a halt in a tiny courtyard. Trembling suddenly, filled with emotions and passions that blazed within me as they never blazed in my Earth-youth, I got down from Oth-Neth's back and stood waiting . . . I knew not what for. Intricately wrought and inscribed glass doors stood open in the granite face of the inner wall; beyond them a maze of mosaic-adorned rooms strewn with cushions glowed in the beams of sunlight striking through a thousand tiny crystal windows all set about the wider casements.

With a sudden snort of impatience and a toss of his dragon's head, Oth-Neth thrust me awkwardly forward. Numb though my legs felt, at least I found them answering my commands, sufficiently to allow me to walk in through the glass doors to the maze of mosaic rooms. Behind me the doors silently closed; one by one the crystal windows, large and small, glowed, then turned opaque; from some-where a chiming music as of færie bells and sighing strings faintly sounded. Now the light grew dim, until quite suddenly the vaulted ceiling glowed with a fluorescence which, while faint, seemed to act upon and fill the maze of rooms with sparkling wineglass translucency.

I stood still, not daring to move lest I ruin the magic by

my intrusion. Gradually the mosaics of the walls faded to be replaced by perfect mirror surfaces in which a thousand images of myself were reflected. Vain as it may seem now to say it, I was not displeased with the looks of these myriad caped giants. Then, even as I stared at the mirror images of myself, suddenly I was not alone. The image of Tiania – a thousand images – gossamer-clad and supple as willow-wands, appeared beside my own.

The sight was enough to burn the retina like a naked sun, containing a beauty to destroy a man's sight forever. At the very least it would make him an addict, drawn forever to seek the purest bliss of such sheer unbelievable beauty, or driven to the dark oblivion of suicide in its absence. A thousand Tianias, but which one was real? Every fiber of my body, my soul and even, I thought, that mechanical heart of mine, ached.

I held out my arms. 'Tiania, which of these dreams is really you?'

'This one,' her warm, trembling voice answered. Then her cool arms were suddenly about me and her eyes, in which I knew I could happily drown, gazed gorgeously into mine. No man of flesh and blood could ever withstand so tremendous an assault on his senses; I made no attempt to but instantly bent to kiss her.

Quickly she put delicately tapered, trembling hands to my lips. Her eyes were wide; her face, even as mine, full of wonder. 'Titus Crow . . . do you love me?'

'Tiania,' I answered, or perhaps my soul answered for me, 'I have loved you forever . . .'

To this day I cannot recall that first kiss. I remember that before we drew apart in mutual wonder the maze of rooms had darkened again, and that Tiania's eyes were veiled jewels in the darkness. Their fire was finally put out beneath fluttering lashes. For a moment we stood like that, until she almost seemed to faint against me. All about us then, as I fiercely caught her up and she as fiercely responded, the færie music swelled to match the beat of incensed pulses . . .

Thus Tiania became mine, and she will remain mine forever.

The morning was synthetic, prepared by the castle itself under instruction from its mistress, for there is no night in Elysia. Gradually the crystal windows lightened, as if dawn glowed beyond them, and slowly the maze of rooms and their mosaic walls began to take on form in the darkness. The twittering of small birds filtered into the castle from the ivied walls outside.

I cannot really say whether I was asleep or not when Tiania's absence impressed itself on me; most likely I was in that half-world between dream and waking. I roused myself, dressed as full daylight returned to the maze of interconnecting rooms and made my way to the open glass doors. In the courtyard a spiderlike creature of roughly human proportions but with an abundance of hairy legs and other appendages moved swiftly, almost nervously about. It was armed with an arsenal of brooms and brushes, dusting, sweeping, polishing the hard cobbles and whistling to itself what sounded like a thoroughly human tune.

Despite the fact that the creature was obviously harmless, a member of Tiania's household, nevertheless I found a certain disturbing similarity between it and certain of the robots on T3RE's world. This was surely, I told myself, only the thing's spindly-leggedness. As I watched, a second spider twitched rapidly into view from around the curve of the castle wall and made straight for the glass doors where I stood. It paused in patent confusion when I made no move to get out of its way.

231

'Er, excuse me,' I said, smiling in what I was sure must be a very foolish fashion. 'Where is Tiania?'

It whistled questioningly, the antennae above its soft brown eyes trembling in peculiar agitation. Then the pitch of its whistling fell. 'Tiania?' it repeated in fluting tones. 'Bathing.' It made to get by me but I stood my ground.

'Bathing, you say? Where is she bathing?'

'Lithard pool,' the spider answered. Then, after a further moment of indecision, it gently but firmly picked me up in surprisingly strong arms to set me down again on one side and out of its way. It shuffled about nervously, awkwardly, peered at me wonderingly and gradually resumed its whistling. Then, as if I no longer existed, apparently satisfied that it had done the right thing, the spider twitched on past me into the maze of rooms within the castle. In another second, in addition to its whistling, I could hear the sounds of its sweeping and brushing as it moved rapidly through the rooms. After that I paid these curious menials no further attention, except to get out of their way when they were busy!

Tiania had told me about Elysia's constant day during our long 'night'. Elysia's dwellings incorporate marvelously intricate computers which make special mornings, evenings or nights to order for their owners. Depending on the worlds of origin of their inhabitants, the dwellings also work all kinds of atmospheric wonders; together with an unlimited combination of special lighting effects and weather conditioning, the homes can be programmed to suit every mood and need. Still, I was surprised and it registered as a shock when I saw that the 'sun' stood as always at its zenith.

Then, shielding my eyes against the orb's brightness, I saw a speck rapidly growing larger among fleecy cotton clouds, and shortly the speck became the outline of Oth-Neth with the glowing form of Tiania on his back. Her wonderful hair, catching the wind, billowed about her shoulders where she stretched out full length along the dragon's neck. As they circled high above the courtyard I could hear her laughter and the joyous booming of her mount. She was clad in a garment that glowed with faint mother-of-pearl, with huge bell-bottoms at her sandaled feet, a top that left her arms and shoulders bare, and a wide belt of silver glowing about her waist. As Oth-Neth commenced hovering above the courtyard like some enormous hawk in the sunlight, she stood up on his neck and put her hands to her belt where the buckle would be – then stepped free of the lithard into thin air!

Down she plummeted like a falling arrow, feet first, her emerald hair a meteorite's tail streaming green fire up from her head. Horrified, I rushed forward, holding up my arms to catch her, knowing that from so extreme a height she must surely kill herself and probably me too. At the last instant I closed my eyes, certain she would smash me down onto the freshly cleaned cobbles of the courtyard. Instead there came only her beautiful voice in worried inquiry, and from on high the beat of great wings and a familiar but questioning booming. As I opened my eyes in disbelief she settled into my arms gentle as a feather.

'Titus, your face . . .' She put the palms of her hands to my temples. 'Are you ill?'

'No,' I answered, realization beginning to dawn, remembering what Oth-Neth had told me about the use of antigravity. I lifted her up and gently shook her. 'I'm not ill, just terribly angry!'

'But why?'

I folded her into my arms. 'I thought you would kill yourself!'

'Surely Oth-Neth told you of the devices we use to – '

233

'Yes, but I had never seen one used, except by Oth-Neth, and that was different. I certainly wasn't thinking of such devices when I saw you step from his back.'

'And you really feared for me?'

I lifted her up above me again, so that she looked quizzically down at me, wide-eyed. 'I've only just found you,' I told her. 'But I don't ever want to lose you!'

'You will never lose me, Titus,' she answered quickly, excitedly. 'We are one now and none may put us asunder. While I bathed Oth-Neth went to see Kthanid far in the frostlands. He sends us his blessing and says that when you have seen Elysia we are to go to him. Kthanid it was who first told me of you; indeed, it was he – '

'Who promised me to you?' I finished for her, smiling.

Her sweet mouth fell open. 'But how do you know that?'

'Oh,' I teased, 'I know many things. Simple Earthman I may be but – '

She laughed at me and kissed me as I put her down. 'No, Titus, Simple Earthman you are *not*!' she said. 'But still you don't know everything!'

I asked her meaning but she shook her head. 'No time now to bother with all that. You shall know later. But this . . . evening' – she formed the word carefully, unused to its sound in a world where natural evenings did not exist – 'many friends of mine are coming to meet you and eat with us. Before then I must show you how to use your flying cloak, and I will need to talk to the computer to ensure that the . . . evening is perfect. So much to do. First you must learn to fly!'

And so I learned to fly! Tiania showed me how I must cross my hands over my chest in front of me, like an Egyptian mummy in his sarcophagus, to reach the buttons set in their brass studs in the harness of my cloak. And she taught me which buttons and combinations of buttons to press in order to achieve elevation, lateral and transverse flight and many other more awkward maneuvers of aerial agility that might have taxed the dexterity of a fly. Because I reveled in this new art I learned quickly, and at last Tiania decided I knew enough to allow me to fly with her over the precipitous edge of her sky-floating island. I took the initiative to speed like an arrow before her, while Oth-Neth hurtled after us and boomed his approval as we tumbled through the sky like human bats in a fantastic game of tag.

Then, as I turned sharply to speed beneath the sky-floating island itself, I heard Tiania's cry of warning and slowed until she flashed up beside me. 'Careful, Titus! See there.' She turned on her side to point out for me a series of vast brass disks, at least a dozen of them, set in the rough rock base of the floating island. Each disk had a black center like an iris, and central in each of the irises was a luminous area that sent a slim white ray of light earthward. These beams soon petered out, but they were plainly visible where they issued from the luminous areas.

'Oh, yes!' Tiania told me later, as we sat beside a fountain. 'The antigravity power which the disks exert is so powerful that to fly into a ray too close to its source would be to die instantly, flattened in a moment and hurled to the fields of Elysia far, far below.' She sipped iced wine from a tiny glass. 'Those engines are tremendously powerful. Just think, they float my entire island here in the air as if it were a feather!'

And then, towards 'evening', Tiania took me with her to the center of the maze of rooms and showed me the computer that governed the life of her castle in the sky. It was quite different from anything I might have expected: a gadget like a large microphone beneath which Tiania sat while she spoke her commands out loud. She explained that really there was no need for her to speak

235

at all but she wanted me to hear what kind of evening she had in mind for our party. Her orders would have been understood and carried out had she merely sat still and thought them to the machine. The device could obey instructions no matter what sort of creature used it, for telepathy knows no distinction between races, creeds or species. Thought is thought.

The evening was to be exotic. No, that simply would not do to describe it. It would be fantastic! Twin moons, one gold, the other silver, would sail the night sky while small warm winds would play all about the castle. Stars as big as a man's fist, so close one might try to pluck them from the firmament, would seem to light up the sky with their twinklings, and meteorites would blaze like fireworks as they fell down from the heavens. Music would play softly in the background, the most beautiful tunes of a hundred worlds, and there would be dancing and singing and good things to eat and drink until 'morning', which would be equally fantastic. The party would go on all through the synthetic night.

When Tiania was finally satisfied, she stood up from beneath the programming device and I took hold of her hands. 'It will go on all night?' I smilingly asked.

'Yes,' she answered brightly, then noticed the look in my eyes and blushed. 'But when our friends have gone then we shall have another night, a long one, to enjoy together. But you must not listen when I tell the castle's computer the arrangements for that night!'

And so we bathed in an indoor pool, dressed and went to the walls to watch for the arrival of our guests. If anything, these arrivals were more fantastic than both the evening to come and the morning put together. First came members of that bird race of linguists, the Dchichis, a member of which, Esch, had been the first being to greet me in

Elysia. Next came a tiny couple that I thought to be small children when I first saw them flying afar. They arrived completely naked and alone, without the aid of dragons or antigravity belts. Only when they actually alighted beside us was I able to see that they themselves were winged, with twin-paired gossamer membranes that gleamed all the rainbow's hues before the little people folded them down along their backs. Then, too, I saw that they resembled insects more than anything else, with slender bodies and limbs and softly furred faces that smiled and blushed as Tiania greeted them warmly, introduced me and then directed them to the castle.

Next came a terrifically tall manlike being in a cape that covered him in fiery mesh from his neck to his feet, if he had any; he climbed up the winds of night to us, Tiania declared, using powers of levitation generated by his mind alone. He was Ardatha Ell, a white wizard from demon-doomed Pu-Tha, who had made his way to Elysia alone. He greeted us in a deep, sonorous voice which, while I studied him intently, I could swear did not issue from his pale lips but yet was not telepathic in the sense that I understood telepathy.

And so they came, creatures and beings from all the worlds of fantasy that a man might ever dream, and all of them plainly loved the woman, the girl, the goddess whose heart was mine. There were two hundred of them, perhaps more, none of them of the Elder Gods proper but all of them chosen ones, Chosen of the Gods. And there were some among them who, like Tiania herself, were very nearly human and yet more than human: beautiful creatures so delicate of form and feature, so exotic in styles and mannerisms, but yet radiating over all such auras of purest love, like Tiania, that they transcended mere humanity.

Of that computerized night, of the party itself and the

237

wonders and mysteries I saw and had explained to me, I will not even attempt descriptions. It is enough to say that despite their various, vastly differing forms and origins, despite the fact that of those who had tongues only a very few of them spoke languages I could understand, despite their coming to Elysia from all the ends of time and space, still a camaraderie of joy and friendship existed between all of them. It existed and grew through the long night, including myself as few friendships have ever included me during a lifetime on Earth. In the utter absence of fear and hate there can only be joy and love!

And so the night, long as it was, came and went. Time flew by and the most beautiful morning I ever saw grew into day, until finally our guests departed. I sorrowed when they went until, as she had promised, Tiania made another night for us, beside which all the beauty and wonder of the last paled to insignificance . . .

3
World of Wonder

(From de Marigny's recordings)

All too soon came the time when, perhaps sensing a germ of restlessness in me, Tiania took me away from her castle in the sky to see Elysia. What little I knew of the home of the Elder Gods was the merest fraction of an amazing total. Tiania told me that if I lived a thousand years and traveled Elysia far and wide I could never behold half of her wonders.

Indeed our travels occupied us for quite a long period. Often we stayed at the houses, castles, nests – on one occasion a hive – of Tiania's friends; at other times we flew back to the castle in the sky. Sometimes we rode Oth-Neth, when there were places and people the dragon particularly wanted to visit. And yet despite the never-ending marvels, the incredible scope and beauty of that world of wonder, always there nagged at the back of my mind an uneasy feeling of frustration. In all truth I was not sure . . . I did not *know* what the nagging feeling was.

How could one know frustration in Elysia, where all of a man's dreams might come true and all fears are put away, dispelled in the atmosphere of well-being that the Elder Gods themselves radiate? And yet there was this worry that I had left something undone, something very important. And just as a forgotten word sits for hours on the tip of one's tongue, so that inchoate thing lurked at the edge of my mind, slipping away whenever I attempted to focus on it.

No, it was not really frustration. Guilt, then? But of what could I possibly deem myself guilty? Had the Elder Gods themselves not found me worthy? Had not Kthanid, the Eminence in the Hall of Crystal and Pearl, bestowed his blessing upon Tiania and her Earthman? No, it was not guilt. What it was of course eventually dawned on me – perhaps I knew it all along but simply did not wish to recognize it, hence my feelings of guilt and frustration – but by then the remedy for this peculiar uneasiness of soul had already been decided.

That, however, is all away from the point. I have seen Elysia; I will now attempt, with totally inadequate words, to describe some of that world's wonders.

There is, for instance, the vast and aerial city of the Dchichis, an aerie of lava crags and spires honeycombed with burrows, silk-lined nests and communal incubators. But if that sounds like some rather grand and elevated North Sea bird sanctuary do not be misled: this island city floats many miles in the sky above Elysia, held aloft by enormous antigravity disks. Its nests are no less comfortable and well appointed than the rooms of Tiania's own castle, and its denizens, Esch's people, are more civilized and sophisticated than any race of Earth ever was or will be. The Dchichi hatchlings, even in their shells, commence learning the arts and sciences – particularly the tongues, the linguistic and other modes of conversation and communication – of dozens of the races and civilizations of an eternally expanding universe. The adults are fearless voyagers in space and time, seekers after knowledge in the fullest meaning of the words.

I saw and was awed at the sight of the Thousand Sealed Doors of the N'hlathi, hibernating centipedes whose slumbers have already lasted for five thousand years and will not be broken for as long again. These great circular slabs of magnificently inscribed basalt, where they line the feet of the Purple Mountain in the Vale of Dreams, are thirty feet in diameter and barred with massive bands of a white metal that no caustic liquid may ever corrode. They are the portals to the burrows of the dreaming N'hlathi, who sleep until the great pale poppies bloom again on the slopes of the Purple Mountains. Only then will they emerge from their deep cavern sanctums, for their food is the seed of the giant poppy which blooms every ten thousand years and then, like the N'hlathi themselves, falls once more into centuried hibernation. And none in Elysia save the Elder Gods remember the ways of these cryptogenic slumberers at the roots of the Purple Mountains, for theirs is a history that was never written and their tongue has never been understood. Not even the Dchichis, whose greatest linguists and calligraphers regularly convene in the Vale of Dreams to ponder the inscriptions of the Thousand Sealed Doors, have been able to decipher their mysteries.

In the mountain-girt Gardens of Nymarrah, Tiania took me to meet the Tree. By then I no longer questioned her with regard to the denizens of Elysia, nor about other matters which had initially bothered me, though certainly there were many questions I could have asked. I had discovered that it was far simpler to wait and see; the answers invariably presented themselves in their own time.

The Tree was a very special friend of Tiania's. She had played in his branches as a child, when he stood to the west of the Gardens of Nymarrah, and had visited him often during his slow journey east. Now he stood in the center of the Gardens, a towering emerald giant twelve hundred feet tall. He had a classical brandy-glass shape, all beautiful yard-long leaves of lush green, with creeper-like tendrils hanging in festoons beneath the branches, and ridged brown bark a foot thick. Serene, silent and sentient!

The trunk of this titan must have been all of one hundred and fifty feet through and through, and as Tiania and I approached him, walking barefoot and hand in hand through knee-deep grasses, the outer branches sighed and bent down and the soft furry edges of giant leaves touched us. At the same instant I felt a thrill of strange awareness deep in my every fiber. A question had been asked, had passed from one living, thinking being to others, but as yet the empathy between the Tree and myself was incomplete. Tiania, on the other hand, had known the Tree all her life.

'It is I!' she cried at once, answering the Tree's question. She darted forward into the shade of massive branches and beneath suddenly mobile tendrils, pressing herself to the rough bark of the great bole and spreading her arms wide as if to encompass that massive girth. 'It is Tiania!'

Should a man be jealous of a tree? No, not even a tree as magnificent as this one. Tiania turned and took my hand as I approached the trunk less hastily. She spoke, but not to me: 'This is Titus, my Earthman.'

Again the Tree sighed and tendrils like slender snakes tentatively brushed Tiania's waist, then wrapped themselves about her. I was watching this so intently that I did not notice the second group of tendrils until I actually felt the first fumblings at my waist. With a startled cry I pulled back against the Tree's touch, and instantly the tendrils sprang away and the leaves above my head furled in on themselves and drew back.

'No, no, Titus. That is not the way,' Tiania chided. 'The Tree loves me, he loves all living things in Elysia and would love you, too, but you must not frighten him!'

Frighten him? I looked up into dim distances of receding green, dappled here and there by soft sunlight penetrating from outside, where shafts of gold showed a myriad scented motes dancing in the air. Beneath one tree, I stood in the green heart of a forest!

'Frighten him?' I asked out loud.

'Certainly. He is very shy.'

'I meant no harm, no discourtesy, but . . .'

'Then you must think of him as a person in his own right, like Oth-Neth or Esch, not just a tree. He is *the* Tree, and he is a very beautiful person!'

Well, no doubt about that last. He was quite beautiful, and indeed as I had pulled away from his tendrils, I had felt in the thrilling energies that filled me a sensation of . . . hurt? So what was wrong with me? I could happily mesh my mind with a machine, the time-clock; feel comradeship toward a robot, T3RE; laugh and swim with dragons and ride one across alien skies. And yet now, this living, thinking – yes, person – shrank from me.

I reached to stroke the edge of a leaf where it curled uncertainly above my head and with my mind I said, '*You are very, very beautiful, and if you love Tiania then love me also for we are one.*'

A sigh that grew into a great soughing of branches filled the Tree as he reached down his tendril arms to lift us up in joy into his midst, swinging us high like bobbins on threads and passing us tendril to tendril all the way up his fantastic length. It was breathtaking, and more so for the fact that now the Tree's empathic aura, its radiations of emotion, were reaching me.

And all the Tree knew or was interested in was beauty! Beauty poured from the titan's soul, enveloping all, swelling out to set the very air trembling in sympathetic joy. And in the center of all that wonder Tiania and I were rushed dizzyingly aloft to finally perch in the topmost branches, there to listen to the Tree's songs of love and joy and beauty.

Peering through those highest branches and leaves,

almost a quarter of a mile above Elysia's soil, I could see a wide gray path away to the west. The great path seemed to lead arrow-straight to the Tree, drawn as if by a ruler, except that this ruler would have to be many miles long. As the Tree's songs finally died away in a vast sighing, I knew suddenly what that great swath of dry sandy soil was: nothing less than the track the Tree had made in his long journey from the west.

'Yes,' Tiania told me when I asked her, 'you are right. The Tree leans almost imperceptibly to the east; he sends out new roots in that direction. To the west, where the soil is dead, there the old roots die. And so the Tree turns himself, ever so slowly, and turning he moves forward. As the new roots turn to the west they grow old. And always the Tree leans toward the east, moving and turning, turning and moving, ever so slowly. He calls it his dance. Such is his size that he requires much nourishment. The earth he feeds in is dead and dry when he moves on, and he sorrows for the dead earth he leaves behind him. But he sorrows rarely and usually only when he is alone. When people visit him, then he fills out with joy.'

As she finished speaking I saw that there were tears in her eyes. I took her in my arms. 'Tiania, why do you cry?'

'The Tree tells me,' she answered, 'that there is a sadness in you. I have known you were restless but did not think it must come so soon.'

'A sadness in me?' I was astonished. 'You did not think it would come so soon? I don't understand, Tiania. What do you mean?'

She threw her arms around me and sobbed openly on my shoulder. 'You do not even know, my love, you have not realized it; but Kthanid said it might be so. You searched so long and hard for your Earth before you found Elysia, that you still – '

'*No!*' I denied it, angrily shaking my head.

She pushed me away and sprang to her feet on the naked branch high above the Gardens of Nymarrah and her hands flew to her belt. 'There must be no pain here . . . the Tree . . .' And drawing back from me as fresh tears flooded her eyes, she flew out through the leaves and was gone.

'Tiania!' Rising in anger – angry because I knew that she was right, and yet still not understanding, or not wanting to understand – I rose to leap after her. The Tree immediately cast quivering tendrils about me, holding me fast. All the fibers of my soul read the Tree's message, which was love, and a great sadness filled me.

'I love you,' the Tree told me, 'and I love Tiania. She loves you, and you . . .?'

'I love her, too,' I answered, 'and always will, but she is right. For a little while at least I must leave Elysia!'

And then I sat down again in that high place and the Tree stroked me with the furry edge of a great leaf and sang songs to my innermost being, songs as sad as my troubled soul, which would not have been soothed by all the joy in Elysia . . .

And so we went to Kthanid, the Elder God who was Tiania's guardian. His palace of crystal and mother-of-pearl lay in the heart of a glacier, in a region where the sun shone far off, as if it were about to sink down behind Elysia and disappear. Warmly wrapped we went, in furs and boots, riding a gravity-defying vessel of silver whose curved crystal screen kept the biting cold from us.

We approached Kthanid's demesne from the sea, across an expanse of blue ocean where icebergs sailed majestic and serene. There, far ahead and glittering in the rays of the distant sun, Tiania pointed out the vast and eternal glacier whose heart housed Kthanid's palace. It was a solitary place, as are all the seats of the Elder Gods, where Kthanid might ponder whichever problems he desired or do whatever he wished in peace eternal.

'I will ask him,' she told me as we flew in through the crevasse that guarded the entrance to the ice-enveloped palace, 'if I may not go with you to your Earth. Perhaps it is possible that – '

'Even if he agreed,' I cut her off, 'I would not take you. There are terrors in the voids of space and time that you must never know face to face. You have risked too much for me already.'

As we alighted from the flying machine at the head of a series of magnificent ice steps she stamped her booted feet, and not, I thought, solely because of the cold we could now feel biting through our furs. 'Are you so soon bored with me then, Titus Crow?'

'Little one,' I told her, my own anger rising, 'Kthanid's palace or not, and him your guardian and all, if you once more hint that I could ever find boredom in your arms – or you in mine, for that matter – then you'll go across my knee! Why, girl, I – '

But she was crying, and if ever a sight was designed to bend, to break my heart, then it was the sight of Tiania in grief. Comforting her while the tears froze on her cheeks, I pulled her furs closer and picked her up in my arms to carry her down the first sweeping flight of ice-hewn steps. Above us the crevasse walls swept up to meet in a splendid arch of icicles, which looked for all the world like the roof of some titanic ice-beast's gaping mouth, but soon this entranceway had dwindled to a mere triangle of light at our rear.

Finally, after descending many flights of the steps cut in ice and arriving at the foot of that tremendous staircase, I saw that we had reached the polished bedrock of the mountain ravine. An ice tunnel, its granite floor worn smooth by centuries of glaciation, stretched away into the heart of the glacier. Sweeping along this passage there came strange and exotic scents the like of which I had never known before, all carried by a warm breeze. It blew upon the face of the now drowsy girl in my arms and caused her to stir. She kissed me, which told me that all was well, and I placed her gently on her own feet. Then, with my arm around her waist, we continued.

As the distance we covered increased, so did the warmth. We soon shrugged off our robes and proceeded clad only in the accustomed dress of Elysia's warmer climes. I would have flown but Tiania stopped me, saying that mortals should show humility in the presence of the gods.

We walked another mile or so until quite suddenly the dim blue light grew brighter, as if here a great source of illumination was hidden behind the soft sheen of ice walls. Then those walls themselves became granite and finally we arrived at a hanging curtain of crystal beads and pearls threaded on gold. Such was the number of golden threads thus adorned that the curtain was quite thick; in width it extended right across the tunnel. Even so, each individual thread of that precious veil was fine enough to allow the whole curtain to move in the warm draft that issued from its hidden side.

'The throne room of Kthanid,' Tiania told me, 'whose wisdom is unequaled and unchallenged among all the Elder Gods!' She parted the curtain and held it open for me, beckoning me to enter. I slipped through the opening . . . into a scene remembered from my dreams!

For of course this was the Hall of Crystal and Pearl, the Palace of the Eminence, the inner sanctum wherein a great being thought Great Thoughts upon its throne in a curtained alcove! It was here that I had stood beside an anguished, frightened girl/woman/goddess who had not known I was present, to watch myself hurtling down to the Black Hole in the time-clock. But while that had been a dream – or at best a vision engendered of some aeon-spanning telepathic empathy between Tiania and myself – this was real, here, now! My mind reeled in the grip of fantastic paradoxes.

Standing just within the curtain, Tiania at my side, I gazed dry-mouthed all around me. I recognized the tremendous hall, with its weird angles and proportions and high-arched ceiling, the titan-paved floor of massive hexagonal flags and the ornate columns rising to support high balconies that seemed obscured in a haze of rose quartz. Everywhere were the remembered white, pink and blood hues of multicolored crystal, even the vast scarlet cushion with its centerpiece that resembled nothing so much as a huge, milky crystal ball. Everything was as I remembered it . . .

No, not quite. There were two things, at least, that were new to me. One of these was that the walls, where they rose up on all sides from the flagged floor, had a regular series of tunnels cut into them. These passageways were similar to the pearl- and crystal-draped shaft which Tiania and I had just used to enter into this great cathedral of a hall. No use, I supposed, to wonder where these tunnels led. The other difference did not become noticeable until Tiania led me to the center of the hall, where the vast silken cushion lay. From there a great wide trail of what looked like jewel-dust was quite conspicuous. It led from the cushion to the huge and curtained alcove wherein I knew the Eminence stirred even now.

This brilliantly twinkling path was at least fifty feet wide, and I felt strangely uneasy just looking at it. It was like –

'Kthanid has been using the viewer,' Tiania told me, her eyes, too, turned to the twinkling path. And I knew

248

then that I had been right: that the jeweled track between the silken cushion and the curtained alcove was nothing less than the – dare I say it? – snail-trail of the Eminence, and my uneasiness returned twofold.

4

Kthanid

(From de Marigny's recordings)

No sooner had the outré realization dawned on me – that
I stood now truly in the presence of a being strange and
mighty almost beyond the imaginings of the world of men
I had left behind – than the curtains of the great alcove
billowed slightly in response to a hidden inner movement.
And then Kthanid's awesome mental voice spoke in our
minds, addressing Tiania but not shutting me out:

*'So, child, it is as I said it would be: for a while you must
lose your Earthman. But I have looked into the viewer on
times to come, and though the possible futures are many I
have seen that all the factors that guide probability point to
his return. However, since you yourself do not appear in any
of this man's most immediate tomorrows, you will not
accompany him but wait in Elysia until he returns.'*

'But why may I not go with him, Kthanid?' she cried.
'Perhaps you have not seen all the possible futures in the
viewer; perhaps if he stays a little longer in Elysia the
futures will change, and – '

*'I have not seen all of the possible futures, no, for that
itself is impossible – as you well know, Tiania. And no use
to argue, child, Titus Crow may not stay longer. Indeed,
he sets forth in a very short time to return to his Earth.
Even now his machine is being readied. I have seen to it
that a weapon is fitted, by possession of which during his
journey he need not so greatly fear the minions of evil,
though certainly they will yet attempt to lure him astray
from his path. Indeed, even equipped with the weapon, his
return to Earth will not be an easy one . . . When the
machine is ready, it will come for him.*

'Now I would speak to Titus Crow alone. Tiania, play with the viewer and find yourself a joyous future to look upon in its depths while we talk, for there are many questions your man would have answers to, and time grows short.

'You, Titus Crow, come and stand by the curtains and I will tell you the things you need to know.'

'But, Kthanid – ' Tiania started forward, and immediately her figure stiffened, then as quickly relaxed again. The contrary frown on her face fell away and she smiled, turning to step up onto the scarlet cushion and throw herself down in its center, head on hands to gaze into the swirling, milky depths of the crystal ball.

It seemed to me that in my mind I heard a sigh, then Kthanid's mental voice saying: *She is only a girl, yet more than a woman. I delight in her for she is of my own flesh. Now come to the curtains.*

And so I walked the space between cushion and alcove, noticing as I did so that the massive flags of the floor were blank now, that the brilliant track which had told so elegantly of Kthanid's passing this way had faded and disappeared. I stopped and waited at the softly billowing curtains, almost hypnotized by the reflected luster of scintillant points of light and color. At once the voice of the Eminence came again:

'Yes, you have been patient and there is much you desire to know. There is much that you should know and little time for the telling. We who are known as Elder Gods, however, have a way of communicating many things in a very short space of time. Were you an ordinary man so vast an amount of concentrated knowledge would surely blast your mind if I attempted to pass it in such a way. But you are no ordinary man.

'Now steel yourself, Titus Crow, and know these things.'

* * *

That command of the Eminence, to steel myself, gave me barely sufficient time to brace my mind before I found it suddenly submerged in a tidal wave of intense telepathic transmissions. I was well able to understand, as my consciousness reeled under that mental assault, how any ordinary man's being might well be blasted! With incredible rapidity a series of facts imprinted themselves on my mind, coming in no recognizable order but simply flashing on me as brilliant bursts of knowledge and often of inspirational truth.

'*Know these things*,' the Eminence had told me, and now –

I knew why in the beginning and after the Great Uprising the Elder Gods had retired to Elysia from all the worlds of space. For the CCD had been Elder Gods too; yes, even the Great Old Ones, but they had realized their power. And their power had been so very nearly absolute that they had been absolutely corrupted.

Then the Elder Gods had locked away their brothers who had grown evil. Lest others of them fall prey to corruption, they had decided to remain and live in Elysia. And knowing that they alone were responsible for the evil they had bred in all the worlds, they elected to take all necessary precautions: the imprisoned forces of evil *must* remain imprisoned and never again gain the upper hand over the various sentient races which inhabited the worlds.

And so the Elder Gods watched over the prisons of the CCD from afar, that the forces of evil might never again prey among the emerging races of the worlds. But as the æons passed those new races grew in wisdom and in folly. Influenced little by little by the mind-sendings of the evil ones imprisoned in or adjacent to their worlds, they began to worship them and seek ways to free them from their prisons.

The Elder Gods were aware of all this, and they knew what they must do. Capable of miscegenation, they would go out and plant their seed in the flesh of the children of all the worlds and thus disseminate their essence down the ages. But in this they had to safeguard their pattern's genetic perpetuation, without allowing their various forms to be repeated in those races with which they intermingled. And in this, too, they were adept.

Thus a subconscious strength – springing of the Elder Gods' own wanting to overcome the evil of the CCD – would always lie dormant in the beings of the children of all the worlds. When strength was needed to oppose the insidious wills of the captive forces of evil, then they would find it within themselves. And yet the Elder Gods had to be careful, for they wished all the races and civilizations to grow according to their own natures, and therefore the seed of the Elder Gods must not be sown too thickly.

And so on Earth the Elder Gods mated with the daughters of men, and there were giants in the world in those days. And among all the spheres they mingled with the children of the worlds, to ensure that when they returned to Elysia there would still be warders to guard the prisons of their brothers lost in great sin.

And I knew that I myself was a throwback to just such matings between the Elder Gods and the daughters of men, that in my blood and body and being an ancient genetic pattern had returned, had swung full circle. I was a man, but part of me had roots in Elysia! I knew that there were many like me, and that one of them was my own Tiania, but Tiania was a very special case for she was also of the Chosen Ones.

Born of man and woman but not on Earth, Tiania had been raised in Elysia when her parents had traveled there from Earth. Her father had been a great scientist of drowned Mu and her mother a Thenopian lady whose blood was imbued with all the æon-spanning properties of the great Beings of Eld. And they had journeyed to Elysia at the foundering of Mu in no vessel but using the power of their minds alone, a power only the Elder Gods had known before them, for in Mu they were far, far ahead of their own time on Earth. Unbeknown to them they had been assisted by Kthanid, who sent them a Great Thought to guide them forward through time and space to Elysia. In his action in this matter the Eminence had felt an obligation, for it was none other than his blood which flowed in the veins of Tiania's mother, and his genetic pattern which, repeating down the ages, shaped her inner being.

Tiania's parents had found favor in the eyes of the Elder Gods and, desiring to do their will, were sent out into the worlds to do wondrous works. So as a child Tiania was left in Elysia and Kthanid watched over her, and thus she grew to strange, beautiful womanhood, more strange and beautiful even than the drowned flowers of Mu . . .

But even as she grew Kthanid had known that the time would come when one of Elysia's young men – of which a small number were of worlds similar to Earth and of very human form – would desire her. This had troubled him, for while the Chosen of the Gods were beautiful in all their diverse forms they were often weak – not in spirit or intelligence or character, not even physically weak. But they were weak in that they had never known the meaning of adversity; their strength had never been tested.

So he had looked into his crystal sphere – that viewer whose surface was a window on a universe of universes, just as the time-clocks are gateways on all times and places – and he had seen a man fighting the immemorial fight against the powers of evil. Following this man's life

254

in his viewer, Kthanid had seen that there was a possible future when he might reach Elysia, and so he had brought the man to the attention of Tiania. And she had looked into the viewer at Kthanid's bidding and had seen this man. And he had been old. Then Kthanid told her, '*Look into his futures, for there is one such future when he might come to you in Elysia, but not as an old man.*'

So she had looked again, and saw the same man grown young and strong, and Kthanid made her a promise that if ever he came to Elysia (for the possible futures were many) then she should have him. That promise was made to a child of twelve tender years who, from that time on and for ten long years more, was to wait patiently for her Earthman in Elysia.

And often she had begged the great being Kthanid to send her mind and thoughts out to this man when dangers threatened him on his long journey to the secret place of the Elder Gods, even when the Earthman went down to the Black Hole. She would have gone to him, too, when he penetrated the blackest veil of all and was driven into Yog-Sothoth's prison dimension, but such was the evil of Yog-Sothoth that not even a Great Thought could carry her there. And so she waited still, unknowing if he lived or died, for Kthanid's crystal could not see into that dark demesne. (Or at least Kthanid would not allow it, lest Tiania see something which might break her mind and soul.)

And Kthanid himself had despaired, for the man was after all only a man despite his heritage. Then the veil was rent and Kthanid called out to the man to come into Elysia. And Kthanid also used the great power of the Elder Gods to throw back the monstrous Yog-Sothoth, who would have followed the man into Elysia . . .

All of this knowledge and much, much more crowded my mind, de Marigny. I knew that you, my old friend of

255

– of how many ages ago? – had lived on when I had thought you dead and gone in unlit abysses; found that even now you were alive and well on old Earth. And I knew why Tiania had never once mentioned your name to me, though she too must have known that you lived. If I was going to leave her to return to my home planet, she was not going to hurry me with any such inducement. But in any case I could not blame her, for even knowing all of these things, I also knew how much she loved me.

And it was as if I looked into Kthanid's crystal ball myself, for I saw that my return to Earth would be hard, despite the ever watchful Tiania, and despite whichever weapon the Elder God Eminence had given me. But I knew now that you, your mind, would be there like a bright beacon to guide and speed me into a safe berth, Henri.

My mind absorbed this knowledge like a dry sponge absorbs water. I knew finally and was ashamed of my own and man's cowardice. Strange knowledge blossomed from depths and storehouses of my mind unguessed, telling me things I had always known but refused to recognize, facts that lie dormant in the beings and souls of all men. I had been a coward, all human beings are; but I knew now that mankind's terrors, since mankind dawned, have never been physical, tangible things.

Make no mistake, what I say is true! Our fears are all of the mind, implanted there by other minds that rule our dismal destinies. Cowards all, I said: we have looked outwards, yes – but how often have we looked inside?

Few minds have been strong enough to bear even a single glimpse. Alhazred, who might have been one of the greatest of men, went insane, and others before and since his time. And some simply died rather than go on living knowing what they knew – their purposes in life! Those few who looked, who saw and yet retained their sanity, they were brought down by the night, destroyed by the atavistic fear of others, fears that lingered on from a time before recorded history. They are no more.

I am speaking of the works of the CCD, yes, and of the fear that the entire world of men knows in the face of them. And that is not as it should be. Their seed is in us all, the seed of gods and the seed of demons of Eld, but we are the new generation of the universe and we ought to decide our own futures. Cthulhu and all the others of his dreadful cycle, they should dance man's tune! Perhaps, in the Wilmarth Foundation, the true foundation is laid at long last.

Finally I knew all of these things and many, many others. The full meaning of Kthanid's sendings burst upon me then, illuminating my whole mind, but in that mental sunburst one fact stood out above all others: I knew why the Elder Gods had not destroyed the CCD after they had put them down in their great sin. Do we murder our poor unfortunate lunatic brothers? No, we lock them up and set keepers over them for their own and everyone else's safety.

The Elder Gods are not their brothers' keepers! Man is the custodian, the warder of all the gibbering horrors of Earth and space. I will tell you what we fear, Henri, and why we are cowards. We fear the awesome task we have been given, for we and no others are guardians of the universe!

With this last revelation, without waiting for his permission or even asking it, I stepped forward through the magnificent curtains that draped Kthanid's alcove, and I stood at the foot of his throne. I gazed at him.

Staggered in spite of having guessed what I must find, I was at first amazed, then horrified. Finally I felt my lips pull back in the beginning of a scream, the hair stiffen at the back of my neck and my flesh creep in shudders . . . I gazed on the face and form of Kthanid, the Eminence, the Elder God guardian and progenitor of my own Tiania.

And madness sprang up in me as I tottered on paralyzed legs within the curtain of the great alcove, gazing at the thing on the throne – at the massive body, the wings folded back, the great head with its proliferation of face-tentacles. For this, except for those eyes, might well have been Cthulhu himself! Kin to the Lord of R'lyeh this being most certainly was, and close to him at that, so that only his eyes saved me from the rushing madness. The very soul of goodness and mercy, those massive golden eyes were lucid depths through which passes all the love and compassion of a father for his children, all the joy of a great artist at the perfection of his composition.

And he reached down to me and touched me, and all fear and awe, all terror of the unknown, all uneasiness of soul and psyche fled me at his touch. When I went out to Tiania where she gazed enraptured into joyous futures that floated on the surface of the crystal ball, I was a man at peace with all things . . .

When Tiania and I retraced our steps, when we climbed the ice staircase to the mouth of that great crevasse in the glacier, we found our flying machine just as we had left it. Beside it, its panel open and softly illumined in a pale blue lambency from within, my time-clock waited.

I kissed Tiania once and promised I would return, and no change came into her bright face, but I saw a tear forming in the corner of her eye. Before that tear could swell and roll down onto her cheek, I entered the time-clock and took my vessel up into icy atmosphere. And below me in the scanners a tiny dot stood by a mighty glacier and watched me go, and thus I began my return to Earth . . .

258

Part Six

De Marigny's Choice

(Random excerpts from de Marigny's diary)

Feb. 28

Today I can hardly believe it but last night I looked down on Earth through the scanners of the time-clock, and the lights of the cities were like tiny candles on a gigantic cake. Yet now I can't help feeling that the cake is made of plastic, false and tasteless.

Still, today's mood can't completely spoil the memory of how we flew up high above the world and looked down on the cities of men. Titus showed me how to reach out my mind telepathically and touch the mind of the clock. It was frightening, awesome, exhilarating! I actually flew that fantastic machine out to the moon and back, but Titus took the controls again to land the clock right back in the study. That sort of thing, he tells me, involves a technique which employs 'a step sideways in hyperspace-time', something that takes practice to master. I'll take his word for it; the alternative would have been for me simply to drive the clock in through the wall or roof!

When we got back we had a brandy – I must say I needed it! – over which Titus mentioned how I should be well pleased with myself; my practice flight hadn't gone badly at all. He seems to think it's all decided now. Perhaps it is . . .

Mar. 2

For the last four days Titus has been away roving the countryside in a rented car. He said he didn't know when he'd get the next chance to 'have a look at Old England.' I can't help wondering if he'll ever get another chance!

While he's been away I've given a lot of thought to what he's told me about his amazing travels. The world seems a very drab place compared with Titus Crow's description of Elysia. It's a funny thing, but the more I try to enumerate them the fewer ties I seem to have here on Earth. And there's a certain phrase of his that keeps repeating in my mind: 'a gateway on all space and time . . .'

Mar. 4

Tonight I'm to try my hand at using Crow's flying cloak, the antigravity device he brought back with him from Elysia. He tells me that it's the most wonderful experience. We must, of course, wait for darkness; it wouldn't do for me to frighten the life out of people by flying over London in broad daylight, like some great vampire bat at noon.

Mar. 7

Crow has gone back to Elysia. I woke up this morning to find his bed empty, barely slept in, a note left for me on the pillow:

Henri –
Forgive me for not letting you know that I was returning to Elysia so soon; I didn't know myself until half an hour or so ago. I couldn't sleep, got up and made myself a coffee, then wandered into your study.

The clock's hands were more than normally erratic; I opened the panel and stepped inside. Immediately Tiania's voice came to me, and her message was in the form of a pretty enigmatic warning from Kthanid. In short, it's imperative that I return to Elysia now, within the hour. Tiania wouldn't tell me what the trouble is, Henri – Kthanid had forbidden it – but something pretty big must be in the air and obviously they don't want me involved in it!

I shouldn't feel torn two ways like this, for while Earth is my

262

home world so is Elysia now, and a goddess waits for me there . . . As Kthanid once told me, she is only a girl, but she's a strange, strange woman – and to me she's a goddess.

I wouldn't wake you, Henri – farewells never come easy between friends such as you and I. And in any case I plan to see you soon, in Elysia.

I've left you my flying cloak; you know how to use it and it may come in handy. I'm leaving you the clock, too, for I don't need it now, except as a gateway to the gardens of Elysia. My mind has *opened*, Henri! The possibilities are infinite . . . I've told you all I can of the clock and its workings, and I've instructed the Old Fellow to wait for you for four days before returning to that vast corridor of clocks in the heart of the Blue Mountains. At that time the panel will open of its own accord, and by then you will know what to do.

You will be welcome in Elysia, Henri, but of course you must make your own way there. You are not yet one of the Chosen. It may well be a dangerous voyage; it will certainly be difficult. But at least you have a weapon that I never had when I first set out in the clock. And when there are obstacles, when you need a helping hand, well, we'll be watching in Elysia. And if you are where I can't reach you without aid, then I'll ride a Great Thought to you. Oh, yes, the pitfalls of time and space are many, but the rewards will be great.

Worlds without end, de Marigny, and all time and space at your fingertips! Strange dimensions and nighted planes of existence – places of myth and legend, dream and fantasy – and all real, existing here and now and within your reach. All this, or Earth, the choice is yours.

You are a lover of mysteries, my friend, as your father before you; and I'll tell you something, something which you really ought to have guessed before now. There's something in you that hearkens back into dim abysses of time, a spark whose fire burns still in Elysia. And one more thing you should know:

I have mentioned places of fantasy and places of dream, and all of them are as real and solid in their way as the ground beneath your feet. Ah, but there are dreams and there are dreams, and there are dreamers and dreamers. Your father was a great dreamer, Henri. *He still is – for he is a lord of Ilek-Vad, where his old friend Randolph Carter is a just and honored king!*

I intend to visit them there one day, in that land of dreams. When I do you can be with me, we two and Tiania – for I know

263

she'll never let me leave Elysia on my own again – and perhaps one other. Who can say?

Yes, the choice is yours, but one more thing I ask you to remember. There once was a time when man's remote forbear swam in warm, soupy oceans and never dreamed of walking on dry land. And then there was a time when he walked and gazed awestruck at the birds which flew. And then he flew in his turn and looked on the moon, the planets . . . In ten thousand years, perhaps, men might have their own Elysia right here on Earth, but you have not got ten thousand years!

Remember, the clock will open. That will be when you must make the final decision.

I will not say goodbye –
Titus.

Mar. 9

I seem to be spending more and more time these days here in my study, and the old clock is really becoming something of an obsession with me. I find myself listening to its ticking, trying to sort out some kind of pattern in the crazy sweep of its four hands. And despite the promise I made myself only yesterday morning – that whatever happened I would remain here on Earth – well, today I've packed all my recordings of Crow's adventures, together with my notebooks and assorted papers, into a strong cardboard carton. All that remains now is to place this diary in the carton with the rest of the stuff and address it. Mrs Adams will do the rest when she comes back. She hasn't been near the place since discovering that Crow was here!

Yes, I'll send all this stuff to Peaslee and . . .

But all this, of course, depends on whether or not I decide to change my mind about going . . . about not going? *God damn that clock's insane ticking!*

Mar. 10

A letter this morning from Mother Quarry, more a note really. She knows Crow's gone again, and she echoes his words when she says, 'Something big is in the air.' But what? I feel it, too, the lull before the storm, a disquiet, an ominous mental depression, an uneasiness of psyche. And I may as well admit it now . . . I've made my choice.

Mar. 11

The door in the clock has opened, Wingate, and I've no time to do more than wish you all the best –

HLdM

Epilogue

At midnight, March 25, 1980, some fourteen days after de Marigny left Earth for Elysia in the time-clock and five days after Wingate Peaslee received de Marigny's parcel, Project X was finalized . . . and the CCD struck back! The unprecedented fury of the destruction that they wrought was Cthulhu's answer to the attack on Cthylla, Dagon and Hydra, for the project of course, had been the attempted destruction of all of these beings. A nuclear-powered burrowing device was sent four and a half miles deep into the earth beneath Innsmouth's Devil Reef and exploded down there by remote control. That atomic explosion, occurring just before midnight, had triggered Cthulhu's direst wrath.

No, that last is an understatement: the prime member of the CCD was not merely wrathful, he was absolutely insane with rage, berserk! Of course he was, for his Secret Seed, Cthylla, in whose darkling womb he planned to rise up again one day reborn, had been threatened. And I fear that she was not destroyed, for if she had been then surely the Fury would have been that much worse. As it was it lasted for three days and nights, a mental and physical onslaught that stopped as abruptly as it began. Foundation telepaths – those few who dared open their minds at all during that time – detected something still alive deep, deep down beneath shattered Devil Reef, something that mewled a demented telepathic threat of revenge as it moved off wounded, finally to disappear into the deeps of the North Atlantic.

The Fury lasted for three days and nights. The mental

266

effects of it were world wide, while its purely physical phenomena were very much localized. Of the former, the hateful telepathic outpourings from R'lyeh and other sunken Pacific sepulchers of the Cthulhi were such as to cause the most frightening outbreaks of unbridled, raging mass lunacy in all the world's mental institutions. Even the most passive inmates became possessed with hideous homicidal urges beyond all the powers of their keepers to control. In more than one hospital home the responsible authorities had to resort to the use of firearms to protect their own lives, but in many others the warnings came too late. Escaped lunatics marauded in the streets of Lisbon, Chicago, London and Köln before the Fury finally, abruptly ceased on the evening of the third day.

By then, too, the old Miskatonic University was no more. Brought down by the earth tremors that shook New England, nowhere more severely than Arkham, Miskatonic was first of all flayed by a tornado to end all tornadoes, then became the center of an incredible electrical storm. I escaped the holocaust by pure luck; many of my colleagues were less fortunate . . .

So the old university burned to the ground, and with it went most of the amassed lore of the Wilmarth Foundation, a vast storehouse of esoteric knowledge concerning the CCD, their minions and their dark works against mankind and the universe. And while Miskatonic blazed Innsmouth suffered a simultaneous and duplicate destruction, in which poor Wingate Peaslee and his team gave up their lives for the safety and sanity of a world they had fought to protect against direst evil.

Even then, however, Cthulhu was not appeased, for on the third day he sent the torrential rains that flooded ruined Innsmouth and Arkham and burst the banks of the brooding Miskatonic in a flash flood that cost many lives before the waters subsided. This was the Fury, in which the whole of New England became a disaster area to rival any other in living memory.

It was not my intention, however, when I first decided to publish this work to chronicle details of the terrible loss of life and the destruction caused by the Fury. Its manifestations were later more than amply discussed in several scientific magazines and journals under the completely inadequate misnomer of unusual meteorological phenomena. And so I will say no more on the subject. What I would take this opportunity to speak about is a matter which at the moment seems to be the standard topic of conversation. It is not only constantly debated among the junior ranks in our ever-expanding Wilmarth Foundation, but also among a minority of the heads of those several governmental departments which we serve and which know us and the importance of our work.

Speaking plainly, Titus Crow and Henri-Laurent de Marigny have been slandered in the cruelest manner by people who choose to see them as cowards and traitors to the Foundation's cause. Titus Crow, particularly, is seen to have fled the Earth at a time when he alone was in possession of a weapon against which the CCD could not stand. Indeed, one of the reasons why those forces of evil were so determined in their efforts to prevent Crow from returning to this world must have been that they themselves feared that he would use his newfound powers against them.

Still I say that these two men have been slandered, and so they have. Both de Marigny and Crow fought the most hideous battles with the CCD behind the scenes long before many of us even knew the Ancient Ones existed. How can one describe such men as cowards or traitors? And yet I have spoken to several people who are dissatisfied with Crow's 'desertion', and it seems obvious to me that festering seeds of suspicion have certainly been sown in their minds – *but by whom?*

Do I have to remind Foundation members of the fact that our fight is far from over? And must I add that just as surely as we are pledged to thwart every effort of the CCD to free themselves from the immemorial prisons of the Elder Gods, so are they equally determined in the discovery of new ways to achieve just that end? And if one of these ways is to breed distrust in the minds of men . . . what then? I am afraid, we are *all* afraid, and in Titus Crow's own words I will tell you what we fear: We fear the awesome task we have been given for we and no others are the guardians of the universe . . .

Always remember, Cthulhu lives and dreams on, yet seeking to rule the minds of men; and through them all of space and time – *and I say to you that already he has gained certain victories*!

Arthur D. Meyer
New Miskatonic,
Rutland, Vermont